Timeswept passion...timeless love.

GUARDIAN ANGEL

"Don't you know who I am? Aren't you here for me?" Maddie asked. Just her luck, she thought. He was probably someone else's escort. She'd no doubt get an aging lady with rolled-down nylons and blue hair.

The breeze caught Devon's black hair, ruffling it against his neck and jaw. The horse whinnied and shifted restlessly. But the man never moved. He just continued to stare at Maddie as if she'd dropped out of the sky into his soup or something.

Maddie saw the twitch in his cheek and felt a twinge of disquiet. Then he said, "This is my property and I want to know how you got here."

"Your property? You mean you get a place like this up here? Geez, I can't wait to see mine."

"Yours?" The stiff features finally softened as he asked the question in a tone bordering on amusement.

"Yeah, do you know where I'm supposed to be?"

"How the blazes should I know where you're supposed to be? I don't have the vaguest idea who you are."

"I'm Madeline St. Thomas. Aren't you my angel?"

The full lips parted and he quickly covered what might have been a chuckle. "I don't think so, madam." His eyes dropped and he seemed to shake off his shock. "Then again, perhaps I am."

Time's Healing Heart

Marti Jones

For Andy, who made it all possible.
For Adam, Amanda, and Drew, who made it all worthwhile.
And in loving memory of Barbara and Denise Nowling.

Book Margins, Inc.

A BMI Edition

Published by special arrangement with Dorchester Publishing Co., Inc.

Printed in the United States of America.

Chapter One

"I'm sorry, Maddie, truly I am."

Madeline St. Thomas stared across the desk at Dr. Joe Phillips, the grandfatherly family practitioner who'd brought her into the world more than three decades ago.

"And I thought all I had to worry about was my biological clock ticking."

"We can hold off the surgery for a while, but I don't want to wait too long. We've tried laser and hormone therapy with no success. The endometriosis is too advanced. There's a real risk of endometrian cancer."

Maddie nodded and suddenly the tears came. Dropping her head into her palms, she let them flow.

A hysterectomy. God, she was too young. And

what about the babies she'd always planned to have one day?

Dr. Phillips didn't try to offer false comfort. He sat quietly behind his desk until Maddie collected her composure.

"You've got a little time to adjust to the idea. Think it over," he said, but Maddie heard the twinge of urgency in his voice. They'd known each other too long.

"Yeah, well. You know me, Uncle Joe. Why put off until tomorrow . . ."

"We can go ahead and schedule it if it will make you feel better."

Maddie didn't think she'd ever feel better. Instantly she chastised herself. A lot of people had worse things to contend with.

"I'll call you in a few days," she said noncommittally. So she still felt a little sorry for herself. Under the circumstances she thought she was entitled.

"If there were any other way . . ." she began, not even sure what she'd been going to say.

"Well . . ."

Maddie's head came up sharply. "Well? Well what?"

"Have you thought about getting pregnant?"

A chuckle escaped Maddie's lips, followed by a forlorn sigh. "That generally takes two, doesn't it?"

"Come on, Maddie," Dr. Phillips said, seeing through her attempt at humor. "I told you six months ago the best treatment for this condition is pregnancy when it's a viable option.

With the lack of hormones during gestation and the disruption of the menstrual cycle for nine months, the endometrian tissue usually disappears completely."

Maddie was listening intently now. "And besides," he added with a smile, "this is the nineties. Sperm banks, artificial insemination. Lots of choices."

All traces of humor fell from Maddie's face. She sat forward almost eagerly.

"You're serious?"

"I don't usually suggest this option unless the woman in question is already planning to start a family. I'm not sure bringing a baby into the world this way is the best idea. However, I know you, Maddie. I know how you feel about Genny's kids. And the truth is, we've tried everything else. If you want a child, Maddie, I'm afraid it's now or never."

Maddie slumped against the back of her chair, a dazed expression on her face. "I always assumed I'd be a mother someday. But like this, I don't know. I'm not sure I could handle being a single parent."

"Of course. It's a big decision, Maddie. This isn't something you want to rush into. I just wanted you to know all of the options before we go any further."

"Yes, I'm glad you told me, Uncle Joe. I'll give it a lot of thought."

Maddie picked up her purse, slid the strap over her shoulder, and rose.

"Oh, don't forget the supplies I collected for

Genevieve. She'll have my hide if I let you leave here without them." The doctor pushed a button on his intercom and called the nurse into his office.

"Genny's something. I don't know if I'd have the courage to do what she's doing." Maddie didn't feel very courageous about her own choices right now. She couldn't imagine flying halfway around the world on a medical mission to administer to people still basically in the Dark Ages. Her sister, the nurse, saw it as an adventure.

"I have no doubt you possess more courage and spirit than you realize." He smiled and slipped his arm around her shoulder, and Maddie understood his silent message. Uncle Joe had faith in her judgment, even if she didn't right now.

The nurse came in with what looked like two cardboard suitcases. Actually they were cartons with tiny plastic handles on one side. In blue letters they were labeled PERISHABLE and PHARMACEUTICALS.

"Do you need some help getting these to your car?"

"No thanks, Uncle Joe, I can manage." She hefted the cartons into her hands. "Thanks for everything. I'll be in touch."

"Maddie," he added, as she headed for the door. "Don't wait too long."

All the way down in the elevator Maddie considered her choices. Basically there were only two. She could have the hysterectomy and maybe one day adopt a child, or she could try to get pregnant and have her own child.

As she stowed the cartons in the back of her Chevy station wagon, her mind took the next logical step. If she were to decide on pregnancy, how would she go about it? Uncle Joe had suggested artificial means. Of course there was always the good old-fashioned way. Except the old-fashioned way had never been that good for Maddie.

One disastrous affair in college had tainted her perspective on sex and the two relationships she'd had since then had been dismal, to say the least. Her passion was her job, interior design. Men made good friends but, as the saying went, strange bedfellows. At least for Maddie.

The drive home passed in a blur as she tried to sort all the thoughts in her head. As she approached her third-floor condominium overlooking the Gulf of Mexico, she knew she was no closer to a resolution than she'd been an hour ago.

The telephone began to ring as she struggled with the bulky cartons and tried to unlock her door. Finally, the key turned and she propelled herself into the room and across the couch to snatch up the receiver.

"This is Madeline St. Thomas," her machine droned. "I can't come to the phone right now. . . ."

"I'm here," she said, trying to talk over the recording of herself.

". . . please leave a message and I'll get back to you as soon as I can."

"I'm here," she repeated, just as the tone sounded deafeningly in her ear.

Maddie cringed and said again, "I'm here, please hold."

"I'm holding," Genevieve's giggling voice came back at her. "Just don't ask me what I'm holding."

Maddie felt the first real smile of the day slide easily across her face. "Either a cuddly baby or a cuddly husband would be my guess."

"Right the first time," her sister congratulated. "It's Sam. He's teething. Still cuddly, though, drool and all."

"Hold that pose till I get there Saturday." Slipping her feet out of the cream-colored pumps she'd worn all day, she tucked her feet under her and settled into the corner of the sofa.

"I hope he'll get the darn tooth before then; I need my sleep. How'd it go with Uncle Joe?"

Maddie curled her toes, closed her eyes, and sighed loudly.

"That bad, huh?" Genny asked, already reading her sister's mood.

"Worse. We talked about a hysterectomy." No beating around the bush with Genny. She'd get to the facts sooner or later anyway.

"God, babe, I'm sorry. Geez, I was hoping for another solution."

Genevieve had walked Maddie through every step since the diagnosis six months ago, so

Uncle Joe's suggestion had come as no real surprise.

"Well, he did mention one other option."

Genny giggled. "Let me guess: pregnancy."

"You know your treatments. Yeah, he said I could still conceive and it would probably arrest the disease entirely."

"So?" The baby fussed and Maddie heard a shuffle, followed by the sound of Genny transferring the phone to her other ear.

"So what? I'm single, Gen. I've got a very demanding career. I've never even considered raising a child alone. I can't imagine anything more difficult."

"That's the cons. Now list the pros."

Good ol' Gen, cut to the heart of the matter. Maddie pulled the barrette from her long blonde hair and ran her fingers through the strands, loosening them from her scalp.

"I've always wanted a family. I can't imagine living my life without ever knowing the wonderful things you've experienced firsthand. I want to hold a child in my arms who isn't my niece or nephew, but my own flesh and blood."

"Pretty strong case for motherhood," Genny whispered.

"I just don't know. It's a major decision. I don't want to screw up. I mean a child isn't something you try your hand at, like watercolors. It's a lifetime commitment."

"Yep, with the highest highs and the lowest lows. No other job can compare. Not nursing, not decorating. Nothing."

"You sound like a recruiter." Maddie laughed and stretched her legs out, already feeling the tension seep out of her limbs. Lord, Genny was so good for her. Sometimes she didn't know how she'd have made it this far without her sister.

"Maybe I am. This feels right to me, Maddie. You've always wanted children. If it weren't for Todd . . ." Her voice trailed off for a moment as they both remembered the awful time after Maddie and Todd split up. "Besides, you'd make a great mom."

The baby sent up another cry and Genevieve cooed and shifted the phone once more.

"You're busy, Genny. We can talk more when I get there this weekend."

"Oh, wait, I almost forgot. Did you get my stuff from Uncle Joe?"

"Sure did," Maddie said, glancing over to the two cartons sitting just inside the door. "Looks like he got a good haul this time."

"I can't believe how great all the doctors are being about donating medicine and supplies. I'm about to burst, I'm so excited. Of course when I think about leaving Sam and Elizabeth I just about cry. Romania's a world away."

"It's only for three weeks, and John'll be with them the whole time. He's terrific, Gen. I mean it. How many men would want their wives going on a trek like this, much less take their vacation so they can be home with the kids?" Maddie suddenly felt like crying all over again. "Sam and Elizabeth are gonna be fine. You'll suffer more than they will, I'm sure."

"You're probably right. I'm sure gonna miss this bunch, though. Oh, darn, Sam's spit up all down my back. I'd better run. Doesn't this sound like fun, sis? Think about it. I'll see you Saturday. Drive carefully."

Maddie didn't even know if Genevieve heard her good-bye. The phone went dead in her hand and she laughed, setting it back in the cradle. Could she live with that kind of chaos? she wondered.

But in her heart she knew the real question was, could she live without it?

The 40-mile drive from the Florida coast to Genevieve's country home over the Alabama state line consisted mostly of slowly meandering two-lane roads.

Maddie settled into her seat, buckled her seat belt across the silk boxer-style shorts she'd chosen to wear, and turned on the radio. A familiar song came over the air from one of the many country and western stations prevalent in the area.

She caught the spur, wheeled onto the interstate for about 15 miles, and then exited onto state road 87.

Her blonde hair was pulled back into a loose French braid, and her rose silk tank top allowed the cool blast of air from the vents to wash over her skin. Another easy-moving country hit poured out of the speakers as she sipped springwater from a little cup in the holder attached to her dash. Behind her the backseat inclined forward all the way to allow room for her sample books of carpet and wallpaper, and the two cartons of medical supplies for Genevieve.

The day itself would have made a good commercial for tourism in northwest Florida. Bright sunshine, small, billowy white clouds, and just a hint of a breeze in the passing trees.

Maddie loved this part of the drive. On either side of the road small, family-owned farms coexisted beside video stores and beauty parlors. People waved as you drove by as if your being there made you a friend. She envied Genny this place sometimes. But there were very few calls for interior decorators this far out in the country and you had to travel at least an hour to get to the next good-size town.

It was about 11:30 in the morning when Maddie caught sight of Crowe Lake, the man-made body of water where most of the citizens gathered every July fourth. She'd gone with Genny and her family last year and they'd had a blast swimming, picnicking, and watching the fireworks display after sundown.

At first Maddie didn't notice the car slowing down. She accelerated at the base of a small hill, and it was then she felt the definite shudder. Letting off the gas pedal, she reached to turn down the volume on the radio and the car coughed to a halt.

"Darn," Maddie cursed, quickly checking her rearview mirror for oncoming traffic. Nothing in sight, thank goodness. She put the car in park and turned the key. It roared to life again and the engine held long enough for her to steer out of the road onto the shelled shoulder.

"Now what," she murmured to the steering wheel, as though expecting the car to tell her what it needed. Several times she tried to turn the motor over, but it was no use. She was stuck.

Suddenly the long stretch of country road looked longer. The lake off to one side reflected the sun, but no one was there to offer her help. She remembered a little mom-and-pop store about two miles back, but she couldn't remember what might be farther ahead. She'd driven this road many times, but somehow she'd never noticed the long stretch of emptiness. Her best bet would be to walk back to one of the stores, where she'd be assured of finding a working telephone.

Unbuckling her seat belt, she collected her purse and keys. As she stepped out beside the car she could feel the heat coming off the pavement seep through her thin leather sandals. "Poor walking shoes, to say the least," she grumbled. She caught sight of the cartons containing Genny's supplies and groaned out loud.

The bright blue letters stood out clearly through the back windows of the car and she didn't have anything to cover them with. The walk back would be trying enough in the rising midday heat; now she knew she'd have to take Genny's cartons with her. She couldn't

17

risk someone coming along and stealing them, and she knew that even small towns had drug problems. Boxes clearly labeled PHARMACEUTI-CALS would be too tempting.

She unlocked the rear door and lugged the cartons out onto the shoulder. Taking a deep breath, she picked them up. No use wasting time complaining. She'd be at a store soon enough and she'd call Genny. She knew her brother-in-law could be there in less than half an hour to help her.

The cartons were heavy, but the plastic handles made them less awkward. She'd gone several yards without even working up a sweat and was feeling pretty good about herself when a car appeared on the horizon. As it headed toward her she considered her options. No doubt they would stop—country folk still did that—and she'd have to either accept their offer or politely beg off.

City life had made her wary and she was thinking of several nice but firm refusals when she saw the car swerve. Maddie froze. She could see the driver slumped over the steering wheel, and she felt her heart leap in icy fear.

She sidestepped, watching in horror as the car tried to make the slight curve. Too late Maddie realized it would never make it. The driver was still as death. Maddie turned to run, but the car was heading straight for her. She'd waited too long; it had been too close before she'd seen the danger. Her sandals slapped frantically on the crushed shells lining the road. She heard the sound of tires on those same shells and cried out, dodging just as the left fender caught her hip.

Propelled over the shoulder of the road, she tumbled end over end down the embankment. Spiraling colors and noises filled her head. Her fingers grasped for a hold, but nothing slowed her descent. She vaguely heard the sound of metal against metal and knew the other car had hit hers.

She splashed to a halt, water from the lake sucking at her bruised body. She felt herself sinking and tried to flail her arms, but everything hurt and nothing seemed to work properly. Her nose and mouth quickly filled, choking off her scream. Darkness funneled out the light of the bright sun until it was nothing more than a pinpoint, and then it disappeared altogether.

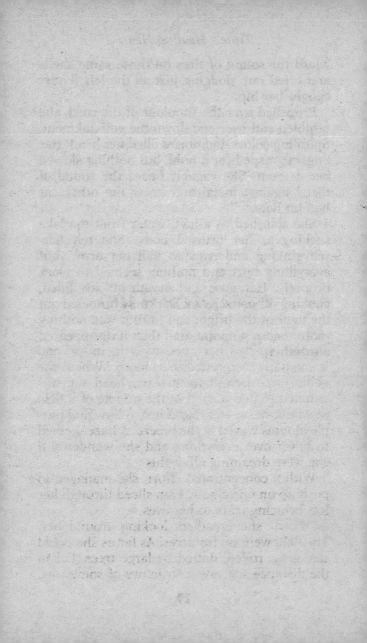

Chapter Two

Maddie opened her eyes, tried to move, and immediately regretted her haste. When she could force herself to turn her head she was stunned to find herself in the middle of a field of wildflowers. All around her, yellow and purple blooms waved in the breeze. A haze seemed to hover over everything and she wondered if she were dreaming all of this.

With a concentrated effort, she managed to push up on one elbow. Pain sliced through her leg, bringing tears to her eyes.

"Wow!" she breathed, looking around her. The field went on for acres. As far as she could see, grass rolled, dotted by large trees. Off in the distance she saw a structure of some sort, but she couldn't make out any details.

Then an odd foreboding squeezed her in its grip. Where were all the power lines? The telephone poles? Her blurry eyes scanned the horizon for acres in every direction, but she could see no sign of anything modern. What kind of place didn't even have paved roads? And for that matter where was the road she'd been driving on? She could see all around her. Not so much as an inch of asphalt in sight. And then it hit her.

Obviously she'd died.

Since she distinctly remembered falling into the lake, she must be in heaven. It was the only explanation. For a moment she felt peaceful, as she always thought she would at such a time. A sense of acceptance came over her.

She'd just lie here until someone came for her. Maybe they were running late. Surely she wasn't supposed to have to lie on the ground in pain for long.

Her eyes popped open. Pain! Oh, Lord, the pain nearly took her breath away. So much for all the stuff she'd learned in Sunday school about there being nothing bad in heaven. The blades of hot agony shooting through her were certainly *not* pleasant.

If she was dead why did it hurt so much? Something wasn't right here.

Her eyes fluttered shut once more and she must have dozed, because when she reopened them the sun was no longer directly overhead. The heavy floral scent of the wildflowers surrounded her, bringing on nausea to add to the pain.

Where was the angel, or whatever, who was supposed to come for her? Surely they didn't mean for her to walk. Not with the hotly throbbing aches searing her body.

She tried to draw her legs up, cried out again, and sank back to the ground, trembling. "Yow, don't do that again. Obviously a big mistake, trying to move." She'd just have to wait for her escort.

A rustling noise caught her attention and she perked up. Finally! She hoped the building she saw was where you got rid of all your pain and such. And she hoped the tardy angel was better at finding the place than he was at being on time.

A shadow passed over her and she looked up. Way up. Past the longest legs she'd ever seen to a well-built torso, broad shoulders, and— wow! a gorgeous face. The man wore boots shiny enough to see yourself in, skin-tight buff-colored trousers, and a loose-fitting white shirt unbuttoned at the throat.

He was frowning at her, his blue eyes wide in surprise. Over his shoulder were what looked like leather reins. She followed them to where they attached to a huge gray horse. She'd had no idea. Angels looked just like Rhett Butler!

"It's about time you showed up. I think I'm about to pass out again. Can we get to the place where they take care of the pain first?"

His eyes blinked comically and his gaze swept over her body. She saw his throat convulse and then he stared at her in what looked like horror.

"I'm sorry if I'm being rude. I don't really know what I'm supposed to be doing. But, ow! As you can see I'm still in a lot of pain. So if we could just . . ."

He didn't move and Maddie felt frustrated. Wasn't this man supposed to help her? Obviously he'd been sent to her; he was everything she'd ever dreamed of. Maybe he wasn't allowed to talk to her until she saw whoever was in charge.

"Can't you talk to me?" she asked.

"Who the hell are you?" The deep, resonant voice, all the more powerful because he'd nearly shouted at her, threw Maddie off balance and she jumped, crying out in pain.

"Don't you know who I am? Aren't you here for me?" Just her luck, she thought. He was probably someone else's escort. She'd no doubt get an aging lady with rolled-down nylons and blue hair. "And I'm not sure you should be using language like that here. I mean, you know, someone might hear you."

The breeze caught his black hair, ruffling it against his neck and jaw. The horse whinnied and shifted restlessly. But the man never moved. He just continued to stare at Maddie as if she'd dropped out of the sky into his soup or something.

"I couldn't care less who hears me," he told

her, every muscle in his body tightening dangerously. Maddie saw the twitch in his cheek and felt a twinge of disquiet. "This is my property and I want to know how you got here."

"Your property? You mean you get a place like this up here? Geez, I can't wait to see mine."

"Yours?" The stiff features finally softened as he asked the question in a tone bordering on amusement.

"Yeah, do you know where I'm supposed to be?"

"How the blazes should I know where you're supposed to be? I don't have the vaguest idea who you are."

"I'm Madeline St. Thomas. Aren't you my angel?"

The full lips parted and he quickly covered what might have been a chuckle. "I don't think so, madam." His eyes dropped and he seemed to shake off his shock. He noticed her injuries for the first time and frowned. "Then again, perhaps I am."

He knelt and eased his hands over her leg where a purple bruise covered half her thigh. Another long discolored area began under her knee and ran all the way to her ankle. Various cuts and scrapes which had since quit bleeding marred her long slender legs. Her arms, exposed by the tank top, had fared about as well. She could only imagine what her face looked like.

"What in the name of all that's holy happened to you?" He tried to turn her leg and Maddie sucked her breath in sharply.

"I was hit by a car."

"A what?" He looked up at her incredulously as he assessed her condition.

"A car. You know, an automobile." His hands grazed over her flesh as though taking inventory of all the injuries.

"That's impossible," he said, quickly looking back over his shoulder. "No one around here owns one of those contraptions. No one I know has actually even seen one except for the pictures in the newspapers."

He'd never seen a car? "You've got to be kidding!"

"I assure you I'm most serious. Now, we've got to get you back to the house. No way you can ride with that leg. I think it's broken."

"At least," Maddie confirmed.

"Well, there's no help for it. I'll just have to carry you."

"What? You're joking. Look, even if you've been up here since before the invention of the automobile you must have some sort of conveyance."

"Certainly. I have several wagons, but I can't leave you here while I go get one of them. In case you haven't noticed, you're seriously injured and, I might add, nearly naked."

Maddie's face flushed. She would have to get an angel with a caveman mentality. Of course, he'd probably been up here since before the suffrage movement.

Without warning, he slipped his arms beneath her, and Maddie felt herself being lifted through the air like a feather. Well, he might not be full of brains, but he was more than compensated in the brawn department.

They started across the field, the horse following docilely behind. Each stride of the man's long legs jarred Maddie, causing her to squeeze her eyes shut and bite her lip to keep from crying out. He seemed to notice her discomfort and he eased into the next step, and then the next.

"You said you weren't my angel," Maddie recalled, talking against his chest as he held her close. "Are you an angel at all?"

"No."

Maddie tossed that bit of knowledge around and then added, "What are you, then, a fantasy? That must be it. Everyone's probably busy here so they send fantasies to collect the new people. Sort of like holograms or something."

The man didn't reply as his legs ate up the distance to the edge of the field. Spongy green grass covered the ground, muting the sound of his heavy boots striking heel to toe.

"You don't talk much. Aren't you allowed to answer questions?"

"Madam, I will answer any questions you might ask, and be sure I'll have a few of my own as well. But you will have to wait until we reach my house, as you are not exactly light as a feather. I can't carry you and carry on a conversation at the same time."

Maddie's mouth fell open. What kind of fantasy was this? He'd actually insulted her. She felt sure the man in charge would not be happy to know he'd sent a rude fantasy to welcome her.

The house came into sight and Maddie suffered another shock. Black men and women lined a field of cotton off to one side while still others were busy applying a fresh coat of paint to a massive, three-story Victorian house.

"Holy cow! What kind of place is this?" Confusion blossomed into full outright horror. "Certainly people don't have to slave like this in heaven."

The man's arms tightened painfully on Maddie's back and legs. "All of these employees are free men and women of color who work, damned hard I might add, for me. And they are very well compensated."

"But heaven isn't supposed to be this way," she murmured, more to herself than to the stranger. Something wasn't right. Heaven wouldn't have cotton fields, would it? And the buildings wouldn't be in need of painting or repairs. And no one, black or white, would be expected to work in the fields that way. Dread crept along Maddie's spine.

"Where am I?"

Her question drifted away as the workers close to the house saw them approaching. Several called out to the stranger and a few rushed into the house, obviously to get help. The front door burst open and a large black woman hurried out, followed by an older, more refined woman who stared past Maddie and the man.

"Sarah, get me a blanket quickly. Aunt Bev, to the parlor."

The black woman moved surprisingly fast, considering her girth, and the older woman whirled quickly and was waiting inside when the man strode in with Maddie.

"What's happened, Devon?" the aged lady asked, her wrinkled face puckered in a worried frown.

"I don't know, Aunt Bev," the man, Devon, answered.

The black servant returned with a beautiful quilt in a star pattern and held it out. "Where's the chile's clothes, Misser Devon?" she asked, aghast.

His aunt gasped and pressed her hand to her chest. "Sarah, you didn't tell me the girl was naked."

"She's not—"

Maddie had had enough. "I'm not naked, ma'am. I'm wearing perfectly adequate clothes. At least they were fine before the accident." She looked down and was pleased to note her shorts and tank top were not revealing anything they shouldn't.

She thought she saw a smile cross the woman's face, but her eyes stared blankly ahead. Maddie realized with a start that the woman was blind. Another piece of this puzzle which didn't fit.

"She is in fact wearing some sort of under-clothing, Aunt Bev. Odd looking, but of good quality."

"These aren't—"

"Does this girl have a name, Devon? Or am I supposed to continue to talk through her as you seem to be doing?"

Now Maddie knew his aunt was smiling. She couldn't help smiling back. Hah! Good for Aunt Bev. "My name is Madeline St. Thomas." She looked past the man and said sweetly to his aunt, "But you can call me Maddie."

"Maddie, what a lovely name. Are you seriously hurt, Maddie?"

"She's—" Devon began, only to be cut off by a sharp frown from his aunt.

"I'm not sure, ma'am. I am in a great deal of pain, though."

"Sarah." Aunt Bev nodded at the servant.

"Yes'm. I was goin' ta fetch my doctorin' bag. Somethin' in there to make her feel better, I know."

"Thank you," Maddie whispered, settling back against the arm of the couch where the stranger had laid her. He continued to hover nearby, but didn't look directly at Maddie even though she was now covered from neck to toes in the quilt.

When Sarah returned, Maddie gave herself over to the woman's ministrations. She accepted the bitter-tasting liquid and felt her limbs grow heavy almost immediately.

The servant began to dab at the cut along

Maddie's leg, but Maddie couldn't keep her eyes open. She slid into blissful unconsciousness once more.

"Where on earth did you find this girl, Devon?"

"I found her in the south pasture. Despite what she told you, Aunt Bev, she's dressed in a pair of brightly colored bloomers which have been cut off at the thigh and a shirtwaist so thin I could see right through it. Not that I looked," he added quickly, seeing the smirk on his aunt's face. "Her arms, legs, and feet are completely bare."

"My goodness," Beverly Crowe exclaimed, astonished by the picture her nephew drew for her with his words. She smoothed the folds of her heavy blue damask day dress. The high lace collar stood against her neck, hot in the late afternoon heat.

"That isn't all," Devon told her in a loud whisper as he looked back to the woman on his sofa. "She's disoriented and hallucinating. She was talking about heaven having automobiles and fantasies." He took his aunt's elbow and led her from the parlor into the foyer.

After closing the door behind them, he turned to her and said, "She asked me if I was her angel."

Beverly's face broke into a wide grin. "And, pray, what did you tell her?"

"I fail to see the humor in this situation,

Aunt. The girl obviously has a severe head injury."

"She didn't seem too badly afflicted when she spoke up a moment ago," his aunt reminded him. "She did seem quite piqued with you, though."

"Don't turn that impish smirk in my direction. I was a perfect gentleman."

"Yes, I'm sure you were. Still, we must find out who she is and where she's from."

"I thought I'd send word to Anthony. He can be here by this time tomorrow and he'll know what to do."

"Splendid idea," Beverly agreed, taking his arm in hers. "And until then?"

"You know the answer to that, Aunt. I'll not send the waif out into the night injured."

"I didn't think for a moment that you would, dear."

Together they went back into the parlor. Maddie was still asleep on the sofa and Sarah was at work bandaging her many injuries.

"She'll be staying with us for a time, Sarah," Beverly told the servant. "Ready the guest suite next to Mr. Devon's room when you finish here."

"Yes'm," Sarah replied, never taking her eyes off Maddie.

Devon's eyes strayed to the length of smooth thigh revealed as Sarah tended the cuts along Maddie's leg. Her skin was neither pale nor soft, but firm and tanned. He remembered the feel of her in his arms, and cursed his body's reaction.

Still, he thought, looking down at her face in repose. He'd have to be blind himself not to notice her beauty.

Chapter Three

"Heaven indeed!" Maddie thought·as she woke in the huge cherrywood sleigh bed. She felt as if she'd fallen onto the set of *North and South*. All around her were antiques, exquisite pieces she'd coveted as a designer but never had the opportunity to buy.

But Maddie knew this wasn't heaven. And she hadn't died. Death couldn't hurt this much.

There wasn't an inch anywhere on her body that didn't ache. Her head throbbed, but the haze which had seemed to hang around her in the field had dissipated. An offensive odor brought on the nausea once again and she realized with chagrin it was coming from her. She pushed aside the heavy coverlet and frowned.

Lifting her arms, she looked down at the gown covering her body. A snowy-white creation of yards and yards of soft fine lawn, it reached from her fingertips to her toes. Experimentally, she began to move parts of her body.

Surprisingly, nothing seemed to be broken. No heavy casts were plastered on her. Only the noxious thick salve which seemed to be everywhere.

"Whew!" Maddie slowly eased her feet over the side of the bed. The floor seemed a long way down and she rested a moment before slowly slipping off the mattress. As her feet touched the glossy parquet floor, pain shot like needles through her body.

The gown settled around her feet in a marshmallowy puddle and Maddie inspected the unfamiliar garment. Across the bodice it was gathered into intricate ruching like a Polly Flinders dress. The sleeves fell full to her wrists, where they were gathered with a drawstring bow. Thick embroidered lace dripped over her hands and adorned the hem. She could have made 15 of her skimpy nightshirts from so much fabric.

Walking with the gait of a tortoise, she limped to the window. Heavy damask draperies were drawn over lace sheers. She pulled back one panel, peered outside, and gaped.

"Holy Christmas!"

Besides the field of cotton, the pasture of wildflowers, and the rolling lawn she'd seen on her arrival, there was a long drive lined with blooming magnolia trees and a wall of azalea hedges shaped into a maze.

And nothing, absolutely nothing else in sight. The cold dread which had begun when she'd seen the house chilled her. Gooseflesh rose on her bruised and battered skin.

"Oh, God, what's going on? Where is this place?"

"Lordy mercy, chile, what you doin' outta dat bed?"

The shriek startled Maddie and she whipped around. Her feet tangled in the gown and her head spun dizzily. She reached out to steady herself, but her fingertips met only air. She tensed for the fall she knew was coming.

But the black maid rushed forward and gripped her arms, catching Maddie to her heavy bosom. Together they sank slowly to their knees, the maid cushioning the jolt.

"Misser Devon! Come quick!"

Another hot poker of pain stabbed Maddie's forehead and bile roiled in her stomach. Bright white pinpoints of light whirled crazily across her line of vision.

"What in the name of all that's holy . . ."

Maddie heard the familiar voice, the quaint expression, and tears filled her eyes. "Oh, God. Oh, God," she cried, clasping her hand to her mouth.

Suddenly familiar arms came around her and she was swept off the floor. "Hush, it's all right. I've got you. You're going to be fine."

37

The warm, gentle words covered her like a cozy quilt, banishing cold reality. Maddie snuggled against the hard chest, her fingers clutching the fabric of his shirt.

"Oh, please," she begged, not certain what she was pleading for, only knowing she could not face this awful, crazy tableau alone.

"Shh," he soothed, lowering her to the bed. He tried to draw his arm from around her, but Maddie cried out and clutched it to her. "All right, relax," he said, sliding his hip onto the bed beside her. His hand came around and caressed her shoulder softly. One leg was trapped beneath her knees, but he didn't try to move.

Maddie chanced opening her eyes. Everything shifted, whirled, and settled into place. The room looked the same but for the maid standing openmouthed in the center of a tapestry rug.

"Sarah, fetch a fresh pitcher of water, quickly." The maid's double chin quivered as she tried to collect herself. Finally she snapped her mouth closed and scurried from the room.

"Where am I?" Maddie asked. "What is this place?" She'd visited Genevieve enough to know no place like this existed anywhere in the area. How could she have gotten so lost?

"You had an accident," he told her, his deep, resonant voice vibrating in the chest pressed against her ear. "I don't know any more than that. I was hoping you could tell me, actually. This place is my home, and rest assured you are perfectly safe here until we can contact your family."

Family! Genevieve must be sick with worry. How long since the accident? Maddie wondered. Had they found her car? What had happened to the other driver? Did they have any idea she was at this man's home?

"My sister, she'll be frantic. I have to call her. How long have I been here?"

Maddie pushed away from the warm comfort and missed it immediately. Her gaze swept up the white shirt to settle on the man's face. This man was certainly no angel or hologram. He was living, breathing, hard-as-steel flesh and blood.

A frown creased his forehead and tiny lines feathered out from the corners of navy blue eyes. Deep concern glowed brightly from the odd-colored orbs.

"You've been here more than twenty-four hours. The doctor examined you this morning but you didn't awaken. To my surprise nothing was broken, but you have sustained severe bruises and several lacerations."

The maid hustled back into the room before Maddie could reply, and Maddie suppressed a grin when her rescuer jumped guiltily from the bed. The maid's eyes widened, huge white circles in her black face.

"Here's da watta, Misser Devon. You bess go on and let me tend the lady now."

"Yes, of course, Sarah." He looked like a chastised little boy as he edged around the rotund woman. At the door he turned back briefly and Maddie saw a flush on his cheeks. "Rest a bit longer, Miss St. Thomas. We'll talk more later."

The door closed behind him and Sarah chuckled gleefully. "That Misser Devon. He done looked like I caught him wit his hand in the cookie jar. Think he'd never seen a woman in her nightgown befo'."

Maddie smiled at the woman. Her ample breasts were jiggling with mirth and Maddie couldn't help the giggle that escaped her. "Do you mean he looked like that because of the way I'm dressed? But that's silly. This gown covers everything but the top of my head."

Sarah poured a glass of water and handed it to Maddie. "Misser Devon's a gentleman. He's been in a woman's bed befo', but he ain't used to being caught in the act by his ol' nanny."

"But he was just helping me. Surely there was no reason for him to feel guilty about that."

"Wasn't the helpin' he felt guilty 'bout. It was the enjoyin'. The man looked plum contented in your bed and he knowed I seen it. Misser Devon, he cain't hide nothin' from me. Never could."

As Maddie sipped the cool water, she wondered at Sarah's statement. Contented? What an odd observation.

"Let Sarah have a look at you now, Miss Maddie." She pulled the gown up and clinically perused the cuts and bruises covering

Maddie's body. "You don't mind me callin' you Miss Maddie, do ya?"

"Well you can drop the 'Miss.' Just Maddie will be fine."

The woman lowered the gown and faced Maddie with an astonished look on her face. "Yes'm, Miss Maddie."

Maddie got the feeling her comment had scandalized the woman more than finding her employer in Maddie's bed.

"You gonna be just fine." The maid settled the gown back over Maddie's legs and tucked the covers to her chin. "Ol' Sarah gonna see to it."

"I'm sure that's very kind of you, Sarah. But shouldn't I be in the hospital?" The woman's eyes bulged and a look of horror twisted her face. "Not that I don't appreciate what you've done for me," Maddie rushed on, thinking she'd insulted the woman. "But I was hit by a car. I might have internal injuries or something."

Sarah's expression went from horror to bafflement. "Dr. Anthony say you need rest. I don't know what you was hit by, but your skin turned every color of the rainbow. You got more black and blue on you than I ever seen on anyone befo'. But it ain't nothin' my liniment won't put right in a week or so. He even complimented me on my stitchin'."

"Stitching? You mean you sutured my leg?" Maddie had noticed the tiny black bits of thread when she'd lifted the gown earlier. Neat

41

little knots lined a cut about three inches long across her thigh.

"And your shoulder." Sarah nodded briskly. "Good thing you was out long enough for me ta finish. You didn't feel nothin'."

"No, I didn't." Maddie's mind spun. What were these people thinking? Why hadn't they called an ambulance? Why were they stitching her and covering her with foul-smelling liniment? It sounded like something you'd treat a horse with, not a human being. This was crazy. They were crazy!

Or were they? Once more she noticed the heavy brown dress the maid wore. Tiny buttons marched up her chest all the way to her throat. The sleeves were long and cuffed, the skirt full to her ankles. Heavy black boots with buttons covered her feet. An apron was tied across her waist and it, too, reached the top of her shoes.

She remembered the other woman she'd met when she arrived. Her dress had been blue, and much better quality, but it, too, had looked old-fashioned. Their hairstyles were odd, their speech accented but formal. Her glance swept over the room's furnishings once more. Antiques, she'd bet her business on it, but not old. An icy sweat covered her skin.

Maddie woke again several hours later. Her outburst had left her drained and emotionally hung over. Tears threatened when she scanned the massive bedroom only to find everything the same.

"So much for hoping it was all a nightmare," she muttered, taking a deep breath and corralling the useless self-pity. More pressing concerns were making themselves known to her bladder and she knew she'd have to find the nearest bathroom quick.

Another wave of dizziness muddled her brain when she tried to stand, but Maddie fought it down. After a moment she let go of the bed and crept gingerly across the floor. The door leading to the hall was closed. A huge cherrywood chiffonier flanked the bed on one side, a writing desk on the other. Her reflection stared back at her from an ornate cheval mirror, and she groaned at the wild array of tangled hair and the various scrapes and abrasions. A tapestry armchair sat at the head of the bed, its mate resting by the small fireplace. Opposite the fireplace was an elaborately decorated silk screen.

"A decorator's dream," she said dryly, walking to the screen. As she poked her head around the screen her mouth twisted in an odd grimace.

"What in the world . . ." A chair?

Maddie crept closer. She bent down and peered beneath the cushioned seat and her eyes widened. Lifting the padded seat, she giggled. "They've got to be kidding. Talk about taking decorating to a new level of authenticity."

As bad as she needed facilities, there was no way Maddie would use this antiquity.

A knock on the door had Maddie scuttling back around the screen. "Yes, who is it?"

"It's Devon Crowe, Miss St. Thomas. May I come in?"

Crowe? Did the man say Devon Crowe? As in Crowe Lake?

"Yes, of course, Mr. Crowe."

She considered getting back into bed, then discarded the idea immediately. Devon Crowe opened the door, bent to the side, and lifted something in his hands. Maddie gasped in surprise when she recognized the cardboard cases of medical supplies.

"I recovered your cases from the field. I thought perhaps you might be in need of them."

"Oh, thank goodness." Maddie hurriedly limped to examine the boxes. One had been smashed in at the corner, the other dented, but neither looked too badly damaged. "I can't believe this. Did you find anything else?"

"Anything else?" Devon Crowe's blue gaze swept over Maddie's gown, then returned to her face. He cleared his throat and turned away.

"My car?" Maddie hesitated as she saw his back straighten. He missed a step, seemed to collect himself, and then proceeded to the chiffonier.

"I saw no automobile, Miss St. Thomas," he said, opening the door of the wardrobe and drawing a frilly garment out. He smoothed the lacy fabric as he came toward Maddie.

He held it out to her and Maddie saw that it was a robe. She slipped her arms into the bouffant sleeves and drew the front together. Tiny pearl buttons paraded up the front and she quickly fastened them. A sash of pink satin cinched her waist, drawing the yards of lace together.

"Thank you," she managed, feeling weighted down by so much fabric and lace.

He nodded. "Shall we sit?" He motioned Maddie into the chair by the fireplace and then lifted the matching one from beside the bed and carried it effortlessly back to its designated place. They took their positions across from each other and Maddie felt as though they'd somehow laid battle lines.

"Now, then," he said, shifting in his chair and crossing his legs. "How are you feeling?"

Maddie watched the skin-tight fabric of his fawn-colored trousers stretch over his thighs. He folded his large, well-shaped hands in his lap and she could see herself reflected in his knee-high boots. His eyes scrutinized her minutely as he held his chin firmly tipped toward her.

"I'm feeling much better," she told him. "I want to thank you for all you've done."

He waved away her gratitude. "No need."

What an odd man, Maddie thought. He looked all cool and composed on the outside, but the muscles of his arms bunched beneath his shirt and she could see a dimple along his jaw that came and went as if he were clenching his teeth.

"No, really. I'm sure you saved my life. No telling how long I'd have lain in that field if you hadn't come along."

He nodded again and forced a grim smile. Maddie's eyes wandered away from the statue-like figure before her and then back again.

Frustration and nervous anxiety built to a crest inside her. Maddie felt disadvantaged by his icy composure, and decided to see if she could break it. Shifting in the chair, she crossed her legs, careful of the stitches and bruises, and let the hem of her gown ride up to her calves. She didn't miss Devon Crowe's quick perusal of her exposed leg.

"What I don't understand," she said, smiling when his head snapped back to face her, "is how I got out of the lake."

"Lake? Um . . ." He cleared his throat. "What lake?"

"After the car hit me I tumbled over the embankment into a lake." Crowe Lake, she wanted to add. But something held her back. Something strange had happened. She didn't know what and she decided to proceed slowly until she had a better idea.

"I'm sorry, Miss St. Thomas, you've lost me. There is no lake in this area. Oh, a pond or two, perhaps . . ."

"No, this was a lake. A very large, man-made lake." Why not just say it and get it over with?

Maddie thought. But something told her to keep that bit of knowledge to herself.

"Man-made?" He shook his head sharply. "No, I'm certain we have nothing like that anywhere near here." He rubbed his thumb and forefinger over his mustache and Maddie followed the movement as if mesmerized.

Suddenly he sat forward as though a thought had just occurred to him. "Is it possible you were injured somewhere else and brought here?"

Maddie had an idea that was exactly what had happened. But the immediate question still remained unanswered. If she wasn't in Genevieve's little town of Brewster, Alabama, just where the hell was she?

Once again her bladder reminded her she'd neglected to find the bathroom and she squirmed in her seat trying to relieve the pressure. But Devon Crowe was too astute. He frowned at her wiggling; then she thought she detected a hint of amusement around his full lips.

"My apologies, Miss St. Thomas," he said, rising from his chair. "I'm sure you must want to freshen up a bit since you're feeling better. If you'd like, there's a water closet at the end of the hall."

He extended his hand and Maddie nodded, preceding him into the hall.

"This way."

He led her down the surprisingly bright hall and Maddie felt the uneasiness she'd been fighting wash over her. The rich, thick wall covering was genuine striped brocade. Scenic oil paintings hung from long wires extended near the ceiling. A few tintype pictures in oval frames were neatly arranged in groupings.

"What interesting decor," she mumbled to Devon Crowe's back as he walked along ahead of her. "Are the photos authentic or copies?"

He stopped and looked from Maddie's tense face to the photographs lining the walls. "I beg your pardon?"

"I mean are they family members or just period pieces?"

Devon scanned the wall and Maddie could see the dimple in his jaw working. Whatever she'd said had set his teeth clenching again.

"Family."

He shook his head and turned away, striding more briskly along the carpet runner stretching from one end of the long hall to the other.

Maddie hurried along behind, deciding not to say anything more to Devon Crowe. After all, what did she know about the man? He'd rescued her after the accident only to bring her to his home instead of a hospital. Everyone she'd met so far had been strange, to say the least. And obviously they thought the same or worse about her, judging by their reactions.

Finally, Devon Crowe stopped outside a narrow oak door, his hand on the tiny brass knob.

"Towels are on the shelf over the bathtub. Make yourself at home. I'm sure you'll find everything you need. We've installed all the latest—uh, facilities."

Again Maddie noticed the slightest hint of a flush on his face. What a man! she thought. She'd never met a guy who blushed around a woman just because he had to show her to the bathroom. Still, she found it kind of charming in an old-fashioned way. Real old-fashioned, she added.

"Thank you," she said, brushing past him. She thought she heard him suck in his breath as her shoulder and hip came into contact with his body. Definitely charming, she concluded with a grin as she swept into the bathroom—and stopped dead.

The grin froze on her face. The door closed behind her and the click was as loud as a rifle shot in the eerie quiet.

"Do da, do da, do da, do da," Maddie whispered, mocking the famous notes of the *Twilight Zone* intro.

A nervous giggle escaped her lips as she scanned the room. A square oak cask was fastened to the wall above an odd-looking commode. A cast-iron pipe connected the two pieces, and a gold chain dangled from the cask. The washbasin was a round porcelain bowl on a stand. Along one wall sat a true, honest-to-goodness claw-footed bathtub with gold detail and an ancient looking spigot extended from the wall.

"Modern facilities?" No way. She'd installed fixtures designed to look old-fashioned. These were no replicas: they *were* old-fashioned.

She shook her head to clear the cobwebs. They'd drugged her; she remembered the foul-tasting liquid Sarah had given her when she first arrived. Between that and the accident it was possible she was hallucinating.

She made quick use of the commode, watching with amazement as she pulled the chain. The spigot on the wall yielded lukewarm water but Maddie didn't care. As she immersed her battered body in the slightly off-color water, she sighed. Never had she wanted, or needed, a bath as much as she did then. On the shelf over the tub she found not only towels but lilac-scented soap, a can of tooth powder—to be applied with a soft cloth or bristled brush according to the instructions—and bath salts. She used it all.

The towels were large and fluffy and smelled of sunshine the way her mother's used to. With her hair washed and the foul-smelling liniment removed, Maddie felt refreshed. Even her aches and pains seemed to have eased quite a bit. She inspected her body as best she could in the small, somewhat distorted mirror over the washbasin. The small cut on her shoulder looked minor. The bruises covering her legs and arms had already turned to a greenish yellow color. Only her thigh, where the bumper of the car had hit her, looked serious. The stitches were small and neat with no sign of infection, though.

No matter how she felt about these people and their methods, she couldn't deny she'd been well cared for. Still, she'd be glad when she could call Genevieve and get back to the real world and out of this place. All these nineteenth-century antiquities were giving her the heebie-jeebies.

Reluctantly Maddie put the gown and robe back on. As she caught sight of herself in the mirror once more, she hesitated. All the frills and lace she'd thought busy earlier seemed almost otherworldly in the wavering glass. Her hair fell over her shoulders and her green eyes sparkled out of her pale face. With a shrug she turned away. Maybe there was something to be said for the Victorian peignoir set after all.

She met Devon Crowe coming up the stairs, a tray in his hands. "Since you seemed so much better I had Sarah prepare you a proper breakfast. You must be famished."

The aroma drifted up to tease her nose as Devon directed her to a room across the hall. She was surprised to see it was some kind of sunroom with long windows leading out onto an upper veranda. The wide French doors were thrown open and a magnolia-scented breeze wafted in.

Her stomach growled loudly and Devon looked over his shoulder and grinned, setting the tray on a low table. Maddie smiled back, a tight quickening fluttering her stomach which she knew had nothing to do with hunger. What a devastating face this peculiar man had when he smiled.

Her gaze drifted over the wicker furniture and she relaxed. At last, something normal. The cushions were covered in a bright, cheerful floral pattern of rose and pale green. The table held a small centerpiece of fresh-cut flowers. A cup and saucer sat beside a newspaper. Someone must have already breakfasted in here this morning. Maddie wondered if it was Devon Crowe.

She ambled over to the paper and casually flipped to the front page. Her mouth twisted as she scanned the curious headings and print. It was a copy of the *Gulf Herald*, a paper she'd read herself a thousand times.

A freezing chill trapped her breath in her throat. "Where did you get this newspaper, Mr. Crowe?" Maddie asked, trying to keep the terror out of her voice. She didn't succeed. Devon turned away from the low table and came to her side. A tremble started in her knees and worked its way up her body until she could feel her teeth chatter. Devon looked from the paper to her ashen face and his eyes widened.

"It isn't fresh, Miss St. Thomas. I'm afraid the news you'll find in there is a bit stale."

Maddie released a whoosh of air and sank into the nearest chair. For a minute there she thought she'd really lost it. A bit stale was obviously Devon Crowe's idea of a joke. The relic dated May 31, 1892 was more than a hundred years old!

"We're quite a ways from Gulf Island, you know. It takes at least a week for the paper to arrive. That one came yesterday evening. As you can see by the date it's nine days old."

The room shifted suddenly and Maddie grasped the table for support. Nine days! Dear God, had she lost her mind? Or had she, as the evidence seemed to indicate, lost a century?

Chapter Four

Maddie flew from the chair like a woman possessed, clutching the front of Devon Crowe's snowy white shirt.

"Why are you doing this to me?" she cried. "What kind of horrible, cruel trick is this? I admit it's all very effective, the clothes, the furniture, the *modern* facilities, but this is too much. You're trying to make me think I've gone crazy. Why, Mr. Crowe? Who are you and why are you doing this to me?"

Devon's face registered shock Maddie was certain mirrored her own. He grasped her shoulders and eased her back into the chair, prying her fingers from his shirt. "Please, calm down, Madeline. No one here wants to hurt you. We've done only what was best for you."

"Best for me?" Maddie leaned away from the man. "What is best for me is just to get to a phone and call my sister." She met his wide-eyed stare and her own gaze narrowed. "Are you willing to let me use the phone to call Genevieve?" She was testing him. If this man had some nefarious scheme, he'd never let her near a telephone.

"If I had a telephone I'd be happy to take you to it. But as I told you, we are a ways out. There are no telephones in this area. If you can tell me who your sister is and where she lives I'll be happy to send word to her immediately."

"I thought as much," Maddie said, slipping from the chair on the side farthest away from Devon. "No telephone, huh? That's a bit odd, isn't it? I mean you have to search pretty hard to find a place without a phone nowadays."

Four tiny lines appeared between Devon's eyebrows and the tic returned to his cheek as Maddie backed away toward the hall. "Odd? I don't know what you mean. Mr. Bell's invention has become commonplace in the city, but here it's still just another contraption we've yet to adopt." One eyebrow lifted sardonically and he added, "Like the automobile."

"I'm getting out of here," Maddie said, turning to flee the room. There was no way this man could keep her. She'd fight her way out if she had to. My God, this was like something out of a Stephen King novel. But she'd be damned if she'd stick around and find out what little surprises they had in store for her next.

"Madeline!"

Devon's voice spurred Maddie on. She slowed outside the bedroom where she'd been kept, briefly considering trying to get her clothes and Genny's medicine. But the sound of Devon's boots hurrying along the hall tapped out a warning. If he caught her now he might never give her another chance to escape. Bunching the cumbersome gown and robe at her waist, she raced for the stairs.

Her bare feet flew over the carpet runner, her calves and knees exposed as she lifted her clothing higher. The stairs loomed ahead, but in her fright they seemed to tunnel, appearing farther away than they were. As she finally reached the first step, the ball of her foot caught on something and her body propelled forward. Teetering on the top step, she struggled for balance, flailing the air uselessly. She was going to fall, and there must be at least 40 steps to the bottom!

Suddenly, strong arms wrapped around her waist and she was snatched back just as her feet left the step. The momentum of the reverse direction sent both her and Devon Crowe tumbling back onto the landing in a heap.

In a tangle of lace and ruffles they rolled. Devon held her in his embrace, supporting his weight so she never took the full brunt of the fall. When they stopped, Maddie found herself pinned beneath Devon. His face was tucked into her neck, hers against his chest. Her arms were caught between their bodies, but his seemed to cover her back in a protective cocoon. Her knees were drawn up and parted and his thigh rode high in the apex of her legs, caressing the exposed petals of her womanhood.

Heat radiated from the friction of their contact and a whirling tidal wave of awareness swept through her. The moment drew out into an eternity, but Devon never moved. Maddie wondered if he'd been hurt somehow. Was he unconscious? Why didn't he get up?

His breath was hissing in and out near her ear, his heart racing against her chest like a runaway locomotive. His hands clenched the material of her robe and his leg shifted, rubbing the already sensitized nub between her legs.

Maddie couldn't breathe. Her head spun, from more than her malady this time. Her body came to life beneath Devon Crowe's. Her breasts tightened and peaked and a warmth stirred in her. . . .

"Mr. Crowe, are you hurt?" Maddie asked, pushing furiously against his chest. Her wounds protested his weight and the jarring knocks of her fall. But still, she knew she had to move him for other reasons. "Get off me," she cried. This was ridiculous! How could she possibly respond to this lunatic in that way? Good God, what kind of drugs had they given her? She'd never responded to any man so instantly and spontaneously.

Devon's head came off Maddie's shoulder and he glared into her face. The look in his eyes stole Maddie's breath and she fell still beneath him once more.

"What the bloody hell do you think you're doing?" he demanded, purposely resting his weight against her lower body. She struggled, but he successfully held her in place.

Had he felt her body's response? Did he know her libido'd gone haywire just because she had a hard, male body draped across her? What could she say? Yes, Mr. Crowe, I'm aroused.

"What—what do you mean?"

"What do I mean?" he said, the dimple in his jaw flashing in and out like a neon sign. His navy eyes blackened with fury and his hands came out from under her and gripped the sides of her face. "I'm talking about nearly killing us both, Miss St. Thomas. I'm talking about that stupid feat you just attempted. What the hell is wrong with you, woman? And this time don't give me any of your folderol and foolishness. Straight talk, Miss St. Thomas, and answers. God knows I've been patient enough."

Maddie saw the anger and fear in Devon's eyes. But more than that she saw the sincerity. He'd risked his own life to save her from falling. If he hadn't been able to steady them they'd both have fallen. She swallowed hard, her body beginning to quiver.

"I just want to go home," she said, willing the shaking to go away.

Devon didn't move and after a moment Maddie whispered, "You're hurting me."

Instantly he pushed himself up, lifting her in his arms. He carried her to the bedroom she'd occupied and kicked the door closed behind him. Depositing her on the chair by the fireplace, he stepped back.

"Now," he said firmly. "I have been patient and as accommodating as I know how to be. But I want answers, Miss St. Thomas."

Maddie could only nod. He deserved complete honesty after all he'd done. Even if his methods were bizarre, he'd taken her in and cared for her. He'd been, as he said, patient and hospitable. And, she now knew, even though she was loath to admit it, he was right.

Devon looked surprised by Maddie's compliance but he quickly recovered himself and fired the first question. "Who are you?"

Maddie swallowed, rearranged herself on the chair, and twisted her hands in her lap. She figured, in for a dime, in for a dollar. If she was going to tell Devon the truth, she might as well tell it all.

"My name is Madeline St. Thomas. I'm an interior decorator from Gulf Island, Florida. I was on my way to see my sister Genevieve Lord in Brewster, Alabama, when my car broke down." She saw the now familiar—and annoying—dimple in his jaw and tipped her chin up defiantly. "I was trying to get to a nearby phone when a car came out of nowhere and hit me, knocking me over the embankment into Crowe Lake."

Devon's eyes widened and he sank into the chair opposite her. "There is no Crowe Lake," he told her, eyeing her closely as though he suspected his announcement might set off another fit. She really couldn't blame him after the incident with the newspaper.

"There is where I came from."

"Gulf Island? I've been there. It's a resort off the mainland of Florida, south of Pensacola, about forty miles from here. There's no lake bearing my name anywhere between here and there."

"Not in May of eighteen ninety-two there isn't," she said, taking a deep breath to steady her erratic heart. "But in June of nineteen ninety-two there is."

As though shot from the proverbial cannon, Devon left the chair and whipped around to stand behind it. "What a foolish thing to say, Miss St. Thomas. How would you know what will be in this area a hundred years from now?"

"Because I live in this area a hundred years from now. That is if the newspaper in the sunroom is accurate."

"Accurate?"

Maddie stood also, feeling slightly intimidated staring up at Devon. Her height put them almost at eye level. "You said it was nine days old?" He nodded. "It was dated May thirty-one, eighteen ninety-two. The paper I read the morning I left for my sister's house was dated June twentieth." She paused and met his eyes with a look of both confusion and determination. *"Nineteen hundred and ninety-two."*

Disbelief and horror crossed Devon Crowe's face and he stepped back, away from Maddie. His hands came up as if to ward her off and she almost smiled. He thought she was crazy and it frightened him. A noise sounded from the hall and, startled, he faced the door, then quickly turned back to Maddie as if he didn't dare take his eyes off her for an instant. She guessed under the circumstances she couldn't blame him.

"Miss St. Thomas." He paused, collected himself, and continued. "Madeline, you mustn't say things like that. Not even in jest. If anyone should hear you you'd be sent to an asylum and there'd be little I, or anyone else, could do to help you."

Maddie's pulse quickened at the sound of her name coming from Devon's lips. He'd changed to the less formal form of address in an attempt to soothe her. Like calming a frightened child, she thought. But the warm timbre of his voice started very adult feelings in the pit of her stomach.

"Maybe I am crazy," she concluded. "Or else you and everyone in this house are, which is unlikely." She bit her bottom lip and turned toward the empty fireplace, shivering and wishing for its warmth. "If it is indeed June ninth, eighteen ninety-two, then I'm in the wrong century. And I don't think its the drugs Sarah gave me or any head injury. I think maybe I died, in my time. And somehow ended up here, in yours." Her voice shook and she crossed her arms to rub her chilled flesh.

Devon came up behind her and wrapped his arms around her. His body pressed tight against her back and he drew her into the circle of his embrace. He massaged her arms and shoulders gently.

"You're trembling," he said, as if to explain his actions. "Don't upset yourself. You certainly are not dead. Whatever happened, I'll help you. You'll be safe here until you get your memory back or until these fantasies go away."

He didn't believe her, Maddie realized with dismay. But then why should he? Would she have believed him if the tables were turned? Not a chance. She'd have run for the nearest phone and called the men in white coats from Chattahoochee Mental Hospital.

His arms were strong and secure and Maddie felt herself relaxing. So what if he didn't believe her? He was offering his help and that was one thing she needed right now. No matter how she'd come to be in this time warp, she was here. And until she found a way out, it seemed she was stuck. A friend would come in handy under the circumstances.

"You're still willing to help me?"

His chin rested atop her head and she could feel the warmth of his breath stir her hair. His arms tightened and then released her. He took her elbow in a gallant gesture and led her back to her seat. Then he did the most astounding thing Maddie had ever seen. He knelt on the floor in front of her chair and took her hands in his. Tears threatened as he warmed her fingers between his clasped hands.

"Don't worry, Madeline. I'd never turn such a beautiful damsel out into the streets when she is so obviously in need of rescuing. I'm nobody's knight in shining armor, but neither am I an ogre."

A small smile crossed Maddie's face and Devon responded with an answering grin. Oh, how wrong he was! she thought. This man had to be from a bygone era. Because such true gallantry had long since died.

She lay on the bed, the covers pulled to her chin. Her eyes were closed, her breathing slow and rhythmic. She slept.

Devon released a ragged sigh and let his head fall back against the chair back. Who was this woman? he wondered for at least the hundredth time. Where did she come from? What was she doing here?

He knew he'd get no answers until she'd had a chance to recover. She'd been badly injured. How, he didn't know, since he didn't believe for a minute that wild tale she'd told about being struck by an automobile.

Even Aunt Bev could outrun those noisy, cumbersome contraptions he'd seen on display at the World's Fair. No, this woman hadn't been run down by an automobile. Then what had happened? And why had she made up that bizarre story? Had someone done this to her? A husband perhaps? The thought sickened Devon. If indeed a man had caused this woman's injuries, Devon would make damn sure he didn't get another chance.

He didn't know what it was about Madeline St. Thomas, but she brought out feelings in him he couldn't deny. Emotions like possessiveness and longing filled him. He kept glancing at her just to assure himself she was all right.

Her outburst earlier had shaken him to the core. If he hadn't caught up with her she'd have tumbled down the stairs and probably broken her neck. He resisted the urge to go to her and hold her as she slept. Even now his body ached to press against hers and feel her heart beat and her chest rise and fall with steady breaths.

Anthony said she'd be fine in a few weeks. Devon wondered what shape *he'd* be in by that time. His heart raced and his loins tightened every time he remembered the feel of her naked flesh pressed against his thigh. Even now he felt his body respond and he shifted to relieve the pressure in his trousers.

She stirred and Devon pushed out of his chair. He eased to the bed and leaned over. Even with the bruises and scrapes on her face he couldn't help marveling at her beauty. Her thick lashes brushed her cheeks, and her lips were full and slightly parted. Her nose was tiny and rounded, a little mound in the center of her face. Her skin wasn't milky white like most women's but had a warm tan. It made her look healthy somehow, despite her battered condition.

The knob on the bedroom door twisted and Devon stood frozen by Maddie's bed, guilt at his actions plainly written on his face. If he didn't stay away from this woman he'd compromise both their reputations.

Aunt Beverly poked her head around the doorjamb and tipped her chin up. After a second she pointed her finger right at his chest. Devon released his breath and she crooked her finger, directing him into the hall.

Knowing better than to ignore her summons, he quietly crossed the room. But he couldn't leave without one long, last look at the woman behind him. He closed the door and went to where Beverly stood awaiting him.

"I thought I'd find you there," she said, a frown creasing her already wrinkled forehead.

"I was just looking in on her," he hedged. "After that scene earlier I·wanted to be sure she'd calmed down."

"Sarah's been taking care of her, Devon. There was no reason for you to trouble yourself."

"The woman's my responsibility while she's here. I'll satisfy myself she's settled."

"What is it, Devon? You haven't been yourself since you brought her here. Do you know something about her?" Beverly's blank eyes stared into his and for a moment it seemed she could look into his soul.

Devon sighed and rubbed his fingers over his mustache. "I know very little," he admitted. "I wish that I knew more. All I know is, there is something strange about that woman."

"Strange? In what way?"

Clearly Beverly thought she'd missed seeing something vital. How could Devon explain it was not something you could see with your eyes? He felt it, though. Deep inside, something stirred each time he thought about Madeline St. Thomas, but it was more than mere attraction.

"I don't know. Perhaps we can learn more once she's rested." He straightened and cleared his throat. It had been his duty to help the girl; he'd had no choice. But he'd waste no time finding out the truth about her. He told himself his urge to know more about her stemmed from his duty to protect his home and family.

"Rest assured, I intend to learn all there is to know about Madeline St. Thomas before very much longer."

"You're keeping something from me," Aunt Bev said.

Devon considered lying but knew it would be useless. She'd see through him if he tried.

"After she fled the dayroom I questioned her and she told the most fantastic story."

Aunt Bev waited for him to continue, but Devon didn't know what to say. Finally, he decided to be frank. "She claims to be from the future, Aunt Bev. She went wild and wove the oddest tale I've ever heard."

"The future? Surely you misunderstood, Devon."

"No, Aunt Bev, that is what she said. I'm afraid she's—"

"What? What are you thinking?"

He saw Beverly's hands twisting in her skirt. She'd come to care for the girl in a short time. Why? he wondered. What was it about Madeline St. Thomas?

Even though Beverly couldn't see him, or read his expression, he looked away. "I'm afraid the woman is touched, Aunt Bev. She went berserk. You wouldn't have believed it."

He raked his hands through his hair and then over his face as if to erase the memory of Maddie racing for the stairs, her hair flying out behind her, legs bare to the thigh as she pulled her gown up to her waist.

He thought of the odd cases, with their strange markings. His fingers had itched to open them and search for some clue to her identity, but the markings stopped him. Pharmaceuticals. He understood enough about the word to know it dealt with medicine. Would he find proof she'd escaped from an asylum? And would that proof force him to make choices he wasn't ready to make yet?

"No, oh, no, Devon. Surely she's just confused. Maybe the accident—"

"I wish that were true, honestly I do. But I'm afraid this woman may actually have escaped confinement somewhere." He confessed his fears to Beverly, confident her reaction would be similar to his own. "Obviously she doesn't want us to know where she's really from, hence the bizarre tale about the future. And the injuries were probably caused by her escape or by something which occurred afterward. Remember, she didn't have decent clothes when I found her."

"What are you going to do, Devon? I can't bear the thought of that child in one of those horrid places."

"Neither can I." He reached out and patted Beverly's back in a reassuring gesture. Keeping his arm draped across her shoulders, he led her to the dayroom. "I'll think it over thoroughly before making a decision. You know how I feel about asylums and hospitals. We won't send her back unless there's no other choice. Perhaps I'll speak with Anthony again, let him know the latest."

"But Devon, he's a medical doctor. I know he's your friend, but won't he feel she should be institutionalized?"

"I don't know. Maybe you're right." He led her to a chair by the open French doors and seated her there, placing a quick kiss on her wrinkled cheek. "Don't worry. I'll take care of Madeline. She'll be fine."

Beverly smiled and turned her face toward the sunshine coming in through the open doors. For a moment Devon stood looking out across the lawn, deep in thought. Could he bear to see Madeline put away in an asylum? He glanced down at his aunt and knew he had to consider her safety first. If it turned out the woman was dangerous, he knew he'd do whatever was necessary to protect the people who depended on him.

"Devon?"

"Yes, Aunt Bev?" He tucked his hands in his pockets and dragged his eyes from the peaceful scenery outside.

"Is it possible? I mean, could she be telling the truth?"

Devon almost wished he *could* believe her. It would make the feelings she stirred in him easier to deal with. But he knew he had to face the facts. No doubt the woman was touched. How else could her odd behavior be explained?

"The truth as she sees it, possibly. That's why she's so convincing." He realized with a start that Madeline had been *very* convincing. The hair on his nape rose and bristled.

"Poor soul," Beverly whispered.

He placed his hand on her shoulder and she covered it with her own. "We'll look out for her. At least she won't be alone."

They shared a brief moment, each thinking of Devon's poor mother, Olivia. She'd gone mad with grief when his father was killed. Devon was a teenager and Beverly had recently been wounded in a carriage accident. He'd gone to her to help care for her, leaving his mother alone. Later, when he returned, she was gone. He'd searched for her, finally finding her in Arrowcreek Hospital for the Mentally and Criminally Insane. A shudder shook him as he remembered the sight and, oh God, the *smell* of the place.

No! Madeline St. Thomas would never again have to face that if he could help it. Unless she proved a threat to his family, he'd find some other way to help her.

Chapter Five

A knock on her door awakened Maddie for the second time that day. She scooted up in the big bed and brushed her tumbled hair out of her face.

"Come in," she called, wondering how she looked and wondering why it mattered. When she saw Devon Crowe's aunt peer around the door she suddenly knew why. She'd hoped it would be Devon.

"Am I disturbing you?" Beverly Crowe asked, stepping further into the room.

"No, not at all. Please, come in." Maddie thought it strange the way the woman looked right at you sometimes, as though she could see. Brushing off the odd sensations, Maddie told herself it must be because the woman hadn't always been blind. Apparently at some time in her life she'd had the gift of sight and her movements now were merely leftover gestures.

"I thought we might dine together. It would give us a chance to get better acquainted."

"I'd like that," Maddie told her honestly, glad for the company. She was quickly growing tired of being confined to this room and this bed, no matter how lovely they were.

Beverly motioned to someone in the hall and Maddie smiled as Sarah entered with a huge tray. "I took the liberty of having Sarah prepare the tray," Beverly confessed with a smile.

Maddie pushed the covers aside and quickly cleared a spot on the bedside table. She glanced around for somewhere to sit and saw that one of the tapestry chairs was once again beside her bed. She went to Devon's aunt and led the woman to the chair, then reseated herself on the edge of the high bed.

"This looks wonderful," she said, smiling at Sarah as she eyed the plates of baked chicken, rice with cream gravy, snap beans, and fried corn. A basket of biscuits made her mouth water as Sarah drew back the dishcloth cover. Even the glasses of milk held their own appeal. "I'll put on twenty pounds just smelling all this food."

Sarah beamed and handed a freshly pressed linen napkin into Beverly's hand. "Get on with you," she teased Maddie, draping her napkin across her lap. Maddie laughed and Beverly and Sarah shared a conspiratorial grin.

"From what Devon tells me I don't think a few pounds would make the slightest difference," Beverly told her. Sarah swept out of the room, her wide, white grin still in place. As the door closed, Maddie realized Devon's aunt probably knew as much about her by now as she herself knew. Blind or not, she was the most observant woman Maddie had ever known.

"He told you what I looked like?" Maddie asked, actually feeling a blush creep up her neck.

"I asked your size when we were trying to find you something to wear. He very politely told me you had the figure of a goddess."

A goddess! Maddie laughed out loud. She'd been a size eight since high school but she knew too well she'd never be able to stay that size eating meals such as this. Still, for some reason she felt a glow of pleasure that Devon had been impressed with her figure. Maybe all those aerobics classes and workout tapes had paid off.

"I hope you don't mind that I questioned Devon and Sarah about you. You'll find I ask a lot of questions. It's how I keep abreast of everything around me. I imagine it becomes tedious sometimes, describing everyday things, but they love me and so they oblige me."

"I don't mind at all," Maddie said, realizing just how true it was. If she were to find herself in Beverly's place, it would be the small things in life she'd miss seeing the most. She looked over and noticed that Beverly had already begun to eat. Her blindness did not inhibit her at that task either, Maddie noticed. Apparently Sarah arranged the food on the plate so Beverly would know exactly where everything was.

Maddie enjoyed her meal, but as she suspected she couldn't even put a dent in the massive amounts of food. Everything tasted so good though, she made an effort to at least taste all the dishes.

"So, Sarah tells me you're healing nicely," Beverly said, after a few minutes of silence.

Maddie swallowed a bite of flaky biscuit and washed it down with the rich milk. "Yes. I don't know what she used on me; it smelled terrible, but it worked wonders."

"Ah, Sarah's famous for her salve. A miracle cure, I always said. I'm relieved you haven't suffered any aftereffects."

Maddie paused with a forkful of rice halfway to her mouth. Was she imagining it, or was Beverly's statement more a question?

"No," she said, carefully watching the older woman. "Not a one. Sarah said she'd remove the stitches tomorrow and I should be as good as new in no time."

"Fine, fine," Beverly murmured, wiping her mouth on her napkin and then setting her plate on the table without even hesitating. Her steady-handedness was almost eerie, and Maddie shivered.

"Maddie," Beverly said, looking directly into Maddie's eyes. "Devon told me about your conversation this morning. He was very concerned."

Maddie froze. Was this it? Would Beverly deliver the message that Devon Crowe wanted the nutty woman out of his house, the sooner the better? She tried to speak and felt her throat tighten. Where would she go if they threw her out?

She knew as surely as she knew anything these days that she'd somehow come to be in another century. Unfortunately, whoever delivered her here forgot to tell her how she was supposed to get by in this forgotten period. Certainly she couldn't get a decorating job. Besides, all she really wanted was to find her way back to her time.

"I've upset you," Beverly deduced, reaching across to touch Maddie's hand. No fumbling, no probing. Her touch was right on target. Maddie jumped. "I apologize."

Maddie studied the woman for a long moment. Could she be faking? Was she truly blind? "It's all right," Maddie lied. "I suppose you both must think you've taken in a real fruitcake."

Beverly surprised Maddie by laughing gaily. "Such a quaint term, Maddie. A fruitcake." She laughed again. "No, not at all. At least *I* don't think you're mentally unbalanced."

"And Devon?" Maddie forced herself to ask.

Beverly dabbed at her eye with her napkin, wiping away a tear of mirth. "Ah, my nephew is a little stuffy at times. He likes things to be neat and precise. Let's just say you've rippled his pond."

This time Maddie laughed with Beverly. She couldn't help but like Devon's aunt. The woman saw without benefit of sight and had probably forgotten more than most people would ever know about human nature.

Maddie set her plate on the table and settled herself more comfortably on the bed. Beverly rose from her chair and unerringly seated herself next to Maddie. She took her hand, looked into her face, and smiled like a child.

"Tell me about the future, Maddie."

A swift, harsh breath escaped Maddie and she snatched her hand from Beverly's grasp. What did this mean? Could Devon's aunt possibly believe her? Maddie's heart soared! Oh, to have someone she could talk to would be wonderful. But her relief was short-lived. She couldn't share her fears with anyone without appearing insane.

"What do you mean?"

"Oh, come on, Maddie. You might disconcert Devon, but I've seen a lot of things in my time and I know some of them were unexplainable. I may not have my vision anymore, but I still have a sharp mind."

Beverly stood and walked across to the dressing table. She fingered the items laid out there as though touching old friends.

"Devon told me about the automobile that hit you and the lake you claim to have fallen into. And I took your clothes from Sarah when she removed them. I may not have been able to see them, but I haven't forgotten the feel of silk in my hands." She turned to Maddie and smiled and again Maddie felt the tension ease from her body. This woman meant her no harm. Somehow Maddie knew that.

"Devon thinks you may have escaped from a sanitarium." She paused and Maddie held her breath. "But I've never known an asylum to outfit their patients in silk. Besides, those were the most interesting undergarments I've ever seen."

Maddie admired the way the woman could "see" with her hands, but she wished this time she hadn't been so astute. Deciding discretion would be the better part of valor this time, Maddie remained silent.

"Are there really machines that fly through the air?"

Maddie cursed her reaction but there was no way she could have suppressed the gasp which escaped her. Beverly smiled triumphantly and hurried back to the bed.

"There are, aren't there? Big silver cigar-shaped things with wings?" she queried excitedly.

"How can you know that?" Maddie demanded, her voice quavering more than a little now. What was it about this woman? She was uncanny.

79

Beverly looked almost childlike as she smiled with anticipation. "Is it true?" she persisted.

Maddie could not lie. If it were a ploy to trip her up somehow, she'd probably fallen right into it, but she couldn't bring herself to outright lie to Devon's aunt. "Yes."

Beverly grabbed Maddie's hands and giggled. "Oh, how I wish I were going to be around when these things are in their heyday. It must be thrilling to live with such miracles!"

Maddie thought how she'd taken such things for granted until now. What a shame people in her time didn't appreciate all the inventions these people would never know. Lord knows, when she got back to 1992 she'd view things differently.

"How did you know?" Maddie had to know. Could Beverly somehow be from her time? Was it possible? Maddie almost laughed. She'd traversed the time barrier and yet she still questioned its possibility. No wonder Devon thought she'd escaped from the loony bin.

"When I lost my sight the Lord saw fit to compensate my loss."

Maddie tipped her head and settled her hands more firmly into Beverly's. The woman's eyes were bright with excitement, yet Maddie sensed she was struggling to remain cheerful. "You have second sight?" Maddie breathed.

Beverly smiled. "No, nothing so dramatic as that. But I have dreams, Maddie. And in these dreams I see the most fantastic things. I've always wondered if I was meant to do something about the things I saw, but alas, I'm no inventor." She lifted her hands in a gesture of resignation. "It remains a mystery why the dreams were given to me."

Boy, Maddie could sure identify with that feeling. Ever since she'd come to the conclusion she'd traveled through time she'd been trying to figure out *why*. She knew next to nothing about history—it had never been her best subject—and she couldn't offer any assistance to these people since she, like Beverly, was no inventor. She couldn't tell them how to build machines, or cars. Face it, Maddie, she thought, your talents aren't exactly in demand in 1892.

"What is it, Maddie?" Beverly asked, frowning at Maddie's silence. "Something's bothering you."

Could she trust this woman? Maddie wondered. It would be great to have someone to talk to. But at the same time Maddie still felt sure anything she said would make her seem totally mad.

"Miss Crowe—"

"Oh, no, Maddie," Beverly cut her off. "We're going to be a lot closer than that. I already feel as though I've known you for years. I'm Aunt Bev."

"Aunt Bev." Maddie tried the name out on her tongue and wasn't surprised to find it flowed off like it was second nature. Yes, she knew what Beverly meant. For some reason, Maddie knew she had landed where she was supposed to be. Somehow, she was connected to these people even before the car hit her. She cleared her throat.

"Aunt Bev, I don't know why I'm here. I feel certain I'm where I'm supposed to be." She hesitated, not quite sure how to continue.

"Of course you are. Like my dreams, Maddie, there are no mystical mistakes. We may not know why we've been chosen, but we must trust that whoever did this, knows their business."

Maddie wasn't so sure. Was she going to be stuck here forever, or was there some way back? And if not, how was she going to support herself in the nineteenth century? What could she possibly offer in the way of help? She'd watched that popular television show where the guy flits through time fixing errors and correcting history. Maddie couldn't do that. Besides, she didn't even know how she'd gotten here. She knew she'd never become adept at century-hopping.

"I'm scared," she finally admitted, looking to see how Devon's aunt would react to her weakness. But the woman merely smiled again and hugged Maddie to her bosom.

"Of course you are, dear. That's why you're here. So you won't have to go through this alone. Together we're going to figure out your place in the scheme of things."

And then what? Maddie wondered. Would she be zapped back to her own time like the guy on TV? Or would she stay in 1892 forever?

*   *   *

Devon heard the laughter from the parlor the minute he closed the front door behind him. Aunt Beverly's rich tones he recognized immediately. But the soft, seductive chuckle took him by surprise. Gooseflesh rose on his arms as the sound seemed to seep through him, centering in his loins. Lord, how was he going to live with that woman in his house if just the sound of her laughter brought him to full mast?

Tossing his hat onto the parson's bench in the foyer, he stepped lightly to the parlor door and peered inside.

"Okay, okay," Maddie said, fluttering her arms in the air. She sat at his piano, the full skirts of a brilliant yellow cotton day dress spread on the stool around her. Her blonde hair was drawn back with a matching ribbon and her green eyes flashed with laughter.

Without warning her hands sank down on the keys and Devon winced as she began to pound out a loud, raucous tune. Her voice pierced his ears as she lifted her head and sang about crocodiles rocking 'round the clock. He automatically glanced behind him to make certain no one else was present to hear the woman's bizarre behavior. It was bad enough his aunt and Sarah were in the parlor, but he could count on them to keep the scene a secret. If only he could shut the woman up before she brought all the workers running.

To his surprise she finished off the ditty with a flourish and Beverly and Sarah clapped as though she'd performed Beethoven. Devon shot the women a frowning look, then turned back to his houseguest.

Maddie noticed him and all signs of humor fled from her face. Like a candle flame, the light in her eyes winked out. Her pretty bow mouth thinned into a tight line and her brow furrowed.

"I—I was just . . ." she mumbled, looking to Beverly, then back to him.

"Is that you, Devon?" Beverly asked, turning toward the parlor door.

Devon stepped into the room. "Yes, Aunt," he said, crossing to her and lightly kissing her cheek.

"I thought as much. No one can rain on a parade the way you do, boy."

Devon stiffened, certain he heard a snicker behind him. Sarah hid her grin behind a cough and excused herself to go to the kitchen.

"I didn't mean to break up your party, ladies, but might I remind you we decided to keep Miss St. Thomas's presence here as quiet as possible to keep down questions."

"*You* decided that, Devon. I said we'd keep the details of her arrival a secret. As far as anyone knows, Maddie is my dear friend Grace's daughter, visiting from out of town."

"Yes, just how far out we aren't sure."

Maddie paled, but she refused to look away from Devon's piercing eyes.

"Devon!" Beverly admonished.

"I apologize, Miss St. Thomas," he said, truly repentant. "That remark was ungentlemanly and uncalled for."

"This is your house, Mr. Crowe. You have every right to say whatever you like."

Devon's guilt doubled. He'd hurt the woman with his remark and succeeded in making her uncomfortable once more when she'd seemed almost happy moments before. Feeling like a cad, he decided to try to make up for his cruelty. After all, he knew it was his attraction to her that had him upset, not the woman herself.

"That is no excuse," he said, walking toward her. He took her fingers and bent at the waist, placing his lips against the back of her hand. The gesture almost undid him as he touched the smooth skin with his lips, smelled the lilac soap she'd used to bathe with, and felt her fingers tremble.

"You look lovely this afternoon," he told her, making the compliment sound casual, though he'd never meant words more in his life.

Maddie swallowed hard. "Thank you," she replied, surprised she could speak past the lump that rose in her throat.

"That's more like it," Beverly said, rising from the sofa. "And since Maddie will be our guest for a while, I think we should all forgo the formalities."

Maddie and Devon stared at one another. Somewhere in her mind it registered that he still held her hand, but she couldn't think of a discreet way to request he release it. His thumb slipped across her knuckles and she sucked in a breath.

Devon seemed to snap out of the spell which held them, and he dropped her hand. "Yes, of course," he said to Beverly, his gaze never leaving Maddie. "Maddie?"

Maddie could only nod her approval. Her heart fluttered from more than the exertion of singing. Her breasts rose and fell rapidly.

"Now, then," Beverly said. "Maddie was showing us some of the more popular music of her . . ." Her voice trailed off and she hesitated. "Where she comes from," she finally finished.

Maddie could see the flicker of annoyance in Devon's eyes. Obviously her origin was a sore spot with her host. She'd do well to play down their previous conversations for the time being and pretend she was exactly what Beverly suggested. A visiting friend from out of town.

"Well then, perhaps she'll play another tune before we dress for dinner."

Maddie almost laughed out loud at Devon's expression. No doubt he had to force the request out. Her musical talent wouldn't win any awards, even in her time. She didn't play the piano very well, really. Genevieve held that distinction. Maddie had always put on skits, though, pretending she was Elton John or Mick Jagger in her teens. There was one song she'd actually taken the time to learn to play and she smiled at Devon Crowe as she seated herself on the stool once more.

Her fingers shook as she gently played the first notes. Her voice quavered as she sang softly.

Devon felt the warmth of desire wash through him anew as Maddie's voice sang about a "desperado." The words were confusing, but the tone was universal. She sang with her heart and Devon felt his own respond to the call of love. He stood, not moving, not even breathing as she closed her eyes, her voice fading out on the last words of the ballad.

Silence filled the room, holding the trio in suspension as the echoes of the piano's last notes drifted away on the sunbeams from the window.

Beverly was the one who finally broke the stillness. She applauded lightly as she stepped up next to her nephew and elbowed his ribs. Devon winced from the unexpected poke and joined Beverly in clapping.

Maddie felt foolish and self-conscious as she rose from the piano stool. Just the way she had when she'd performed that song in front of her whole high school at the annual talent contest. But she knew now, as she had then, that she'd earned a blue ribbon. Devon might not appreciate her music, but no one could deny the feelings present in that particular song.

"That was truly wonderful, Maddie," he said, holding her gaze again as he had earlier. Maddie decided she'd have to watch out around Devon. The man exuded masculine

appeal and she seemed particularly suscep-
tible to his charm. Odd, since she'd never
been one whose head could be turned by a
handsome face.

"Yes, indeed," Beverly concurred. "Now, I
think we should change for dinner, as I'm sure
Sarah will be calling us anytime now."

Maddie allowed herself to be led out of the
parlor by Devon's aunt and she was halfway to
the massive stairway before she remembered
she was being directed by a blind woman.
Slowing her steps, she kept pace with Beverly
as they reached the first step.

"I have a picture of this house in my head
that is as clear as any drawn map, Maddie.
I have lived here many years, so don't fret
about my falling down those steps and doing
myself in."

"How did you know I was wondering about
that?" Maddie asked, deciding she would not
try to hide anything else from Devon's aunt.
Obviously it did no good anyway.

"Everyone wonders the same thing," Beverly
told her. "In that, you are no different."

They climbed the steps without incident and
Beverly stopped directly outside Maddie's bedroom.

Maddie spontaneously leaned over and
kissed Aunt Bev on the cheek. "Thank you,"
she whispered. "For everything."

Beverly nodded and proceeded down the hall
to her own chamber. Maddie slipped into her
room and was astounded to find another two

dresses altered and ready to wear lying across the foot of her bed. They belonged to Beverly but she'd given them to Sarah to be fitted for Maddie. One was lavender with yellow stripes and a flounce of crocheted lace across the bodice. The other was rich, jade green silk.

Maddie decided the silk would be the best choice for dinner and she quickly began to change. Her reflection in the cheval mirror looked as though she'd been wearing petticoats and camisoles all her life. No one would know looking at her now that she'd grown up in jeans and sweatshirts, or tank tops and jogging shorts.

How quickly they'd transformed her into a genteel Southern lady, she thought. If only it were that simple. If only she could forget who she really was and where she'd come from.

But Maddie knew she'd never accept that life, as she knew it was out of her reach. And she'd never, ever, stop searching for the way home. No matter how long it took.

Chapter Six

Maddie stared across the table at all the food and wished for a salad.

She could eat very little of the rich beef and broth, mashed potatoes, or buttered vegetables. Lunch still sat heavy in her stomach and she'd be a blimp inside of a week if she started eating the way her hosts did. Not to mention the cholesterol!

"Is anything wrong, Maddie?" Devon asked, obviously concerned about her lack of appetite. He'd been a perfect gentleman since the incident in the parlor and it was hard for Maddie to remember all the reasons she shouldn't be attracted to the man.

"No, not at all," she told him, smiling. "I'm just not used to eating so much."

He quirked an eyebrow curiously, but resisted comment. The brief flash of distress on his face told Maddie he thought she'd come from a place where food was scarce.

"Shall I have Sarah prepare you something else? Perhaps something simpler?"

Maddie couldn't imagine how long it must have taken the servant to fix all this food; there was no way she'd ask for anything else. "No, thank you."

Devon nodded. "As you wish, Maddie." He smiled, a small tipping of one side of his mouth, and Maddie knew he was still perplexed by her. They'd somehow come to a silent understanding after the incident in the parlor. Since then he'd treat her as "Grace's daughter" and she'd try to act the part. It was a thin truce at best, but under the circumstances Maddie couldn't think of anything else to do.

"Were you expecting company, Devon?" Beverly tipped her head, her fork poised in midair. Maddie looked at Devon and saw a range of emotions flit across his face as he recognized the sound of a carriage outside. Confusion, concentration, and finally dismay.

"Dear Lord," he said, tossing his napkin onto the table and scraping his chair back hurriedly. "I forgot to collect Elaine from the station!"

Maddie saw Beverly suppress a wicked grin and she watched the dismay turn to annoyance on Devon's face.

"Not becoming conduct for a bridegroom-to-be, nephew." Beverly clucked her tongue in mock disgust. Devon gave her a hot look and turned to Maddie.

"I apologize," he said. "It will take a good deal of soothing to smooth my fiancée's ruffled feathers. If you'll excuse me."

He left the room before Maddie could form a reply. Not that he'd expected one. The look he'd given her spoke volumes. His fiancée would not be happy about being left at the station, and somehow she felt as though her presence were being blamed for Devon's forgetfulness. Or was it her imagination? Perhaps she felt guilty that she'd been attracted to the man without even inquiring whether he was otherwise attached.

Maddie wanted to leave the table before Devon returned with his fiancée. But Beverly made no move to end the meal so Maddie sat silent. In a moment she heard the front door open and close and Devon's resonant voice reached her ears.

"I have already apologized, Elaine. Do not continue to berate the issue."

A high-pitched reply followed, but the woman was not close enough for Maddie to make out the words.

"Lower your voice," Devon told her. "I told you we have a guest."

"No doubt the reason I was delegated to the far corner of your mind. Where is she?"

Maddie had no trouble understanding the woman now. And it was obvious Elaine had no intention of doing as Devon asked and lowering her voice.

Beverly frowned and pushed her plate aside. Maddie longed to escape to her room, but by now the pair had reached the hall outside the dining room.

"You invited yourself here in the first place, Elaine. Don't expect me to put my life on hold to entertain you."

Maddie nearly gasped at the hard tone Devon used with his fiancée. How rude! She couldn't believe the man who'd shown her, a stranger, such tenderness, could be addressing his beloved with such disdain. And why, for that matter, hadn't anyone mentioned the woman before now? Was there some problem between the pair? she wondered. Perhaps they'd had a spat? It seemed likely as Elaine's next words shrilled through the heavy wood of the door.

"How dare you imply I'm not welcome here," the woman shrieked. "We're to be married in less than two weeks."

"I certainly didn't need you to come all this way just to remind me of that fact, Elaine. I'm not likely to forget it." The sound of a door slamming shut made Maddie jump in her chair. The voices faded away to nothing and she set her napkin aside, prepared to make a run for her room while the couple were otherwise occupied. Beverly's heavy sigh stopped her.

"I'm sorry you had to hear that, Maddie. My nephew isn't at his best around his intended."

Was that why he and Beverly hadn't spoken of her before? Two weeks, she'd said!

The man should be occupied with preparations, not with a convalescing houseguest. Maddie couldn't stop herself from asking, "Then why on earth is he marrying the woman?"

Beverly shook her head. "He doesn't have a choice."

"What are you talking about? Didn't arranged marriages go out of vogue by the end of the nineteenth century?"

Beverly smiled, whether at the question or the way Maddie phrased it she wasn't sure.

"Devon's engagement isn't arranged. At least not in the way you mean. He chose Elaine of his own free will."

Maddie didn't want to hear any more. Putting on clothes and letting Sarah style her hair was one thing, but she had no intention of becoming embroiled in these people's lives any more than necessary. She thought of her attraction to Devon Crowe and silently added, any more than she already had.

"No, that's all right. You don't have to explain anything to me." She stood up, intending to excuse herself and get away while the coast was clear.

"Wait, Maddie." Beverly held her hand up and motioned Maddie back into her seat. "I want you to know why Devon spoke as he did. My nephew is really a kind man."

"You don't have to tell me any of this," Maddie assured her. "Devon's been wonderful, really. If he and his fiancée have some problems, I'm sure they'll work them out in good time."

"No, they won't," Beverly stated baldly, successfully halting Maddie's escape. Curiosity built to a crescendo in Maddie, but she fought the desire to know Devon's story. It was none of her business, she told herself. Still . . .

"They will never work out the problems between them because Devon does not want to. He chose Elaine for the simple reason that she is cold-blooded enough to go along with his plans. Plans, I might add, that I have tried repeatedly to talk him out of."

Okay, Maddie thought, sinking into her seat once more. No one could walk away from a statement like that. "Tell me," she said, knowing Beverly was the one who needed a confidant now.

"Devon's thirty-fifth birthday is in exactly twelve months. According to his father's will he must have an heir on that date or forfeit everything his father left."

"How cruel," Maddie whispered, leaning closer to the table, engrossed now in the tale.

"Not at all," Beverly contradicted. "In fact, Devon suggested the idea himself just a year prior to his father's death. You see, Maddie, so many homes were lost following the war that Devon and his father decided to make sure all their holdings stayed in the Crowe family. To that end they set up a trust specifically for taxes and upkeep which cannot be touched for any other purpose. And they established the terms of the will specifying whoever inherits the estate must have a living heir on their thirty-fifth birthday or forfeit everything to the next male relative with an heir. That way, the lines of inheritance would be soundly established and there would be no chance of the property being sold out of the family should someone die without issue."

"I don't understand. If Devon knew the requirements, why did he wait so long to get married?"

"For a while it looked as though Devon had nothing to worry about. He married a wonderful girl when he was but twenty-five. I suspected all was not as it should be between Devon and Crystal. Their relationship went along, polite and friendly for a time, and I thought they'd eventually work things out. I didn't know that Crystal was in love with someone else."

Maddie felt a wave of shock hit her. Had Devon's wife betrayed him?

"Crystal cared for Devon; they'd grown up together. But she truly loved another man. And then she learned she was expecting a child. The baby belonged to her lover and Crystal knew she could not deceive Devon any longer. She confessed the truth. Devon agreed to forget the incident and claim the child as his own, but Crystal knew she couldn't live with the lie. She planned to leave Devon, divorce him." Beverly stared into empty space, her glassy eyes filled with tears. "She tried to sneak away in the night but there was an accident and Crystal was killed."

"Oh, God, I'm sorry," Maddie whispered, uncomfortable with the older woman's grief. Beverly looked her age for the first time since Maddie had met her. The lines and wrinkles on her face deepened with sadness.

"Devon never forgave himself for not allowing her to leave when she'd asked it of him. And he never forgot her betrayal. He'd have never married again if it had been up to him. But he knows he must produce that all-important heir or forfeit his home and his fortune. And so, he decided on this arrangement with Elaine."

Maddie remained quiet, still unsure what kind of reply to make to such a tale.

"Why Elaine, though?" she finally asked, wondering why Devon would choose to marry someone he obviously held no regard for.

"Quite simply, because there is no chance he will ever lose his heart to her. Child or no child, he is not in danger of falling in love with that woman."

The way Beverly spoke the last two words made Maddie think they were a generous description of Elaine. Suddenly she wanted, no needed, to know more.

"If she's so awful how can he allow her to raise his child?"

Beverly's sharp laugh was without humor. "Elaine has no intention of being saddled with a whelp, as she calls it. She is doing it for the money Devon has agreed to settle on her upon the birth of the child. After that, the marriage will be dissolved and Elaine will be free to go her own way."

Maddie thought it all sounded cold and cynical. She felt the now-familiar knot in her stomach that had become her constant companion the last six months. Every time babies were mentioned, her gut twisted as though she'd been kicked.

"How awful," she said, not able to hide her disgust at the thought of them both using a baby to gain wealth. "They both deserve whatever they get."

"Oh, Maddie, don't judge him so harshly. I thought, since you'd seen his other side, you'd be more understanding."

Maddie bristled at the accusation. She had no reason to be ashamed. Devon Crowe and his fortune-hunting fiancée were the ones acting callous here, not her. But Beverly's frown clearly showed her disappointment. Obviously the woman could see no fault in her nephew and Maddie decided it was not up to her to point it out to her. She'd been right about not getting involved in the first place.

"You're probably right, Aunt Bev," she lied. "I'm sure they think they have good reason for doing something so . . ." she bit her tongue on a word she was sure Beverly would find highly unsuitable for the dinner table and finished with, "unorthodox.

"I really am tired, now. Would you like me to walk you to your room on my way up?"

"That won't be necessary, dear," Beverly said, not fooled for a minute by Maddie's abrupt change. "You go on ahead. I'll be along shortly."

Maddie knew Aunt Bev could find her own way up, so she pushed back her chair and stood. She considered trying to talk with Devon's aunt some more, then decided against it. Her place in this house was tenuous at best; she had no intention of rocking the boat as long as she was stuck in this time warp.

"Good night, then," she said, leaving the dining room and beating a hasty retreat to the sanctuary of her room.

But Maddie could not find peace, even alone in her room. As she stood by the window looking out at the quiet stillness of the night, thoughts of Devon kept her awake.

Her first reaction to his arrangement with Elaine had been based, more than a little bit, on her own emotions. She'd decided to go through with the artificial insemination Joe Phillips had suggested, and she'd even stopped one afternoon to look through the infant section of her favorite department store. She'd planned to tell Genevieve the news when they saw one another that Saturday.

But fate had decided once again to stand in her way. Maddie would probably never have the child she longed for now. Not if she couldn't find a way back to her time, and modern medicine. In fact, she could really be at risk of serious consequences if she didn't return soon. Dr. Phillips had mentioned cancer if she went untreated too long. Didn't whoever was responsible for this wild trip of hers know that? Or was there no divine intervention? Was her time-travel just an atmospheric quirk, a wrinkle in the fabric of history? Either way her plans were on hold.

That thought brought her back to thoughts of Devon and his plans. The man was making a mistake. Maddie could have told him that, but of course he wouldn't be interested in the opinion of a daft woman. Still, he'd been very good to her and she'd seen his kindness and generosity on more than one occasion. He deserved someone better than his fiancée.

Any woman who'd give up her child for money was indeed coldhearted. And Maddie could well imagine the years ahead for Devon. His life would be a steady string of demands for money from his ambitious wife. And if he thought Elaine would divorce him after the baby was born, Maddie suspected he was in for a surprise. The child would be Elaine's meal ticket. She might even blackmail him over custody.

But it wasn't her problem, she reminded herself. Lord knows, she had enough to deal with on her own. Like how she could get back to her time, and what she'd do for a living if she couldn't get back. It suddenly occurred to Maddie that maybe a mistake *had* been made. Maybe she wasn't supposed to be here. If she'd stayed where she was, in the field, maybe she'd have woken in her own time.

Fueled by her desperate hopes, Maddie quickly dressed in her shorts and tank top. Sarah had had them washed and put them in the drawer of the bureau. Maddie smiled when she recalled how the woman had tucked them toward the back, beneath her undergarments.

Maddie pulled her hair back in a French braid, just the way she'd worn it that day. Her sandals were lost, but she decided that little detail couldn't matter. Almost as an afterthought, she wrapped the elegant robe around her in case she met anyone on her way out. Silently, she left her room, tiptoed quickly through the house, and sneaked out the front door.

A full moon rode high in the sky, clearly lighting the way for Maddie. The night was cool and quiet. Eerily quiet. She realized she'd never been anywhere that present-day sounds couldn't reach her, and she listened to the absence of traffic and machines.

So odd, not to hear horns in the distance or the steady drone of a refrigerator or air conditioner. As she picked her way across the yard to the edge of the field she briefly wondered if she'd ever hear those sounds again.

Other noises soon filled her ears, but they were anything but comforting. The first few she'd identified as crickets and frogs. But there'd been a wail, and a cry she could only hope emanated from a hoot owl or other such creature. A rustle in the bushes startled her and set her feet to racing.

Soon she reached the approximate area she thought she'd been in when Devon found her. She walked around a bit, saw a patch of beaten down grass, and decided she was in the right place. There was nothing to sit on save the ground, so she removed the robe and spread it like a picnic blanket. Curling her legs beneath her, she sank down to wait. And wait. And wait.

Sometime later she dozed, awoke with a start, and decided to try something else. She sat up, crossed her legs, and placed her hands on her knees. She'd briefly practiced the art of visualization, a fad she'd been caught up in during college, and she tried it again now. She focused on Genevieve until she could see her sister as clearly as if she stood before her. But time passed and all she got for her efforts was a headache. No matter how hard she concentrated, the field surrounding her never wavered. Not willing to give up, Maddie decided to try another angle.

As daylight turned the sky gray, then purple, then pink, Maddie's frustration built. Finally, in desperation, she called out, "What am I supposed to do?!"

Tears threatened, but she was tired of feeling like a helpless victim of fate. She forced her chin up and directed her questions to the dawn-tinged sky, knowing if she were seen she'd never be able to convince Devon she wasn't a raving lunatic.

"I'm here," she called, looking over her shoulder to make certain no one was within hearing distance. "Now what?" she asked. "If I'm going to be stuck here at least give me a clue as to why. Don't just drop me here and leave me in limbo."

Of course no reply came; she hadn't really expected any. But somehow she felt better for her outburst. A tired laugh bubbled from inside her and she shook her head. If she was trying to appear sane, she was doing a poor job of it. She decided she'd better return to the house and sneak back to her room before anyone saw her.

The grass was damp as she made her way back to the Victorian structure. Her thigh ached, stiff from sitting in cool air. She'd put the robe on and clutched it around her. As she entered through the front door she stopped to listen, hoping no one was up yet.

Luck was with her and she made it up the stairs undetected. But suddenly she stopped. Voices, raised in anger, reached her ears. She crept forward and listened.

"Of all people, why Edward, for God's sake," she heard Devon demand. The door to the master suite was open and she'd noticed the matching doors on her way down the hall that first time. Obviously, his bedroom adjoined some sort of sitting room and the voices were coming from there.

"What do you care? You told me I could do as I liked."

"After you'd fulfilled your end of the bargain, dammit."

Maddie wanted to slip away, but she brazenly inched forward, not sure why she needed to hear the words Devon and his fiancée were hurling at one another.

"You and I have had our fun in the past," Elaine taunted. "It isn't my fault your interest waned."

"Isn't it? I got tired of waiting in line for your favors."

A sharp slap sounded loudly, causing Maddie to start. She could almost feel the sting of such a blow.

"Don't think to make a habit of that during the months ahead, Elaine. I won't stand still for being struck."

"You'll bloody well stand for whatever I want. You have no choice."

"You overestimate your position, madam. We are not yet wed."

"No, but we will be," she told him confidently. "You don't have time to find another woman who'll agree to your terms. If you called it off now you'd have to admit defeat. And Edward would step right in to claim all this for his own."

"I'd see him dead first," Maddie heard Devon remark, a coldness to his voice she'd never imagined him capable of. Obviously Elaine brought out the worst in the man. If only . . .

As though a burst of sun suddenly lit the sky, Maddie felt the warmth of knowledge fill her. It was no disembodied voice answering her question, but she knew she'd received her response all the same. It occurred to her that spending the night out in a field wasn't conducive to rational thought, and she quickly pushed away the crazy notion. But it returned, relentlessly demanding she acknowledge the possibility that she'd discovered her reason for being here.

"Even now you could be carrying that bastard's child. Our wedding is only two weeks away. That isn't time enough to guarantee he hasn't planted his seed before mine. Damn you, Elaine."

"Oh, stop acting the part of the wronged husband. You were more than willing to claim another woman's bastard before. What do you care who fathers the whelp as long as he's legally yours? The damned inheritance is all that matters. And if Edward's child helped you assure your position, your victory would be even sweeter."

Maddie cringed and pressed her hand to her mouth. How horrible! Knowing Devon's history, Maddie realized Elaine had struck a felling blow this time.

"Get out," she heard him say, loathing evident in his words even from a distance.

Elaine merely laughed. "You aren't about to call off our wedding, darling, so stop fussing. You need me to assure your future, and you know it as well as I."

"No." His voice was firm and Maddie almost cheered his decision until she realized what he was doing. He'd never marry Elaine now, and he'd lose everything. Could it be her wild notion hadn't been so wild after all? Devon's next words seemed destined.

"I'd sooner marry the devil as align myself with you," he said. "And it isn't as though there aren't any other women around. Why, there's one in the next room even now."

Maddie knew with certainty now that the time had come to act. Somehow she'd been sent here and now she knew why. It was crazy, mad, but she didn't question it any longer. She stepped forward into the doorway of the sitting room.

Elaine saw her first and sneered. "Well, here is your chance, darling. It seems we woke your *guest* with our discussion."

Devon whipped around, his eyes black with rage. The tail of his robe fanned out with the force of his movements and Maddie had to force herself to keep from taking a step back. Elaine had guts, she'd give the woman that. Maddie wasn't sure she could have faced the look Devon wore without cringing.

"Maddie," he finally managed to force out. He stepped forward. "I apologize." His look told her he meant for more than waking her. "I didn't mean to imply . . ."

Maddie could have told him it no longer mattered. She knew she'd have probably said anything to shut Elaine up if she'd been in his position. She smiled.

"I couldn't help overhearing," she lied.

"I'm sorry we disturbed you." Devon's voice chilled her.

"I'm not disturbed," she told him frankly. "I heard what you said."

He made to apologize again, but she raised her hand. "I accept."

Devon stared at her blankly, his face expressionless. They might have stood that way for hours, gazing at one another, if the sound of Elaine's sharp laughter hadn't roused them.

"Oh, that is rich, Devon. Did you hear her? She thought you were actually proposing." She laughed again and Maddie longed to cut her a scathing look, but somehow she couldn't drag her gaze from Devon.

"Maddie, I didn't—"

"Of course he didn't, you little fool. Devon, we still have things to settle. We need to make arrangements if everything is going to be ready on time."

"You may not have been proposing, Devon. But I am." Elaine's laughter sounded forced this time. Obviously she'd noticed the way her fiancé hadn't taken his eyes off Maddie. And Maddie suspected her own feelings were clearly written on her face. What a shock! To discover she'd gone back one hundred years to find the man who'd be the father of her baby.

"You what?" Devon croaked.

"I'm proposing. Aunt Bev explained your situation to me and I understand." She added silently, and I wouldn't like to see you murdered in your bed after you've been so kind to me. This time she forced her eyes to turn on Elaine and the woman glared in outrage.

"But Maddie—"

"I know what you're thinking," she assured him, her smile telling him she didn't blame him for thinking she'd lost her mind. "But the fact is you have little choice. If you took time to try to find someone else, you'd lose for sure. So, it seems you only have two choices. Elaine, or me."

"Yes, darling," Elaine drawled, coming up beside him to link her arm through his. "That does seem to be the situation in a nutshell. Tell her we've made a bargain and her *services* will not be needed."

Devon looked deep into Maddie's eyes for a long moment. She thought he'd do as Elaine suggested, but he never spoke the words. She grew uncomfortable under his scrutiny and her throat went dry. Her lips felt parched and she ran her tongue along them nervously. So close was Devon's perusal that his eyes followed the pink tip across her lower lip and back. Without blinking he disengaged Elaine's arm from his.

"Leave us," he told Elaine.

Elaine's gasp echoed around Devon and Maddie. "Devon, you're being ridiculous. Everything has been decided. . . ."

"Go, Elaine. My plans no longer concern you. Be ready to leave within the hour. I'll have my driver take you to the station."

"Oh, no!" she cried, snatching his arm and pulling him around to face her. "You can't do this. We had an arrangement."

"You broke it, Elaine, not me. I told you I'd never marry you now, and I meant it. Be ready in an hour or I'll have you escorted off my property."

Maddie couldn't see Devon's face as he confronted Elaine, but she could see the burning hatred the other woman made no move to hide.

"You will live to regret this, Devon," she vowed. "Both of you." She swept past Maddie, knocking into her shoulder so hard Maddie nearly fell. Her shoulder burned with pain where Sarah had stitched it and she felt Devon reach out and steady her. She refused to look at him for a minute, afraid he'd dismiss her now as well.

After a moment she looked into his eyes. Confusion, doubt, disbelief. They were all present. She tried to look confident, but now that the moment had come she couldn't seem to stop trembling.

"Shall I go?" she asked, trying to pretend everything wasn't riding on his answer.

After a long silence he shook his head. "No," he said. "We have plans to make if we're going to be married soon. We are, aren't we?" he asked, offering her a final chance to run from the room, and her proposal.

She straightened proudly. "We are," she confirmed, taking her destiny in her own hands.

Chapter Seven

Vaguely Maddie heard a door slam along the corridor. But she couldn't seem to focus on the sounds of Elaine's outburst. A steady trembling had taken hold of her legs and she thought she might actually crumple to the floor in a minute.

Her eyes remained locked on Devon's face, and she drew courage from the strength she saw there. It helped that she also saw compassion and a certain measure of vulnerability.

Finally, all other sounds died out and the silence of dawn filled the house once more. The quiet seemed to draw him out of his stunned state.

"Now," he said in a painfully patient tone. "Elaine is gone so you can speak freely. What the blazes did you think you were doing coming in here with such a ridiculous offer?"

Maddie flinched. "You thought I was joking? I assure you—"

All signs of tenderness left his face. "Of course you were. Or else you thought I needed an excuse to throw Elaine out, and so you pretended for her benefit, as I did. But as I said, she's gone now."

"Yes, she is," Maddie confirmed, still smarting from Devon's dismissal of her offer. She'd offered to marry the man and have his child and he was throwing her proposal back in her face. All the old insecurities Todd had left her with roared to life, scratching and clawing their way out into the open once more. With an effort Maddie managed to tamp them down long enough to add, "And so is your chance at inheriting."

"That isn't your concern," he told her sharply, still holding her gaze with uncanny deliberation.

"I just made it my concern. Are you refusing?"

He shook his head and finally their eye contact was broken. Maddie almost sagged with relief. Those odd blue-black eyes had studied her like a bug under a microscope.

"It isn't a question of refusal," he said, speaking slowly, as though talking to a backward child.

"Then you accept?" She wondered for a moment if his reluctance was due to his doubts about her mental stability and so she added, "I assure you I'm not insane. You don't have to worry about that aspect."

"Miss St. Thomas, Maddie, why in the world would you agree to such a thing? You don't know anything about me. And the conditions are far from ideal."

"I understand the situation. I do. And I'm willing to accept that this marriage will not be exactly conventional."

"Why would you do that?"

He turned so sharply Maddie's eyes widened. Once more he pinned her with his stare. She didn't even consider lying to him. Maybe it was the fact they were about to align themselves and she didn't want to base a relationship on lies. Or maybe it was because she couldn't look him in the eyes and tell an untruth and she couldn't seem to look away.

"I don't have any other choice."

"Of course you do. You're a very lovely—"

"No," she cut him off. "I don't. I can't explain everything to you now, and you'd only think I was crazy again if I did. But believe me, I wouldn't have made such an offer if there'd been any other way."

He looked relieved that she didn't bring up her arrival or her origins. But at the same time she could see he was far from convinced she was completely sane.

"I appreciate your willingness to help. I'm honored," he said with a small bow. "But I must refuse."

"If you do, you will lose everything. There's no one else."

"As I said, that is my problem and I'll find a way to deal with it."

"I've just given you the only reasonable answer. I don't understand why you're hesitating."

"I can't take advantage of an injured woman suffering from amnesia, or worse. Not even to save my home."

"You're an honorable man, Devon. I suspected it from the moment I first saw you. But don't let your honor bring about your ruin."

He looked away again, threading his hands through his black hair. He strode to the window and looked out. "I don't want to upset you, Maddie, but I haven't totally lost my reason. I'm not looking for a love match or a woman to share my life." He turned to face her and his eyes were black chips of granite. "I'm looking for a breeder."

Maddie knew he'd meant to shock her, but her emotions were on steady ground now. Resolve and a sense of rightness lent her the strength she needed. She nodded her understanding.

"I cannot ask you to fill such a position. You are a gentle woman, a lady with heart. You have love to give and you deserve a man who will give it to you in return."

"What better qualifications for the mother of your child?"

His eyes narrowed in thought. The lady was smart, Devon thought. And she was right. That

114

was why he'd made Elaine agree to allow him to raise the child. He knew she'd have made a terrible mother and as much as he wished it weren't true, he knew he'd never be able to produce a child without caring for its well-being.

Before he could even put his thoughts into order, she continued. "I don't plan to stick around any longer than I have to," she assured him. "So you needn't worry about me crimping your life-style."

Devon almost smiled at the woman's unusual speech. She was still an enigma to him he hadn't been able to figure out. He ignored the part of him that longed to learn more about her. "Then how do I know you'll stay and see this through?"

Maddie told herself it wasn't exactly a lie to evade the question. She wouldn't tell him she seemed to have little choice in the matter. Instead, she countered with a question of her own.

"Do you have any other choices besides me?"

Devon shook his head.

"Then I suggest you consider my offer again. However," she added, knowing this would be the moment of truth. "I want something besides money."

Alas, Devon thought, the real reason a woman such as Maddie would consider doing something like this.

"I will stay as long as I can, and I will make every effort to fulfill my part of the bargain. But when the time comes for me to leave, the child will go with me." Maddie felt certain that would be the case. After all, if she'd been sent here to make this deal with Devon, it stood to reason she'd get something out of it. Devon needed a child for a brief time. She wanted one for all time.

A look of shocked disbelief crossed Devon's face. "Never," he said firmly.

"You need this child in order to collect your inheritance and that's all. I want it for a far different reason."

"Nevertheless, I can't allow you to just disappear with my child."

"If you want more children at a later date, I assure you I won't stand in your way. However, in the meantime, you need an immediate solution to the problem of the will. And that's all I'm offering you, a short reprieve. If you're looking for an heir to inherit when you die, you'll have to find one after we've parted company." Again she avoided the whole truth, which was that she'd be long gone back to her own time by then. At least she hoped she would.

"He or she will stand to inherit a great deal of wealth. Are you telling me you would simply walk away from that?"

"I'm not doing this for the money, I told you that."

"And what of the child's future? Would you deny him his birthright?"

"I promise you this child will want for nothing in his life. And I swear, no matter what, there will never be a child more loved or wanted than this one will be. Those things are far more important than money. Don't you agree?"

Devon wished he could argue with Maddie, but she was right this time. All his father's money had not guaranteed him a happy life. His father's death, his mother's illness, had all affected him. If it had not been for the certainty of their love, he wasn't sure where he'd be today.

"Indeed," he whispered, awed by the depth of feeling he read in Maddie's eyes. This woman would love and care for his child—for any child, he suspected. A warmth swept him and for the first time since Crystal's death he wished he were still capable of giving and receiving such love.

But to turn the child over to her totally? He didn't think he could bring himself to do that. She might be loving, but he still wasn't convinced she was stable. At the same time, Devon knew he had no choice. He had to agree to Maddie's offer, or pretend to.

Besides, he told himself, the child would be his heir no matter where Maddie chose to live. He'd be able to keep a check on her and the child. She talked of leaving, but anywhere she could get to by train, boat, or carriage, he could get to as well.

The only problem still remaining was one he'd have to deal with in time. His heart had never been threatened by Elaine. Her body had tempted him for a time and her wiles

117

had succeeded in arousing him to passion, but he'd never felt anything more than lust for her. Already, Maddie stirred protective instincts in him. It would not be easy to remain detached from her once he'd made her his wife.

Devon wavered once more, considering his options. Finally, he had to agree they were limited. With a vow to keep his emotions separate from their relationship, he nodded.

"All right, Maddie, I agree," he said. "God knows you'd make a far better mother than Elaine, and you will probably prove to be the better parent in the end," he added, thinking of the way he'd suppressed his emotions to the point he wasn't sure they could be called upon to respond now, even to his own child. "I still don't understand your reasons, but, as you pointed out, I have no choice."

He stepped toward her until she could see the pulse beating in his neck above the lapel of his robe. She tried to avoid looking directly into those disturbing eyes, but he was having none of that. With a gentle fingertip, he lifted her chin.

"Maddie, will you do me the honor of becoming my wife?"

Maddie choked back the frightening urge to run now that her idea was becoming fact. Why did he have to look at her that way, so sincerely, so longingly? It was almost as though he were proposing for real, and Maddie felt doubts assail her. Was she making a mistake? The biggest one of her life?

"Maddie?"

She swallowed, her gaze dropping to his chest and then slowly returning to meet his. She cleared her tightened throat and whispered, "Yes, Devon. I will."

For better or worse, she thought. Devon could provide what she needed, and she'd made a choice based on those needs. Her decision to do this came from her desire to have a child, the importance to her health that she do something soon, and her belief that this was the right choice. The only choice, in this time period. Her goal now was just to produce a healthy child and find a way for her, and her baby, to return to her time. And right now, having a plan helped her keep from losing her mind amid the madness of her situation. She forced a smile for Devon's benefit.

Devon returned her smile and bent closer. Maddie held her breath. He was going to kiss her; she could read his intent in his eyes. She tried to tell herself this was only the beginning. He'd expect far more than kisses as soon as the ink was dry on the marriage certificate.

With infinite tenderness, his lips came down to feather across hers. He held her chin with fingers so gentle it almost seemed like a caress. The soft brushing of his mouth lingered, drawing out the moment until she couldn't stop her own lips from parting. With a soft sigh, she tipped her head to deepen the kiss. Devon complied, letting his arms drop to her back where he rubbed his hands along her spine.

His tongue teased her lips, finally slipping past them to probe the warmth beyond.

Maddie felt a jolt shake her. Without warning, passion and longing suddenly filled her. Her body fit against Devon's and all she could think was that there'd been no awkwardness. That moment of adjustment, where two people try to come together for the kiss, hadn't happened.

And never, not in her entire life, had she ever been so moved by a mere kiss. It was frightening in its intensity, and Maddie shivered.

When they parted Maddie felt breathless and shaken. And aroused. Extremely, hotly, passionately aroused. The feeling was one she couldn't remember having in a long time, if ever.

With his fingers threaded through hers, Devon led Maddie to one of two matching settees in the sitting room and drew her down to sit beside him. Lord, but the man had charm. Even knowing theirs wasn't a love match, Devon sought to make the moment romantic for her. As though to make up for the lack of true feelings.

"Elaine insisted on time enough for a large, resplendent wedding. She put off the marriage for months to prepare. I'd like to offer you the same, Maddie, but the fact is we don't have time. As it is—well, let's just say my deadline draws nearer every day."

Maddie shook her head, trying to keep her mind off the warmth and security of Devon's large hand grasping hers. He absently caressed her knuckles with his thumb, sending gooseflesh up her arm. She considered pulling away, but immediately decided that would not set a good tone for what was to come.

"It doesn't matter," she told him. "There's no one I'd invite anyway. We can have a simple ceremony right here, with just a J.O.P."

"A what?" Devon's frown snapped Maddie's attention back to their discussion and away from the tingles of desire needling under her skin.

Didn't they have justices of the peace in 1892? she thought frantically. They must have, they always had them in the old westerns.

"A justice of the peace?" she queried, hoping she wouldn't see the dimple on his jaw that usually followed one of her slipups.

To her relief, he smiled. "Well, I *can* do better than that, Maddie. We have a preacher in Lawrence, about thirty miles from here. I'm sure he'd be happy to do the honors."

"That will be fine," she agreed, surprised at the pleasure his offer brought her. She'd never thought much about what kind of wedding she'd like, and because of the circumstances now she wondered why it should matter, but it did. And it felt right knowing their union would be properly blessed.

"You'll want to have a gown made. That will take time."

Maddie could see Devon mentally clicking off the time left in his mind. She shook her head. "No, that isn't necessary. I'll wear one of

121

the gowns Aunt Bev gave me."

"Aunt Bev?" He seemed to realize for the first time that Maddie wore only a robe as his eyes scanned her. He cleared his throat and glanced back to face her, but she noticed he made no move to put distance between them. His leg brushed her knee and his arm lay across the back of the settee along her shoulders. "I thought that gown you wore at dinner last night looked familiar, but I couldn't place it."

"It was Aunt Bev's. She had Sarah alter three of her dresses so I'd have something to wear." She flushed with embarrassment that she didn't even have clothes of her own. If she'd needed reminding of all Devon and his aunt had done for her, she'd certainly gotten it.

"But your cases," he said with a frown, as though he'd just remembered them himself. "I brought them to you."

"They didn't contain clothing, I'm afraid," she said, wondering what she'd tell him if he demanded to know what they did contain. He didn't, and she breathed a relieved sigh.

She thought of the silk tank top and shorts beneath her robe and she instinctively drew it closer to her chest.

"I apologize, Maddie. Once I found the cases I'm afraid it never occured to me that you had nothing to wear. I should have been more attentive."

Maddie thought it would have been difficult for Devon to be more attentive than he had. But once more she reminded herself she wasn't dealing with a modern man. This man believed he was responsible for meeting the needs of the people under his care, and he'd willingly made her one of those people the moment he'd lifted her into his arms in the field of wildflowers.

"You've been wonderful, Devon." She squeezed his hand and their eyes met and held. Did she see the same flash of desire light his eyes that she felt? Or was it merely a reflection of her own expression?

"I have an idea," he said, rising from the settee. He tugged her hand and drew her up beside him. "You get some rest. When you wake I'll have a surprise waiting for you."

Maddie couldn't suppress the pleasure she felt knowing Devon longed to please her. Theirs might be an arranged marriage, but he'd not be throwing that fact in her face. He obviously meant to make the best of the situation and project an outward image of domestic bliss. In every sense of the word, she would be Devon Crowe's wife.

She couldn't help thinking Elaine was a fool to have jeopardized her position in Devon's life. Maddie found it hard to believe any other man's attention would be worth what it had cost Elaine. But still, Maddie thanked her. For now she'd be the woman Devon took for his wife. And when this man passed his good qualities onto his child, she'd be the one to reap the benefits. She'd be the one that child called mother.

Chapter Eight

"I can't believe this," Maddie cried, looking at the mounds of clothing strewn all around the morning room. The French doors were thrown open to catch the afternoon breeze and to dispel the smell of dust and mothballs. The surface of every piece of furniture was covered with gowns, petticoats, chemises, camisoles, stockings, shoes, nightgowns, and cloaks. Even several cases of jewelry lay open for her perusal.

"I know, I'm so thrilled," Bev said, taking Maddie's hands in hers. "Devon hasn't even mentioned his mother's belongings since we put them away in the attic after her death. I've never been so astonished as I was when he told me he wanted them all brought down for you. He said he was only sorry there wasn't time for you to have your own trousseau made."

"What on earth could I want that isn't here?" Maddie exclaimed. "I've never seen so many beautiful things." Her face lost some of its animation and she turned back to Aunt Bev. "Are you sure it isn't going to bother Devon to see me wearing these?"

Aunt Bev smiled and briefly hugged Maddie to her. "It was his idea, Maddie. He wouldn't have suggested it if he hadn't wanted you to have them."

"But under the circumstances . . ."

"I didn't ask Devon how you two came to the decision you did," Bev confessed. "And I won't ask you now. That is your business. But I will tell you, Maddie, that it makes me very happy. Elaine would have made Devon's life miserable."

"But it isn't as though this is a love match. Maybe I should just wear one of the gowns you gave me."

"And disappoint my nephew? I won't hear of it. Devon wants to do this for you, Maddie. Let him. Please," she added, squeezing Maddie's hand. "It's been a long time since he's allowed himself to care for another person, besides me."

Maddie glanced from Bev's pleading expression to the mounds of garments and accessories surrounding her. She didn't feel right taking Devon's mother's belongings, but Maddie knew she had little choice. She couldn't very well stay here for any length of time without clothes to wear. And she couldn't wear her silk tank top and shorts in front of these people.

"I's found it!" Sarah declared from the doorway, surprising Maddie from her musing. "I knowed it was up there somewheres."

"Thank goodness," Bev said, sweeping toward the door to meet Sarah. She took the large box from the servant's hands and made her way back to the table. Sarah cleared a spot on the table and Bev set the box down. After a moment's hesitation, she lifted the lid.

Maddie and Sarah gasped and Bev turned worried eyes in their direction. "Is it all right? It hasn't been damaged, has it?"

For a long minute Maddie couldn't speak. Then she reached out slowly and touched the gossamer fabric of the wedding gown. "It's exquisite," she breathed, reverently lifting the dress from the box. "I've never seen anything more beautiful."

"I remember," Bev said, her eyes taking on a faraway look as she saw the dress once more in her mind. "Olivia looked so beautiful in it I don't think anyone in the church that day so much as breathed during the ceremony."

Maddie could believe it. The yards and yards of spiderweb thin silk looked like what she'd imagine angel's wings to be made of. Beneath that was a pearl white satin underdress. The bodice had a design of flowers and leaves made from tiny seed pearls. The sleeves were slashed, allowing the white satin beneath to show through like a medieval gown.

"Devon specified we work on this one first, but Sarah and I couldn't find it right off. I was afraid it might have been lost or damaged over the years."

"No," Maddie whispered. "It's perfect."

Bev and Sarah beamed their approval at the wonder in Maddie's voice. Bev hid a secret smile as she stood by, because she knew, even if Maddie and Devon didn't, that it wasn't the dress that would make this wedding perfect. It was the couple. She'd had another dream. And she couldn't be happier about what she'd seen in the future for these two people she loved.

Maddie ached from standing. She'd been pinned and tucked and twisted for more hours than she could count. Her initial excitement had given way to boredom and finally irritation, but she held on. Only one more and they'd be finished, Sarah assured her.

Trying to keep her back straight and her chin up, she willed away the itch that nagged her lower back. She didn't dare move. The last time she had, Sarah accidentally speared her with a deadly looking sewing needle.

"One mo' second," Sarah promised, her words muddled through the supply of pins tucked in her mouth. "I's jus' 'bout done."

Maddie focused on the far wall and tried to remember why Bev had insisted she needed so many of the dresses. On one's honeymoon you never know what activities you might need specific clothing for, she'd said. And so, Maddie had agreed to five day dresses, three dinner dresses, an outing suit, a yachting toilette, a tea gown, a garden party dress, and even a bicycle costume. She'd drawn the line at the ridiculous-looking dress and bloomers Aunt Bev had called a bathing suit. Maddie swam in the Gulf regularly, but there was no doubt in her mind she'd end up at the briny bottom if she tried to swim in that getup.

Devon's mother had been bigger in the bust from nursing Devon, Bev pointed out, and a good bit shorter than Maddie. But fortunately all the dresses had been designed to be worn with a hoop and so they'd ended up being a bit too long when Maddie put them on without the cagelike contraption Devon's mother had worn.

A nip and tuck in the bust and a bit off the bottom and all the outfits would be perfect, Sarah had assured her. Maddie just wished she could get out of the musty-smelling clothes and into her own comfortable shorts and tank top.

"There now," Sarah said, pushing herself from her knees. She plucked the pins out of her mouth and nodded once for effect. "You's all done. I gots one of the other girls from the field to help me and we should have 'em all done by the time you leave on Saturday."

Saturday, Maddie thought. One short week after her arrival she'd be married to Devon. It still didn't seem possible, or real. Maybe that was why she hadn't been plagued with panic. She'd waited for the realization of what she was doing to hit her, sending her into a frenzy, but it hadn't happened. Perhaps her subconscious still believed this was all some sort of dream. Soon she'd wake up, probably in a hospital bed, and they'd tell her she'd had a nasty bump on the head but that she would be fine. Genevieve would be there, and they'd enjoy a laugh when Maddie told her about the wild dream she'd had while she'd been out.

Suddenly Maddie felt a wave of sadness. Her eyes drifted to Sarah, adjusting one last seam on the dress, and then to Bev, sipping tea in the slice of afternoon sunlight coming from the terrace. She thought of Devon, his hand tenderly caressing hers as he asked her to be his wife. If it was all a dream, she'd be sorry to wake up and find them gone.

Of course, it would be good to see Genevieve again, to get back to work. But as long as she was here, she might as well make the most of the adventure. How many people got to experience all she had in the last week?

For the first time she truly considered what she'd gotten herself into. Months of old-fashioned ways and rules. Months of no modern conveniences. Months of missing Genevieve and being away from her business. She might not even have a business when, or if, she ever got back to her own time.

Bolstering her courage and determination, Maddie told herself she'd had no other choice. Marrying Devon Crowe and agreeing to bear his child had its advantages. She'd get the baby she longed for. She'd be taken care of until she could find a way back to 1992. And besides, she thought wryly, it beat pounding hundred-year-old pavement in search of a decent job in a time when women had few choices.

"Arms up," Sarah ordered, shaking Maddie free of her wanderings. Stripped of the dress, Maddie stood in her frilly camisole and petticoat and let her fears and doubts seep in. What if she were completely wrong? What if she hadn't been sent here to help Devon? Was she being unfair to him to agree to terms she wasn't certain she could fulfill? What if she were whisked back before the baby was born?

A chill shook her. What if, she thought, she *didn't* return to her own time after the baby was born? Or worse, she did, and the child didn't?

The water soothed Maddie's jagged nerves somewhat, but nothing seemed to rid her of the anxious, queasy feeling which had plagued her all morning. In less than two hours she would become Devon Crowe's wife. She wondered if the marriage would truly be legal. After all, she hadn't even been born in 1892, so how could she be bound by a piece of paper from that time? However, she'd signed the marriage certificate Devon had sent up to her and her name had certainly looked legitimate next to his. All that remained now was the actual ceremony.

She'd thought of nothing else for two days. Why did she suddenly feel so antsy? What was this creepy, skin-crawling sensation that bedeviled her now? As she stood to leave the tub, she noticed the red smears on her thighs.

"Oh, Lord, no," she cried, grabbing a towel and bolting out of the water. This couldn't be happening! Every bride's nightmare come true. And how much worse would it be for her without a corner store to go get what she needed. Maddie wrapped the towel around her and tucked the corner in under her arm.

Muttering an unladylike oath under her breath, she knew there was only one thing to do. She'd have to explain the situation to Aunt Bev and hope the older woman could help her.

Two hours later Maddie eased off the bed and winced. Since her bath she'd been overtaken by cramps and nausea. The more uncomfortable symptoms of endometriosis were diarrhea and vomiting. The way she felt at that moment she knew they weren't far off. How was she going to get through the rest of the evening without collapsing?

Her head hurt from the tugging and pinning Sarah had done to fashion her hair into a becoming coiffure. Her back ached and she couldn't get her breath in the corset she'd had to don in order to get Devon's mother's gown on. Obviously the woman's waist at the time she married had been much smaller than in later years and the wedding dress had ended up being too snug in the waist.

A knock alerted Maddie it was time to go down for the ceremony and she clutched her stomach as another cramp seized her. Damn, why did this have to happen today?

"Maddie?" Aunt Bev poked her head around the door. "Are you all right, dear?"

"I'm fine," Maddie lied, trying without success to keep the pain out of her voice.

Bev frowned and came further into the room, closing the door behind her. "I spoke with Devon, Maddie, and he assured me he understood. He said to tell you he could postpone the honeymoon until you felt better."

"Oh, that's not necessary," Maddie quickly assured her. Ever since Devon had told her they would be going to Gulf Island for the honeymoon, Maddie had been anxious. Finally, she'd be going home. Or, at least, she'd be going back to the island where she'd lived. She couldn't wait. "I'll be fine tomorrow, I'm sure. The worst usually only lasts one day." She prayed that would be the case this time. There'd been months, especially lately, when she'd had these bouts recur on the second or even third day.

"Well, if you're sure. I know it will be a bit inconvenient for you, but I know you'll have a lovely time in Gulf Island. The sun and rest will be good for you."

Maddie stepped forward, cursing the pains in her body, and took one last look in the cheval mirror. All in all she thought she looked fine. Sarah had arranged her hair, the gown was

133

beautiful, and no one would know how awful she felt if only she could manage to stand upright.

"Thank him for me, will you, Aunt Bev? And tell him I apologize for the bad timing."

Bev smiled and reached to take Maddie's arm. Linking it with hers, she patted Maddie's hand. "You won't be the first bride to spend her honeymoon seeing the sights *outside* the hotel room."

Maddie laughed, winced, and then smiled back at Devon's aunt. "No, I guess I won't."

The walk to the parlor sapped Maddie of every ounce of strength she possessed. Bev left her standing in the hall, propped against the parson's bench, while she went in first. When Maddie heard the strains of music Aunt Bev had volunteered to play, she was supposed to enter and walk to stand beside Devon. Silently she prayed she wouldn't fall facedown at his feet.

She missed the first cue Bev gave her as she choked down a wave of nausea. Once more Devon's aunt played the key notes and Maddie forced herself to straighten and walk into the parlor.

Devon took one look at Maddie's face and almost rushed forward. Her skin was so pale as to be almost transparent and her hands trembled. Could she be that frightened? he wondered, thinking he might have made a terrific mistake in agreeing to her proposal. But as Maddie stepped closer, he could see the distress in her eyes. Those beautiful eyes which had always let him know how she felt from the moment they met.

Good grief! She was really sick. He broke convention and took two steps to meet her, not realizing how eager the action made him seem. Putting his arm around her back, he offered her support as they walked back to the decorated piano. Beneath his arm he could feel her body shaking as though she had a chill. He clasped her right hand in his left and frowned down at her with concern. She offered him a weak smile and together they faced the preacher.

Somewhere in her mind Maddie cataloged the flowers and ribbons that decorated the parlor, thinking what a fine job Sarah and Beverly had done. She also noticed a few guests skirting the edges of the room. She'd been told ahead of time that Devon had invited ten or twelve neighboring friends for the ceremony when he'd gone to inquire about the minister. Maddie prayed she wouldn't disgrace herself in front of Devon's friends.

Afterward, Maddie couldn't remember a word of the ceremony. She didn't even remember speaking the vows that made her Devon's wife. All she knew was that he'd come to her and his arm had felt so good against her aching back, his hand so welcome in her own. Within minutes the wedding was concluded and Devon placed a tender, lingering kiss on her mouth. Maddie tried to return it with all the emotion she felt, but she was simply too ill.

"Maddie, are you all right?" he asked as they parted. Maddie nodded, immediately regretted it when the nausea returned, and forced a smile.

"I'm fine."

"Sarah has prepared a wedding supper in the dining room," Bev broke in, her beatific smile filling the parlor. "Shall we go in and have a seat?"

Maddie dreaded the thought of seeing or smelling food, but she knew she couldn't disappoint Sarah and Beverly, not to mention the preacher and other guests.

For a little more than an hour Maddie smiled, picked at her food, and tried to carry on polite conversation with the guests. Four couples had arrived: the Georges, the Elkinses, the Brewsters, and the Franklins, who all owned neighboring property. Then there was an older woman named Clair Roberts who'd been good friends with Olivia Crowe when they were children, and the preacher from Lawrence.

Halfway through dinner Maddie's symptoms eased off enough for her to manage a few bites of the creamy broccoli soup Sarah had prepared, and the respite lasted through the cutting and sharing of a piece of lemon wedding cake. But too soon, her malady returned and she felt sweat bead on her lip as she struggled to keep the food down.

Devon saw her discomfort and he managed to rush through the rest of the ritual. When the guests began to clink their silverware against the crystal tumblers, Maddie sat up sharply.

The racket made her head pound anew. Devon shot her a worried look and then hid his concern behind a mischievous grin.

"They are calling for the groom to kiss his bride, Maddie. Are you sure you're all right?"

At the thought of Devon's arms around her again, his lips soothing her with soft nips and brushes, she had to admit she felt a bit better. She smiled and nodded.

Taking her by the hand, Devon drew her up to stand beside him at the head of the table. He smiled in turn at each person seated around the table and then proceeded to take Maddie's mind off her ills. At first it was a simple touching of two mouths. But when Maddie opened her lips to him, he deepened the kiss. All around them the clinking of silver against glass rose to a swell of tinkling music. But Maddie could not think of the others in the room. Devon's arms enclosed her in a warm embrace that chased the pain from her body, and his tongue and lips playfully teased her to a tingling awareness.

When he finally drew back, she felt breathless and flushed. He seemed to notice her high color and he frowned again. With a sweeping bow to the guests he said quickly, "And now, if you will excuse us."

The guests giggled their approval as Devon swept Maddie off her feet and carried her out of the dining room. Sarah stepped out of the kitchen as they approached, and Devon paused only long enough to say, "She's sick, Sarah, come along."

The servant hastily sped back into the kitchen and returned with towels, a glass, and a brown glass bottle.

"Thank you," Maddie whispered, laying her head against Devon's chest as he carried her up the stairs to her room.

"I told you, I'm no knight in shining armor, but I know a lady in distress when I see one."

"I'm sorry I spoiled the evening," she said.

"Nonsense. If we'd have stayed down there much longer they'd have thrown us over their shoulders and carried us upstairs themselves. It's customary for the bride and groom to leave first. By tomorrow it will be all over the county that my bride and I barely made it through the first course."

Maddie tried to laugh, but her body ached too badly. Devon laid her on the bed and stepped back to allow Sarah to help her.

"I'll say good night for now," he whispered, brushing a kiss across her forehead. "Sarah will take good care of you."

Maddie watched him go, more confident than ever that she'd done the right thing in marrying Devon. She only wished their wedding night hadn't turned out so disastrous. If only he'd stayed with her.

A moment later she was thankful he hadn't as the nausea took hold and she lost her wedding supper in the chamber pot.

Chapter Nine

Maddie took the hand Devon offered to her and stepped down from the old-fashioned train. The short trip to Gulf Island had been hot, dusty, and cramped, and she stopped for a moment to take several deep breaths of the refreshing salt air.

For the first time all morning her nausea subsided and she prayed it wouldn't come back. Sarah had given her a dose of whatever was in the brown bottle as soon as Devon left the previous evening, and Maddie had slept through the night. But she'd awakened this morning still feeling the effects of her condition. Uncle Joe had warned her the endometriosis would only get worse. It seemed he was right.

Before the endometriosis Maddie had been healthy as a horse. She hadn't had so much as a sniffle in over five years. But for the last six months, one or two days a month, her illness laid her low. Still, she wouldn't have put off seeing her island again for anything.

Maddie studied the scenery that should be so familiar to her. She'd lived in this area all her life, but the only thing she recognized so far was the train station. Of course in her time it had been converted to a museum. It fronted a high-rise glass and steel hotel and no trains stopped there anymore. She'd bid on the job to decorate the lobby of the museum, but a larger decorating firm had beaten her out.

She would have liked to study the interior of the station but Devon drew her toward a row of waiting carriages.

He escorted Maddie to the nearest one and saw her seated inside before he went back for their luggage. He'd told her they would stay on Gulf Island for two weeks before returning to his home. Maddie assumed it was so they could become comfortable with their intimacies without family and servants looking on. The idea brought her both anxiety and, she had to admit, anticipation.

The trip through the dockside streets did little to settle Maddie's queasy stomach. Strong odors of fish and rotting wood could not be kept out of the carriage. Even the small breeze off the bay didn't help. By the time they reached the ferry that would take them across the bay to the resort island, Maddie's face had lost all color and her legs turned to jelly beneath her. The nausea returned with a vengeance.

Devon hired a man to carry their belongings onto the ferry and then assisted Maddie to a bench seat at the front of the boat.

"I'm sorry, Devon. I'm almost never sick," she told him, trying to stem the embarrassment she felt at her continued weakness.

"No need to apologize." He smiled and took her hand, his arm going around her shoulder along the back of the bench. "I believe the vows said 'in sickness and health.'"

Maddie's head snapped around and she eyed him closely. Was he making fun, taunting her because theirs was not a normal marriage? She was surprised to see nothing but sincere concern in his dark eyes.

She faced the front of the ferry, catching the breeze off the bay as they chugged toward the island. Gone was the six-lane concrete and steel bridge that spanned the bay in 1992. In 1892 the only way onto the island was by ferry. Maddie had always thought the bridge a necessary evil, but next to the interminable boat ride, she'd have given anything for the modern structure.

As the shore of Gulf Island came into view, Maddie gasped. She didn't know what she'd expected to see, but the miles of empty shoreline shocked her to her core.

All the condominiums, all the high-rise hotels and resorts had never existed in this time. The sand dunes and sea oats rose up, undisturbed by construction. A rough wooden dock greeted them, and Maddie could see a coarse, shelled road leading further into the center of the island.

"We'll be staying on the other side of the island, Maddie. Do you think you're up to another carriage ride?"

Maddie swallowed her stunned disbelief and turned to Devon. "What did you say?" She fumbled through her mind, trying to tell herself she'd accepted her journey into the past. But now, looking up to where her condo should have been, panic and amazement seized her all over again.

"The carriage." He motioned past the pier, and Maddie saw several carriages lining the dock. They all had shiny crests on the side with the name of a hotel emblazoned in gold letters.

"Yes, I'll be fine," she said. Actually, she was anything but. Finding herself in Devon's field had been nothing compared to this. Facing her home and finding it all gone boggled her mind. Numb with shock, she somehow managed to climb off the ferry onto the dock and make her way toward the carriages. Devon went through the routine of collecting their luggage once again and then they proceeded toward the other side of the island.

Maddie stared out the window in awe. At first she hadn't seen a single building anywhere on the island, but as they drove on she noticed several residences tucked beneath the thick canopy of moss-shrouded trees. They even approached what she guessed to be a town, though compared to the town of Gulf Island she'd lived in, it looked more like a hamlet. Shopping centers in her time were bigger than this whole place!

They left the town, and all its rustic, nineteenth-century occupants, behind. The carriages, several in all, traveled on for another couple of miles and then drew to a halt outside a sprawling, white building, perhaps three stories high, with a main entrance in the center, and east and west wings sprouting off either side.

The architecture and ornamentation were exquisite and Maddie couldn't help wondering what had happened to the hotel in later years, for she distinctly knew that the land they stood on would become a national park around the turn of the century.

"Let's get registered and then you can rest. You're still pale, although I think the Gulf air has already put some color in your cheeks."

Devon smiled at her reassuringly and then the baggage boys arrived and Maddie and Devon were swept into the hotel, registered, and escorted to their room. A suite!

There were two bedrooms, she saw, separated by a small salon. Devon tipped the boy with the luggage, hauled her trunk into one room, and then placed his in the other.

So, that's how it's to be, Maddie thought. She thanked whatever code of mores prevented Devon from sharing her room under the circumstances. She'd been humiliated enough

143

knowing Aunt Bev had explained her problem to him.

"Why don't you lie down for a while? We'll go down to the dining room if you're feeling up to it later."

Maddie thanked Devon for his kindness and went into her room. Two doors faced her across the large room and she went to the first one and opened it. A closet. She opened the other and felt like shouting hallelujah. A bathroom!

Quickly closing and locking the door behind her, she stripped off her clothes, ran a tub of blessedly warm water, and sank to her neck.

Maddie didn't move until the water had turned cool and her body's aches had subsided. The medicine Sarah had given her the night before had made her sleep, but it had long since worn off.

Refreshed and feeling somewhat better, Maddie took Devon's advice and lay down on the big, comfortable bed. Vaguely, she heard the sound of a door closing in the other room, but already her eyes were drifting shut.

"Wake up, Maddie," a husky voice teased Maddie's consciousness. A whiff of mint-scented breath wafted across her cheek and she reached up to fan it away. Her hand touched a hard, firm jaw, slightly rough with stubble, and she bolted awake.

"Devon!"

"Were you expecting someone else?" He laughed, brushing a lock of hair behind her ear.

"No, I . . ." She quickly scanned herself, found everything safely covered by the Victorian robe she'd donned, and settled back against the pillows. "I wasn't expecting anyone at all."

"I tried to wait until you woke up on your own, but my stomach had other ideas. Do you feel like going down to the dining room or should I order something to be brought up?"

Maddie took a mental inventory and found she felt considerably better, for the moment. "I'd like to see the dining room," she told him. What an understatement! she thought. She was dying to see the furnishings and decorations in the grand hall they'd passed briefly on their way upstairs.

"Good," Devon said, rising from the bed. "I'll go and let you get dressed. I'll be waiting for you in the salon." To Maddie's surprise he leaned over and placed a quick kiss on her open mouth. With a smile, he was gone.

She sat dazed for a moment, wondering what the future held for her and Devon. Would they remain distant after they'd shared the final intimacy of marriage? Devon's actions seemed to discount that idea. Since she'd agreed to be his wife, he'd tried to pretend theirs was an ordinary situation. Of course it was an act. He hadn't forgotten the scene where she'd confessed to being from the future. He couldn't have forgotten her promise to leave after his inheritance was assured.

*   *   *

Devon poured a drink from the stocked bar in the corner of the salon. Sipping the brandy slowly, he tried to put the image of Maddie out of his mind. But when he closed his eyes all he could see was her face, beautiful in repose, lying against the pillow. Her blonde hair, shorter than current fashion, was spread out in a golden fan around her head. And her body, outlined in the lacy robe, had tempted his hands to touch her.

He took another long sip and swallowed his desire. For days he'd thought of sharing a bed with Maddie. His feelings vacillated between arousal at the mere thought and sheer torment. Somehow he knew Maddie wouldn't be like the other women he'd known. She had too much vitality, too much fire, to be just another lover. Fear gripped him. How would he keep his heart out of her reach?

With a snort of disgust, he slammed the glass down on the bar. He just would, he told himself. He'd learned his lesson with Crystal. He wouldn't risk feeling anything for Maddie except the desire necessary to pull off his end of their bargain. He'd had other lovers, and he hadn't fallen in love with any of them.

Of course he hadn't married any of them either, his mind argued. A husband, even a husband in an arranged marriage, was expected to show some measure of tenderness and affection for his wife. Besides, seeing Maddie ill had aroused all the protective instincts he'd felt when they first met.

Still, Devon couldn't, *wouldn't*, allow their relationship to progress beyond the arrangement they'd agreed to. He didn't know how he was going to accomplish such a feat, but he knew he must. Not only for his own sake, but for Maddie's as well. Neither of them needed that complication added to the burdens they already carried.

Maddie stared in horrified dread at the crystal chandeliers, the silver and china, and the rich cherrywood tables and chairs.

"Maddie." Devon's voice drew her back to the present, or past as the case might be, and she followed the maitre d' to a table in the corner. "Are you all right?" he asked for perhaps the hundredth time.

Maddie wanted to tell him—NO! she was far from all right. If seeing her island this way wasn't bad enough, she'd just realized why the Island Breeze Hotel wasn't in operation in 1992.

The national park she remembered from her time had been built on the site of old ruins. The ruins of a grand hotel which had been blown away in a hurricane sometime around the turn of the century!

Blood drained from her face, only to return with enough force to start her temples pounding. She glanced at all the people dining, laughing, and enjoying themselves and felt like a passenger on the Titanic. How had they felt when they knew their ship was going down with all the

147

marvels it contained? Maddie wanted to grab the silver candlesticks and antique crystal goblets and carry them back safely to the mainland.

Of course she couldn't do that; they weren't even antiques yet. But the decorator in her felt like crying at the loss of such beautiful ornaments. The humanitarian in her wanted to run from table to table and tell everyone what was going to happen. These people needed to be warned so no one would be on the island when the hurricane hit.

Reason held her in her chair. She had no idea when the hurricane was due to hit. It might be years away yet. Besides, if she did that she'd look like the lunatic Devon had suspected her of being.

"Maddie?"

Maddie looked up to see the waiter standing next to their table, an expectant expression on his face. With chagrin, Maddie realized she hadn't even opened her menu. Apologizing to all the women's rights activists, she turned to Devon.

"Why don't you order for me."

He nodded, not the least surprised by her request. Of course he wouldn't be surprised; women allowed men to speak for them all the time in 1892. She had to get a handle on her situation, and quickly. She thought she'd accepted the truth before, but she had been hiding under the security of Devon's house. Now, she had to face the real world. The real *old* world.

Dinner passed without further incident and Maddie enjoyed the fresh seafood Devon had ordered for her. After dessert he asked if she'd like to walk along the shore. Maddie was still a bit queasy and achy, but she couldn't refuse an opportunity to see the beach, her beach, up close once more.

Devon had been quiet through dinner and he remained that way as they made their way down the wooden steps leading to the shore. At the bottom of the steps was a deck, stretching the length of the hotel. She realized the other guests were strolling along the deck, not in the sand, and she felt her heart sink.

"Devon, could we walk by the water?"

Devon's eyebrows rose in surprise. "You'll get your gown wet, Maddie, and the sand creeps into your shoes and stockings. I don't think you'd enjoy it very much."

Maddie glanced around and then pointed. "If we went to the end of the deck and walked from there we could take off our shoes and walk barefoot."

Another flash of surprise lit Devon's navy eyes, but he quickly squelched it. "If that's what you want, Maddie."

They walked as far as the end of the deck, and Devon stepped into the sand first. He lifted Maddie down beside him, took her hand, and helped her through the deep drifts.

Devon looked irritated with the sand that slid out from under his boots, seeping over his ankles to suck his feet down. But Maddie didn't mind at all. As soon as they were out of sight of the other guests, she sat down, lifted her dress, and removed her shoes. She looked up and caught Devon eyeing her ankles. Smiling, she hiked the skirt further and rolled down her stockings.

"Now," she said, slapping the skirt back into place. "Let's go."

They took another few steps, but Devon's heavy boots kept burying themselves in the sugar white sand. With a challenging glance, Maddie dared him to remove them. Giving her a wicked grin, he sat down and tugged off the shiny black boots.

"We could be arrested for this, you know," he told her with mock severity. Maddie thought of the thong bikinis and the stretch of topless beach in 1992 and laughed out loud.

"I'll take my chances," she teased, hiking her hem up higher to free her feet.

Together they made their way to the water. When the first wave washed up to touch her toes, Maddie sighed with pleasure. From here, at the shoreline, looking out at the stars and endless sky, she could almost forget where she was.

With her back to the island, she could imagine the familiar sights she was used to. The unbrellas dotting the beach, the canopied tents selling everything from frozen yogurt to suntan lotion. Even the occasional jet-ski rental.

"You look deep in thought," Devon said, drawing her attention back to the pristine beach. No garbage collection areas, no soda cans or abandoned toys littered the expanse of sand. No buildings rose up to touch the sky.

"Yeah, I guess I was." Her voice sounded sad, even to her own ears. She'd always hated those things, she told herself. The soda cans had been a thorn in her side for years. The rental jet-skis weren't always safe and the noise disturbed the peace she'd always found walking the shore. So why now did she find herself brooding over their absence?

"It really is a shame the beach can't stay like this," she said, feeling the warm water wash over her feet once more. The white foam of cresting waves glowed in the moonlight, soothing her jangled nerves and relieving her tense muscles.

"Are you saying you don't think it will always be as it is now?"

She turned to look at Devon's profile, outlined in the dim light, and wondered how much anyone should know of the future.

"I was just thinking progress would certainly catch up to us all sometime. Even the beaches can't hope to stay the same forever."

He rocked back on his heels, seeming to consider what she said. Then he turned his head, and his eyes caught her gaze. Such marked intensity reflected in the near-black orbs she couldn't look away.

"Are you guessing? Or are you warning me?"

Maddie's breath rushed out in a whoosh. What could she say that wouldn't drive a wedge between them? How could she tell him what she knew to be fact without reminding him he'd married a woman of questionable sanity? Knowing it would not help in any way to confess the truth, she smiled benignly up at him.

"Just speculating, is all," she lied.

Chapter Ten

Hot fingers of pain crept around Maddie's sides, gripping her abdomen in their branding grasp. Moaning, she rolled to her other side, but nothing eased the steel bands of agony. A wave of nausea shook her and she retched into the chamber pot beside her bed.

"Maddie?"

A soothing voice drifted to her but Maddie burrowed deeper, seeking the blessed relief of sleep. Another sharp pain rocked her and she cried out.

"My God, Maddie, what is it? What's wrong?"

"Devon?"

"Yes, it's me. Tell me what to do, love."

"Hot bath," she managed to say, curling her knees closer to her stomach.

A light shone from the bathroom, throwing oddly distorted shadows across the walls and floor. The sound of running water penetrated the fog of pain, and Maddie struggled to sit up.

"Let me help you," Devon said, next to her bed once more.

"No, please," she whispered, determined not to submit to that particular humiliation after everything else. "I can manage. Just leave me alone."

"But you're sick. Maddie, I can't just walk away and leave you."

"Yes, you can," she told him, pushing off the bed and heading toward the relief she knew she'd find in the tub.

Closing the door behind her, Maddie stripped off her gown and sank into the water, moaning with pleasure.

By the time Maddie emerged from the bathroom, Devon had their suitcases packed. A chemise, petticoat, and plain day dress were laid out on her bed.

"Are you all right?"

Maddie swung to face the door of her bedroom, squinting at Devon's dark form in the doorway. The only light came from the bathroom behind her, so his face was in shadow. "What's going on?" She motioned to the empty closet.

"We're leaving." He stepped further into the room and she could see the drink he held. As he walked toward her he took a long sip. "I've hired a carriage to take us to the ferry, another to ride ahead with our bags and alert them we're coming. From there we'll be driven straight home. We should reach the house before daybreak."

"But Devon . . ."

"No, Maddie. Aunt Bev told me the cause of your illness, but I thought it had passed or I would never have brought you here. Besides, I've been married before, remember? Crystal was uncomfortable sometimes, but never as sick as you've been. I'm afraid something serious may be wrong and I'm not taking any chances. Once we're home I'm sending for Anthony."

"Anthony?"

"Anthony Riley. He's a physician, and a friend of mine. He examined you after I found you in the field, but you were still under the effects of Sarah's sleeping draft."

Maddie remembered Sarah's mentioning a doctor. But she didn't need Anthony Riley to tell her what was wrong with her.

"Here," Devon said, holding the glass out to her. "Drink this. It will make the trip more comfortable for you."

Maddie took the glass of brandy and sipped it. The combination of the liquor and the hot bath went to work on her cramps, easing the pain to a tolerable level.

"I'll be fine, Devon. I know what's wrong with me; I don't need a doctor to tell me. And I'll be better by tomorrow."

"I hope you are, Maddie. But we're still going home and I'm still sending for Anthony." He offered her a weak smile that didn't reach his eyes.

Maddie finished off the drink, knowing there was no point in arguing with Devon. She should have postponed the honeymoon until she was sure this bout of symptoms had passed. He poured more brandy into her glass and she dressed without assistance.

By the time the boy arrived to carry down their luggage, she felt a buzz in her head. Devon led her to the other carriage and together they left the Island Breeze Hotel behind. Maddie couldn't help being depressed. This wasn't exactly the honeymoon she'd always thought she'd have when she finally married.

Devon must have thought it best to keep Maddie intoxicated all the way home, because every time she awoke he tipped a glass of brandy to her lips and instructed her to drink. This kept her soothed and sleepy all the way home and she didn't open her eyes again until he lifted her out of the carriage and carried her to her bedroom.

Tired, and more than a little tipsy, Maddie snuggled into the soft mattress and was immediately fast asleep.

When Maddie awoke, the sun was blazing through a part in the drapes, and her eyes felt too big for their sockets. The cramps and nausea had disappeared during the night, but now she had the remains of a hangover.

Her ribs ached from lying in her dress and petticoats and she quickly removed the restraining clothing. With a sigh of relief, she pulled on her own shorts and tank top.

Brushing her hair until it shone, she tucked it back in a French braid. Using the basin of water by her bed, she washed her face and cleaned her teeth as best she could.

Feeling her old self for the first time in a long time, she did some stretching exercises to try to relieve the last traces of her headache.

Sitting on the floor with her legs spread in an open scissors fashion, she bent slowly toward one toe and then the other. This was how Devon found her when he walked into her room a moment later.

"What the blazes . . ."

Maddie scampered to her feet and glanced around for her robe, remembering too late that she had taken it with her on the trip to Gulf Island and had not unpacked it yet. Deciding to brave it out, she turned back to Devon with a bright smile.

"Good morning," she chimed.

After blinking several times, Devon took a good long look at Maddie, from her feathered bangs to her bare toes. His eyes lingered on her long, tanned legs, the length of arm exposed by the sleeveless top, and her neck above the scooped front. He pushed the door closed behind him.

"You certainly look much better today than you did last night," he commented, letting his eyes drink their fill of her scantily clad body.

Maddie could see the flash of desire light Devon's eyes as he spoke. She swallowed hard and nodded.

"I told you I would," she reminded him.

"So you did. What I can't understand is how you did it. I would have sworn you were about to greet St. Peter last night."

"It happens that way sometimes. I apologize again for ruining the trip."

Devon walked slowly around to her side, his gaze never leaving her. Maddie turned to keep her eye on him.

"No matter," he said, waving away her apologies. "We can always go back. When I'm sure you're all right."

Maddie held her hands up at her sides. "As you can see, I'm fine."

"Indeed." He stared at her body another long moment, then let his eyes meet hers. "Nevertheless, Anthony is here now. And since he's come all this way you might as well let him have a look at you. He'd like to assure himself you've recovered from the accident anyway."

"All right. If it will make you feel better."

"It would."

They stood staring into each other's eyes for another long minute; then Devon surprised her by reaching out and fingering the silk of her shorts leg. His heated fingers brushed her thigh and she felt her breath catch in a gulp.

"You really are a curious creature, Maddie Crowe."

Maddie eyes shot wide at the sound of her name linked with Devon's. His words brought a flush of pleasure that warmed her flesh and made her heart flutter. How strange, she thought.

Devon left the room, returning a few minutes later with her robe. He helped her into it and then admitted a tall, lanky man he introduced as Anthony Riley, his physician.

Anthony smiled at Maddie and she immediately felt comfortable with him. His eyes were soft nut brown, his face thin and angular, but not unattractive. Close-cropped blond hair and a thin mustache only made his cheeks and jaw appear thinner.

Devon excused himself, leaving Maddie and Anthony Riley alone. Maddie didn't feel like crawling back into the bed now that she'd recovered so she waved the doctor toward the twin tapestry chairs by the fireplace.

"Well, Maddie, you look much better than the last time I saw you. And let me add my congratulations on your marriage. I'm sorry I wasn't able to make the wedding, but one of my patients decided to arrive ahead of schedule."

"Thank you, Dr. Riley," Maddie said, not sure why his words should make her uneasy. Suddenly she felt the urge to squirm in her seat. Obviously Devon's friend was curious about the circumstances of the wedding, but was too much of a gentleman to ask. He looked away and cleared his throat.

"Devon seemed very happy when he came by to invite me to the wedding, but I must say he was terribly worried this morning when he called on me."

"I'm sorry I worried him. I tried to tell him it was nothing serious."

"You're probably right, Maddie. But the symptoms Devon described could be signs of a problem."

Maddie didn't see any way out of telling Doctor Riley about her condition. She hesitated only because she knew he'd wonder at the diagnosis. But Uncle Joe had always encouraged Maddie to be truthful with doctors. He said it was the only way they could effectively help you.

And since Anthony Riley seemed to be the family physician here, she decided to just explain everything to him and hope for the best.

"I have a condition called endometriosis, Dr. Riley. That's why I was so sick."

A frown furrowed Anthony Riley's brow. "I don't believe I've ever heard of such a thing, Maddie. Who diagnosed this?"

"My family physician, Joe Phillips."

"I thought Devon said you were from Gulf Island?"

"That's right."

Again he frowned, shaking his head. "There isn't any doctor in these parts by that name, Maddie. There are only two other doctors between here and Gulf Island and I'm acquainted with them both."

"It's difficult to explain," she said, certain she was in deep trouble. If Anthony Riley was already suspicious, what would he think after she told him about her illness?

"Well, did this doctor explain your condition to you? Because I must admit I've never heard of such a thing. What did you call it again?" He took a little pad of paper and a pencil stub from his pocket. He licked the lead and looked up at her.

With a resigned sigh, she told him again, pausing to spell it out to him.

"And do you know what this endometriosis is?"

"Yes," she said, marveling that there was a time doctors would diagnose a patient without telling the patient the details of their illness. Thank God, those days were over.

"In normal circumstances, tissue collects in the uterus during the month. This tissue is released once a month, causing a woman's menstrual cycle." She glanced up to see if Dr. Riley was shocked or offended by her plain speech, but he only nodded for her to continue. "Endometriosis occurs when the tissue migrates outside of the uterus, to the ovaries, fallopian tubes, and even other organs. This causes extremely painful cramping during the cycle, nausea, diarrhea, and bleeding between cycles. If left untreated it can cause sterility. . . ."

"Sterility?" His eyes widened and he stared at her in shock. Too late Maddie realized that Anthony must be aware of Devon's situation. No doubt he was wondering how she would produce the much-needed child now.

"Eventually, yes," she admitted. "And even endometrian cancer."

"Amazing," he murmured, scratching notes on his pad. "And this doctor, Phillips, he told you all this?"

"Yes, he's a close friend of the family and he's been my doctor all my life. He's been treating me for endometriosis for about six months."

Anthony leaned back in his chair and studied Maddie, the gleam of knowledge shining in his scientific eyes. "I can't believe they've made strides like this in women's medicine and I haven't heard of them. I try to keep abreast of everything that will help my patients."

She nodded, wishing she could ease the man's mind. Obviously the doctor took his responsibilities seriously and she could see he was disturbed by what he saw as his neglect. Maddie felt sorry for the man. She couldn't tell him that these developments wouldn't come about for some years. And she couldn't explain that he'd had no way of knowing about them because they didn't exist at this time. And she'd never be able to explain to him why he'd found no record of them in his journals and articles.

"Did he offer you any reason for this condition, or any cure?"

"They still don't know what causes it," she said, glad she could finally tell him something that was completely true. "And the cure is . . ."

She hesitated. How could she explain hormone therapy and laser surgery? No, the only cure available to Anthony Riley's patients was the one she'd chosen for herself. Pregnancy. Could she admit to him why she'd agreed to marry his friend? Could she tell him the treatment without him drawing that conclusion for himself?

Maybe she could just say she didn't know any cure. Would he buy that? And if he did, what would it mean to other patients he might come across with the same symptoms?

In the end she knew she had to tell him all she knew. She couldn't hold back information that might help someone else.

"There are only a couple of possible treatments. None of which, I'm afraid, would be viable in these times."

"I'm sorry to hear that," Anthony said, his breath issuing from his lungs on a long sigh.

Maddie saw his distress and knew he was concerned on her behalf. She had to assure him she would be all right.

"There is one thing that is supposed to arrest the condition," she admitted, looking away. Her gaze locked on the empty fireplace and she couldn't face him as she said, "Pregnancy is the best treatment there is."

She looked back and saw shock, confusion, and then realization slowly dawn. He cleared his throat and nodded. "I see."

She was afraid he did. And what he saw was a woman who'd agreed to marry his friend in order to rid herself of an illness. Somehow, it sounded cold-blooded even to her own ears. Never mind that Devon wanted a loveless marriage. That he'd have been married to Elaine and probably miserable by now.

Maddie knew what was bothering her and she confronted her own deceit. At least Devon had been totally honest with her. She hadn't told him any of this before the wedding.

"The tissue would of course not be present during gestation, and therefore the disease would retard."

"Yes." Anthony Riley might be out of touch with nineteen ninety-two, but he was very adept for the nineteenth century.

Maddie could see something was still bothering the doctor. She thought she knew what it was. It was certainly a less than ideal environment to bring a child into. Normally, she'd have agreed with him. Of course he had no way of knowing she didn't expect to stay with Devon after he inherited and so the child wouldn't be exposed to his parents' loveless marriage.

Somehow, that thought did nothing to brighten her spirits and when Anthony left the room she couldn't even muster a warm thank-you.

Maddie stepped from her bath, the scent of lilac soap clinging to her damp hair and skin.

She slipped on one of the white lace-and-ribbon gowns Sarah had altered for her and covered it with a matching robe. As she caught her reflection in the mirror she felt angry tears well in her eyes. She might look the part of a bride, but it would do her no good without a groom.

She'd completely recovered, Anthony Riley had gone back to his practice, and Beverly had tried to pretend nothing was amiss. But it had been four days since she'd seen Devon. For some reason her husband was purposely avoiding her.

She closed the bathroom door behind her and started to her room, determined to put thoughts of Devon from her mind.

But as she reached out to open her bedroom door, he appeared at the top of the stairs. He saw her and froze, a scowl immediately lining his face.

His hair was rumpled, his face unshaven, and his clothes looked as though he'd slept in them. But all Maddie could see was the wounded look in his eyes.

Devon glared, made a rude sound in his throat, and made to walk past her. Maddie's hand shot out, stopping him.

"Devon, wait," she pleaded, still not certain what was wrong, but knowing she had to find out. Once and for all.

"We need to talk."

For a moment he didn't move, didn't speak. Then he turned and the look she saw in his eyes cut her to the quick. "Talk will not give me back what you have cheated me out of."

Maddie gasped, startled into silence for a second. "What," she finally managed to ask, "have I done?"

He shook off her hand and took a step away from her. Maddie's hurt turned to anger. In a flash she'd grasped his arm once more. This time he refused to face her.

"We had a bargain," she said. "If you plan to renege on it, I think you owe me an explanation."

"I am not the one who entered this arrangement under false pretenses. I owe you nothing."

He took another step but Maddie held firm to his arm. Finally, he turned back to her.

"What false pretenses?" Maddie asked.

Devon's sharp bark of laughter took her by surprise and she stepped back. "Name one thing," he sneered, "that you have told the truth about since you arrived here."

"Everything I've told you was the truth."

"Ah," he said, lifting his hand so quickly Maddie almost flinched. "And what about what you didn't tell me?"

Maddie recalled her conversation with Anthony Riley and suddenly the light dawned. "I didn't lie to you about being sick. I told you I'd be fine in a day or two."

"But you forgot to tell me your condition could prevent you from keeping your part of our bargain. I had to hear from Anthony that you have a disease that causes sterility. Dammit," he cursed. "You knew how important it was for me to have an heir; you knew without one I'd lose everything."

"I'm not sterile. And even if I didn't tell you the whole truth, I never lied," she said, still smarting from the unfair accusation.

"Didn't you?" he accused, whipping around to face her. He brushed her hand from his arm with a grimace as though her touch disgusted him. "It looks the same from where I'm standing."

"Well, it isn't," she said, growing angrier the longer she had to stand in the hall defending herself. "And I'm not going to discuss this in full view of your aunt and servants."

"Why not, Maddie? Afraid Aunt Bev and Sarah might see you for the lying opportunist you are?"

Maddie fumed. How dare the man accuse her of being an opportunist! She hadn't come here looking for a way to trap him into marriage. She hadn't asked him for a dime. She wouldn't even be here now if she could figure out a way to get back to her own time. And besides, he was the one who'd been willing to marry a woman just to beget an heir, so where did he get off calling *her* an opportunist?

The urge to slap him built to a fever pitch inside her. But she'd never slapped another person in her whole life and she refused to let him goad her into it now. She turned away and entered her room, slamming the door behind her.

But the door flew open, startling a sharp cry from Maddie. Devon entered, slamming the door behind him with enough force to rattle the glass in the window. Maddie stepped back.

"Get out," she demanded, pointing a trembling finger to the door.

"You had something to say to me, my lady wife, say it. I'm anxious to hear how you will explain yourself this time. I must say, in the past you've come up with some of the most entertaining stories I've ever heard."

"Oooh," Maddie cried, clenching her fists by her sides. "I have nothing more to say to you."

"No? You mean you're not going to tell me how an automobile came out of nowhere and ran you down? Or how a lake appeared where there is no lake and swallowed up your home?"

"You're being cruel," she screamed. "Those things really happened. I can't prove it, but I'm telling the truth."

Her words seemed to propel him into action and he swooped down on her, catching her by the shoulders. "You wouldn't know the truth if it hit you right between those gorgeous green eyes of yours. Did you know my cousin Edward stands to inherit if I don't provide the necessary heir? Well, let me tell you he won't be interested in providing for Aunt Bev, Sarah, or any of the others. We'll all be out in the streets, you included."

"I didn't lie to you," she repeated, suddenly comprehending his rage. Her anger was quickly deflated by the real concern she read on his face.

He felt he'd failed in his effort to keep his inheritance, and he blamed her. His responsibility to Bev, Sarah, and the others was weighing heavily on him. She reached up and closed her hands around his, meeting his accusing stare with one filled with understanding.

"I would never have deceived you that way. I know what this heir means to you. And I swear," she said, determined to ease his mind, "I swear, there will be no problem with my fulfilling my end of the deal."

He stared down at her. Anger, disbelief, and desire suddenly mingled in his eyes, turning them as black as the moonless night. He shook off her hands and his fingers fell to the front of her robe.

"We'll see about that," he told her. Deftly he began slipping the tiny pearl buttons out of their holes. "We'll see about that right now."

Chapter Eleven

Desire battled nervousness in Maddie as Devon pushed aside her robe to expose her bare shoulders. He bent his dark head and pressed a kiss to the exposed flesh of her neck, stubble from his unshaven face chafing her skin. The friction sent tingles along her nerves.

"What do you say, wife?" he taunted, running his lips along her jaw to her ear and back down to her shoulder. "Shall we see whether you are willing, or able, to keep our bargain?"

Maddie longed to push Devon away. When she and her husband made love for the first time she wanted it to be special, not an act born of his anger.

But she couldn't push him away. She'd made a deal, and she would stick to it. Even though she knew she could not yet become pregnant, she suspected Devon hadn't heard of the 14-day span between menstruation and ovulation. And if she tried to explain, it would look as if she were avoiding his advances.

"Fine, Devon. That is, after all, what I agreed to."

He looked up at her and she could read the passion behind his anger. He might pretend he only wanted her to produce a child, but she knew he found her desirable, and that knowledge only served to rekindle the flames of her passion.

"No hesitations, no second thoughts?" He tested her, and Maddie met the challenge.

"Of course not. If you had given me time to explain I would have told you that I not only want a child, but I'm still physically able to have one. My doctor assured me of that." She took advantage of his silence and decided to explain the whole situation to him.

"He said if I wanted a child I would have to become pregnant right away. Before my illness progressed any further. I'm sorry I didn't tell you all this when I agreed to marry you, Devon. Under the circumstances you had a right to know. But I didn't set out to deceive you."

"I see." He backed away, releasing her from his hard grasp. He turned, rubbing his hand along his raspy jaw. "So, you had decided to have a child before you met me?"

"Yes. I knew if I waited I'd probably never be able to have one. It was a difficult decision, but children are important to me and I wanted a child of my own."

"And did you have a father picked out for this child?"

"In a way," she hedged, not about to get into the intricacies of frozen sperm and donors.

"But you decided after you arrived here that I would suffice."

It sounded cold and calculating coming from him, but she nodded. Devon turned at her silence and saw her quiet confirmation. He cleared his throat.

"That's why you insist on keeping the child with you? You want children that badly?" His tone softened perceptibly.

"Yes, I do." Her voice was firm, solid, and she made the admission without hesitation. Suddenly a weight lifted from Maddie's shoulders and she realized she hadn't been sure until that second that she really did want a child of her own. But now she knew she'd made the right choice.

"Well," he said, his features smoothing out, his lips tipping up. "It seems I owe you an apology. All things considered, I can understand how you feel. And besides, your motives are far purer than mine."

Maddie didn't know how to reply to his sudden attitude change, or his odd statement, so she remained impassive.

"Forgive my behavior, Maddie. And the way I treated you," he added, looking down at the empty buttonholes on the bodice of her gown.

173

"If you'll excuse me I'll see to a bath and a shave. I'll return when I'm more presentable."

Maddie nodded again, feeling the nervousness of a new bride overwhelm her. She drew her robe more tightly against her throat.

Devon bowed his head slightly to her and left the room without another word.

The wait seemed interminable to Maddie. She climbed in bed, thinking she'd wait for her husband there, only to jump out a moment later, afraid of appearing too forward. Smoothing the spread back over the mattress, she erased the indentation her body had made.

This is ridiculous, she thought, going to the dresser and picking up the silver-handled brush. It wasn't as if she'd never been to bed with a man before. She'd lived with Todd for months.

But Maddie couldn't even picture Todd clearly now, much less remember how she'd felt making love with him. It had been a long time. And besides, this was different. She was married now, but she barely knew this man who was her husband. How would it feel to make love to him? To have his hands and lips caress her. To have his . . .

She plopped down on the stool and ran the brush through her hair. The attraction she'd felt for Devon since the first moment they met assailed her. He was a handsome man. Gentle when gentleness was called for. Kind, even to a stranger. His kisses aroused her, his touch heated her blood. With a small smile she realized all in all she was a lucky bride.

The door opened and she froze. Devon entered, carrying a tray with glasses and a bottle of wine. Maddie felt her heart soften and she couldn't stop her smile from covering her face.

"What is this?" she asked shyly.

"This," he said, setting the tray on her bedside table, "is how these things are supposed to be done."

"Is that right?" Her voice rasped and she choked back the emotion tightening her throat.

Devon held out his hand and Maddie walked forward. He clasped her fingers, drew them to his lips, and kissed them.

"Thank you for honoring me by becoming my wife, Maddie. I will do my best to make you happy, and I promise to see to it you get what you want from our arrangement."

Maddie knew Devon's Southern upbringing and manners had more to do with his change in attitude than anything else, but it no longer mattered. He meant to honor their agreement, and assure her happiness in the meantime. What more could she have asked for?

"Thank you, Devon, that was beautiful. And I promise I'll do my best to see that you get everything you need or want from our marriage. I'll never make you sorry you chose to accept my proposal."

Devon handed her a glass and they toasted their vows. The fruity flavor of wine filled

Maddie's mouth, and she swallowed hard. Already the lump had returned to fill her throat, threatening to cut off her breath.

Slowly, Devon removed the glass from her hand and set it aside. He placed his beside hers on the table and took her hands. With infinite tenderness, he bent his head to place his lips on hers. Her mouth flowered, and the kiss drew out, long and sweet.

Maddie let her hands slip around Devon's neck, her fingers automatically finding the soft waves of hair at his nape. Sensations assailed her. The softness of his lips, the texture of the dark strands against her sensitized fingertips, the feel of his body aligning with hers.

His hands crept over her back, down her hips, and then up to her waist. Fitting his lower body more closely against hers, he bent her over his supporting arms. Maddie moved, coaxing the hardness of his desire into the matching hollow between her thighs. Devon groaned and she felt a shiver pass through his body.

He pressed her down onto the mattress. Devon never allowed their bodies to part as he followed her to the bed. He shifted her leg for better access and Maddie sighed as their bodies rubbed intimately.

Reverently, he parted her robe, finding the softness of her bare shoulders. He pressed kisses to her neck, shoulder, and the hollow of her throat. Slowly, he unbuttoned the tiny pearl buttons on the lace bodice of her gown. As each button slipped out of its matching hole, he pressed a kiss in its place until a slice of her chest lay exposed.

His black eyes met hers as his fingers pushed aside the material to reveal her creamy breasts. Maddie's breath was coming in short, sharp gasps now. His hands crept up just under her breasts and stilled.

She didn't know why he hesitated, but desire made her bold and she ran her hand down his shoulder, along his arm, to his hand. She eased it up to cover her aching breast.

A long, low sound issued from deep in his throat. He looked down at her body. His hand caressed her hardened nipple, teasing it with a maddening circular motion. First wide, sweeping circles, then small, tight ones fanned the flames of her passion. Warm waves of arousal rippled out from his touch to heat her body.

His hand left her breast to push the robe and gown off her shoulders. The lacy fabric puddled at her waist. Devon slid off her to lie by her side and tugged the clothing over her hips and buttocks. He dropped them over the side of the bed as his leg draped across hers.

Placing another long, hot kiss on her lips, he let his thigh ride up to press against the core of her desire. Maddie clenched her legs together tightly and arched to meet the pressure.

"Yes, love," he whispered, drawing her knee up to his waist. "That's the way."

Devon's hand caressed the back of her knee, holding it gently against his side so his thigh could ride higher. Maddie felt her body go rigid under his. Between his deep, thorough kisses and the friction his movements were creating, her passion threatened to peak.

She reached out with desperate hands to stop him. Her fingers went to the front of his shirt. She unfastened the buttons and let her hands slide over the hard muscles of his stomach and chest as she pushed it off. Her trembling fingers found the buttons on his trousers and, with his help, Devon soon joined her on the bed naked.

Their gazes locked and held as each explored the other with eager, arousing hands. Maddie felt swept away by the incredible longing Devon coaxed from her usually unresponsive body. Her heart whispered that no other man had ever made her feel so deeply, or want so strongly. Only Devon could draw forth such wild yearnings. Only Devon. Only her husband.

Too soon Maddie could feel the pressure building in her again and she tried to rush. But Devon held her hands still and let the sound of their heartbeats soothe them. He stroked and kissed and touched every inch of flesh his hands could reach. Maddie felt a warmth pool at the junction of her thighs and she cried out.

"Devon," she begged, "now."

His mouth came down over hers and she thought he'd deny her, but his thighs slid between hers and he met her eyes as he drove into her.

The tempo could not be held back after that and together they rose to the highest high, and slowly descended.

Their hearts beat out a crazy tattoo as the lights and sounds around them came back into focus. Devon rolled to his back, drawing Maddie with him. Breathless, she rested her head on his chest and settled her leg across his. She listened to the sound of his pulse as it slowed to normal, thinking how intimate so simple a thing seemed to her now. She studied his hand as it lay on her hip and remembered the pleasure it had given her. She fell asleep with the memory of his kiss still on her lips.

Sometime later she woke, cold and confused. The covers had slipped off her, although she remembered having their warmth against her bare skin earlier. She glanced around in the dim light of the room and frowned.

The spot beside her was empty, the pillow cold. The clock told her it was still night, not yet morning, and she wondered where Devon had gone. Rising, she reached for the nearest article of clothing she saw and found that it was Devon's shirt. She slid it on and fastened the buttons.

The garment fell to her thighs, the sleeves long and belled. She snuggled into the warmth and inhaled the scent of Devon still clinging to the fabric.

Where could he have gone? she wondered. Had he stepped out for a snack or had he left as soon as she was asleep?

She couldn't be sure but something told her he hadn't slept beside her. Even though she'd listened to his breathing, still erratic from their loving, as she dozed off.

Why had he left? He'd seemed to enjoy their coupling as much as she had, although she had to admit he spent more time on her pleasure than any other man ever had.

Just thinking of his caresses made her warm. She returned to her bed and snuggled under the covers, still dressed in Devon's shirt. Surely he'd just stepped out for a moment. He'd be back shortly. She longed to feel him beside her again, drawing a response from her she'd never suspected herself capable of.

As she drifted off to sleep once more she dreamed of all the nights yet to come. It could take a while for her to conceive a child. By then, maybe this need he'd aroused in her would have been fulfilled.

Chapter Twelve

In his study Devon sat with his chin resting on his palm. Anthony was vigorously discussing the latest developments on the project he and Devon were involved in, but Devon's mind was not on the new hospital. Memories of Maddie, loving him so thoroughly the past seven nights, refused to be pushed to the back of his consciousness.

". . . still agree to donate the land, if we will name it after Seth." Anthony's voice cut into Devon's thoughts momentarily and he realized he'd lost the trail of the conversation again.

"What did you say?"

Anthony stared quizzically at his friend for a long moment, cleared his throat, and patted the rolled drawings against his palm.

"I said the Brewsters are still talking about donating the land for the hospital if all the other members of the board agree to the name they've chosen."

"No one had a problem with that, did they?"

Anthony shook his head, eyeing Devon curiously. "No, everyone liked Seth well enough and they don't really care what we name the hospital so long as we get it built without asking them for more money."

"Are we still short of funds?" Devon toyed with a silver letter opener on his desk and strained to hear Maddie's voice. Occasionally her laughter or Beverly's would drift through the heavy door of his study and he'd wonder what the women were up to now. Their antics never ceased to surprise him.

"Yes," Anthony said, following Devon's gaze to the door. Not seeing or hearing anything, he continued. "And we're down to only a few more possible investors. The rest we've pretty much bled dry."

"I thought I'd ride out and talk to Jeb Franklin. He's still sitting on the fence about investing. Maybe I can get him to come down on our side," Devon said absently.

"I'd offer to go, but Milly Elkins is about to deliver and I planned to ride out and see how she's doing tomorrow."

"You see about Milly," he told Anthony, trying to keep his mind off Maddie. "I'll talk to Jeb. I think he's about to give in anyway."

"Well, that's settled. With the plans complete

and most of the backing secure we can break ground as soon as the land is cleared."

"Fine, fine," Devon mumbled, his attention drawn to the door once more as the sound of Maddie's laughter drifted to his ears. He took a moment to let the sound bathe him in its warmth. Maddie's laughter was something he hadn't often heard. Not that he had anyone to blame for that fact but himself.

He avoided Maddie much of the time for fear he might grow accustomed to her presence in his house and in his life. At night, they shared the deepest intimacies. They made love, they touched, they clung. But no matter how she pleasured him, or he her, he refused to stay the night in her bed. And he hadn't suggested she move into his room although it was what he wanted.

It was damned hard to leave her each night, but Devon knew it would make their final parting easier. And they would part, finally, when she'd produced the child. For even though he intended to keep track of them, he'd agreed to let her and the baby leave once she'd fulfilled the terms of their arrangement.

Devon closed off thoughts of his life without Maddie. He wouldn't think of it until the time came. Until then, he'd keep his heart and his soul out of her reach and hope his body could forget all the exquisite pleasures she'd given him.

"Devon?"

Devon blinked away his musings and realized

he'd been thinking of making love to Maddie. His body had grown tight beneath his trousers and he shifted in his chair.

"What did you say?"

"I said, how are things between you and Maddie? I couldn't help noticing you both seemed tense earlier."

"No," Devon lied, perking up with false joviality. "We couldn't be happier."

Anthony looked doubtful, but he nodded. "Good, good, that's nice to hear. I must say I was more than a little shocked by all this. First you tell me you don't know Maddie, you hint she might be slightly unbalanced, and the next thing I know you've called off your engagement to Elaine and married Maddie, who just happens to have turned out to be the daughter of a good friend of Beverly's. You must admit the situation gets stranger steadily."

"Not really," Devon said, pretending to take offense at Anthony's rehashing of the whole incident. "Besides, you never liked Elaine, so you can't tell me you're disappointed about my broken engagement." His words and tone were harsher than necessary, but it was the only way Devon could think of to discourage Anthony's questions about Maddie. His friend was astute enough to see through the thin story Devon had woven for the other acquaintances in the area.

His ploy worked and Anthony immediately backed down. "Whoa, don't get me wrong, Dev. I think Maddie's a wonderful lady. And it is no secret I never wanted you to marry Elaine. I just want you to be happy."

Devon smiled at Anthony and dropped the letter opener onto his desk. "Well, I am. So you can stop worrying about me now."

He tried to put thoughts of Maddie from his mind as Anthony spread the plans across his desk, pointing out important changes. But Maddie's image refused to be banished. Memories of their nights together had him growing hard again. Closing his eyes, he could see her as she looked at night, naked and beautiful on the bed beside him. His mouth went dry. He knew it would do no good to let his desires overrule his good sense.

More than anything he wanted to go to her, take her in his arms and kiss her, carry her back to his room, and vow never to let her go. How was it possible he'd let a woman become so dear to him that the sight of her, the sound of her laughter had him acting like a love-struck newlywed?

And even more frightening was the fact that it wasn't simple desire. He could have battled that. But Maddie had continued to surprise and delight him with her ability to turn any situation to her advantage. She adapted with amazing alacrity. She brought joy and entertainment to his life. Her vivaciousness brightened even the darkest corners of his house, and his mind. She'd all but banished the black veil of pain and betrayal he had harbored in his heart since Crystal's death.

Yes, he thought, that was what had him at sixes and sevens. He'd let her get too close. Always before, he'd kept women at a distance. But Maddie had caught him off guard and had slipped right past the iron gates of his determination. Too late he realized what a fool he'd been. She'd already stolen his heart. Already laid claim to a large portion of his soul like a poacher on forbidden property.

More fool he, Devon thought bitterly. A long time ago he'd loved a woman. And she'd left him lonely and bitter. Now, after all the barren years, Maddie had brought the sun back to shine in his life. But for how long? She'd made it plain she didn't intend to stay. His wife had been honest about her needs and desires. And it wasn't him or his love she wanted. It was a child. His, or any other.

He'd made a fatal mistake and he felt sufficiently doomed. Once more he'd let his heart lead him, and as before he would pay with the pain later. How could he have fallen in love with her when he knew—was forewarned this time—that she, too, would leave him?

He cursed himself as ten kinds of a fool, and doggedly dragged his attention back to Anthony and the revised hospital plans.

Maddie lay in Devon's arms, listening to the slowing cadence of their hearts beating in rhythm. As usual their lovemaking had left her physically and emotionally drained. Devon was a fabulous lover, never missing an opportunity to give her pleasure. He touched her, caressed her, manipulated her body to his will until she could barely speak. And only when he'd assured himself that she was replete did he join her in seeking his own satisfaction. He'd changed all her ideas of intimacy; he'd destroyed all the fears of failure she'd harbored since the disaster with Todd. Devon loved her thoroughly and completely.

Without love, she thought sadly. He could make her mindless with passion and he seemed as affected by the hot, flowing feelings as she. But she tensed in anticipation of his departure. She'd long since stopped hoping he would stay the night in her bed. Even the few times she'd thought he'd fallen asleep, he would stir and slip out of the bed, gathering his robe or donning his trousers before leaving her alone.

She listened to his steady breathing and thought she detected the soft sound of a satisfied snore. His hand rested against her breast possessively, his other one stretched behind his head. Her cheek settled against his chest and she let her fingers roam his torso at will. He never minded her touching him. In fact, she was almost certain he'd been pleasantly surprised at her ardor. He encouraged her explorations and never failed to respond to her gentle persuasions.

But tonight he slid his hand up to cup hers, stilling her seductive caresses. He linked his fingers through hers and drew them up to his lips, where he placed a light kiss on her knuckles.

"You have well and truly satisfied me, wife," he whispered close to her ear. "And I am astounded at the glory I never fail to find in your bed."

Maddie sucked her breath in sharply and turned her head to stare up into his face. By the fading light of the moon she could see his eyes were closed, and a pained expression crossed his features as she watched.

"Then stay," she offered, trying to keep the longing from her voice. She'd refused to make the request before, certain he'd read her true emotions in her words. And Maddie wasn't yet ready to admit, to him or herself, how deep her feelings really went. She had to remind herself time after time that he was merely fulfilling their bargain.

His eyes slowly opened and a look of hope faded, replaced by the familiar pain she'd noticed before.

"Ah, I would only keep you awake with my tossing and snoring," he said, trying to force a casual smile.

Maddie had sworn to herself she'd not beg him to stay. As much as she needed him with her during the darkest, coldest hours of the morning, when her doubts and fears slunk in to chill her with their presence, she wouldn't plead.

"I would sleep soundly in your arms," she told him, erasing his excuses without losing her dignity.

He smiled at her, but the bleakness never left his eyes. He released her hand and Maddie felt cast adrift. He would leave her again.

"You say that now, but you would berate me later for disturbing your sleep."

He placed a last kiss on her mouth and slipped from the bed. He never even glanced back as he poked his arms into the sleeves of his robe and drew it closed. He left without another word.

Tears filled Maddie's eyes, but she blinked them back. If her husband didn't want to share her bed for the duration of the night, she would learn to live without him. She tried to tell herself that she knew next to nothing about men of Devon's century. Maybe this was the norm. She might have scandalized him by suggesting they share a bed all the time. Yes, that was probably it, she thought. But her despondency seeped into the empty spot where Devon had lain and suddenly the bed seemed too cold for comfort.

Devon slung his robe across the room, but the action gave him no pleasure. His sheets were cold and stiff as he slid into bed and he couldn't keep himself from longing for the warmth and comfort of Maddie's bed. His pillow smelled of soap and sunlight; hers had held traces of musk and desire.

Damn, damn, damn, he cursed, pounding his frustrated fist into the hard, unyielding mound. What was he going to do? He couldn't keep inventing excuses to desert his wife. Tonight, her pleas had almost won him over. Only a strong, desperate dose of self-preservation had kept him from giving in. For he knew, as surely as he knew he loved his wife, that to stay would be a grave mistake.

Wasn't it enough he stayed away during the days, hardly seeing his home or his aunt any longer in an attempt to avoid Maddie? He almost never dined with them, since he felt his respect for her intelligence grow every time they conversed. And he never, ever, allowed himself to touch or kiss her during the day for fear he'd spill the truth about his feelings and be laid bare to her rejection.

He confined his passion to the few hours they shared each night, covering his deep desires with the justification of fulfilling their bargain. But how much longer could he go on without revealing to her the true depth of emotion he felt for her?

He stretched, placing his hands behind his head. The covers shifted across his nude body, evoking heated remembrances of Maddie's daring touches. Lord, but the woman knew what to do to drive him wild with wanting. She poured everything into the act of making love as though she'd sought release for years without success. And her responses never failed to send him over the precipice of good judgment. Throwing all his good counsel aside, he could not deny her, or himself. And for those few precious hours, he let himself imagine what could have been if he hadn't agreed to let her go away. He lied to his heart, deceived his mind, and let his body confess to her how he truly felt. He loved her.

Chapter Thirteen

With her immediate future secured, Maddie settled into life in Devon's home. She awoke each morning and dressed in one of the many outfits Devon had given her. She breakfasted with Beverly, took a walk around the beautifully manicured lawns, and inspected the articles of furniture which she had never had an opportunity to see up close before.

It never ceased to amaze her when she found a rosewood cheval fire screen or an elaborate urn-shaped knife and fork case in satinwood. Some of these she sketched in an attempt to imprint them on her memory for use when she returned to her business, which she continued to assure herself would eventually happen. Such lesser-known pieces would draw a hefty price in any decorating job. She might even start a trend.

She'd taught Beverly how to make pizza, and in exchange Beverly had shown her how to needlepoint pillows. Maddie had been more interested in the embroidery stand than in learning the different stitches, but in the end she'd produced an acceptable piece of work.

Devon hadn't returned to her room that first night and a pattern had been set. He continued to come to her room each night and Maddie looked forward to the hours they'd spend making love. He never acted as though the encounters were a duty or a chore, and their passion had not dimmed one whit in the last two weeks. But he always, without exception, left her bed and her room as soon as the last ember of desire was banked.

They had little time for conversation, either during their nightly encounters or at other times. He left the house each morning before she awoke and didn't return until just before supper. He often took that meal in his study, claiming an overload of paperwork. And yet, each night he came to her, made her feel things she'd never dreamed of feeling. She hadn't asked him to stay since that last disastrous attempt, and he continued to return to his own room each night, leaving Maddie cold and bereft and more than a little confused.

She'd passed her scheduled date of ovulation; now she could only wait and see if they'd been successful. Each morning she arose, hoping for a sign that she'd conceived. So far nothing out of the ordinary had occurred. However, she'd felt better the past few days than she could remember feeling in some time and she wondered if that were a positive sign.

Genevieve had often made the comment that the St. Thomas women could get pregnant if a man looked at them crossways. Maddie prayed it was true.

As she pulled on a pretty day dress with a yellow print bodice, gray skirt, and rows of three red bows along each sleeve and the lapels, she found herself looking forward to the day. Beverly had offered to teach her how to bake cinnamon-raisin bread, a favorite of Maddie's, in exchange for Maddie teaching her a pop song Beverly had taken a particular liking to.

Pinning her hair into the proper twist expected of her now that she was a married woman, she went in search of Beverly.

She found Devon's aunt still in the dining room, and Maddie poured herself a cup of coffee and took a piece of dry toast from the sideboard.

"Good morning," Beverly said, waving Maddie over to give her a kiss on her cheek. Maddie leaned down and offered the peck on the old woman's cheek and then seated herself in one of the satinwood elbow chairs ornamented with roses and a peacock feather border.

"Shall we start the morning with the baking and then work on the song you promised to teach me, Maddie?"

"That sounds fine, Aunt Bev," Maddie agreed. "Would you like to join me on my walk first?"

"Umm, a walk sounds nice, but I don't think so. Maybe another time."

Every morning Maddie visited the place where Devon found her. Curiosity made her poke and pry through every blade of grass, every clump of brush, in an effort to find the "door" through which she'd passed.

She always asked Beverly to accompany her, but every morning Beverly declined. Maddie suspected Beverly refused in order to give Maddie time to go to the field alone. Devon's aunt never asked where she'd been, but sometimes Maddie thought she saw the older woman breathe a sigh of relief when Maddie returned.

Today, Beverly was already in the kitchen, gathering the ingredients for their cooking lesson. Maddie enjoyed learning how to use the wood-burning stove and usually her attempts turned out well, thanks to Bev. Afterward, she offered to clean up while the other woman went ahead to the parlor.

As Maddie approached the door a short time later, she caught the first few notes of a song she'd performed for Beverly the day before and smiled. Devon's aunt liked all kinds of music and she kept Maddie at the piano for hours trying to remember more and more of the "modern" music.

Some of the tunes were neither modern nor particularly classic pieces, but Beverly didn't seem to mind. Anything Maddie could think of entertained Devon's aunt.

"Very good," Maddie called, clapping as she stepped into the parlor.

Beverly laughed and finished off the last few notes with a flourish. She nodded her head in lieu of a bow, and shifted to make room for Maddie on the bench.

Maddie let her fingers trail over the keys and played snatches of several different songs, everything from an old Beatles tune to a Frank Sinatra ballad. She ended with a fairly new piece by Rod Stewart. Beverly's smile was wide as she tried to keep up with Maddie.

"How do you know so many different ones, Maddie?" Beverly asked. "You must have attended a lot of performances."

Maddie laughed. "Oh, Aunt Bev, I didn't go see all these people in person."

"You didn't? But how else could you have heard their music played?"

"With things called radios, stereos, and tape players. Even, now, compact discs." Beverly's eyes widened. She knew she was about to hear another exciting tale of the future from her new niece and she stilled in anticipation.

Maddie tried to explain to Beverly how music reached listeners in her time. Maddie's not being an expert in electronics seriously hampered the discussion, but Beverly didn't seem to mind when Maddie couldn't clarify the details.

Finally, Maddie finished by saying, "And of course we do have concerts. I used to go to them when I was younger. But they aren't like the classical performances I'm sure you're used to."

"Tell me what they're like."

Beverly's curiosity was insatiable. She longed to know everything Maddie could tell her, and the telling helped Maddie through some bouts of homesickness. She appreciated Beverly's interest, without which she'd have no outlet for her loneliness.

"My favorites though," Maddie said, "were the live performances on television." She'd already explained that invention to Beverly, and Devon's aunt nodded. "From the time Genny and I were about eight or nine, we'd watch 'American Bandstand.' That was a show where singers would come on and perform and the audience would dance. It was great, a real American tradition. After the show we'd go to our rooms and practice doing the numbers just like we'd seen them done. God, we had a blast."

"What do you mean, the way you'd seen them done? Do you mean the performers didn't sit at the piano the way you do?"

Maddie laughed again and it was a long minute before she could answer Beverly. "Oh, no," she said, giggling. "They would usually stand, move their hips a little, or sway back and forth. Some of them would even choreograph steps to songs and they'd move in time with the beat."

"Amazing."

"There was one—oh, you'd have loved him,

Aunt Bev—who wasn't allowed on television because he moved his pelvis so much the producers thought it indecent."

"My word!"

"He was the best, the king," Maddie said solemnly. "I'll never forget where I was the day they announced he'd died."

"Show me."

Maddie pushed thoughts of the idol from her mind and turned back to face Devon's aunt. "What?"

"Show me how they danced, Maddie. Especially the ones they did to the beat of the music. I'm trying to picture it all in my head but I simply can't."

"But, Aunt Bev . . ."

Maddie didn't know how to *show* Devon's aunt anything. The woman was usually amazing when it came to getting along with her infirmity, but Maddie had no experience with sensory techniques. She thought for a long minute and finally the answer came to her.

"Stand up, Aunt Bev."

Beverly did as directed and Maddie stood behind her. She began to hum the tune Beverly had asked Maddie to teach her and took hold of Beverly's elbows.

"Bend your knees, sway forward and then back, now lift your arms over your head like this."

The instruction went on for close to an hour and Maddie and Beverly were both breathless and giddy when finally Maddie pronounced

Beverly adept at the routine.

Sarah came in and stopped dead at the sight of the older woman swaying and flapping her arms. Her mouth dropped open comically and she watched in amazement.

"Oh, Sarah, this is perfect. We need another person to do this right." Maddie swept down on Sarah and dragged her into the room.

"These girl groups always had three or four members."

"What you two been doin' in here? I'm gone check the liquor cabinet afore Misser Devon gets home."

"We're not drunk, Sarah. I'm teaching Beverly how singers performed in the sixties and seventies. Now, come on and help me."

Sarah still looked unsure of the two, but she'd do anything for Beverly. Maddie had endeared herself to Sarah as well, and the servant couldn't refuse them.

"Now, you stand on the other side of Beverly and just do what we do."

Maddie tapped her foot a couple of times and she and Beverly broke into song. They stepped twice to the side, twice back, turned around, and threw their arms up, making a wide circle in the air in front of them. Together they sang. . . .

"My momma said you cain't hurry love—
No, you just have to wait, she said love
don't come easy, it's a game of give and
take. . . ."

They did pirouettes, clasped their hands to their breasts, and pointed their hands out in front of them.

They sang louder and louder. Sarah had picked up the chorus, and they continued on when the song should have ended, singing it one more time.

Maddie turned from a spin and saw Devon and Anthony standing in the doorway of the parlor, twin looks of shock and amusement on their faces. Knowing she couldn't be any more embarrassed than she already was, she kept singing and advanced toward Devon. She took the position of lead singer and stepped right up to him.

Anthony laughed outright as she ran her finger along Devon's shoulder, circled him, rubbed her back against his arm, and then tapped the tip of his nose.

Sarah stuttered, stopped, and looked decidedly uncomfortable. Beverly, if she knew the men had arrived, ignored them altogether. As the song wound down, Maddie and Beverly took a deep bow. Sarah missed the first bow but she dutifully bent double for the second and third.

Devon and Anthony clapped enthusiastically and the four began to laugh as Sarah scampered out mumbling about crazy white women and what they make their servants do.

"Well, if I'd known how much fun y'all had around here, I'd have come back sooner,"

Anthony said, hugging Beverly and placing a welcoming kiss on Maddie's cheek.

He looked at Devon oddly, and Maddie's husband awkwardly came forward to greet her.

"Darling," he whispered, placing a brief peck on her cheek. "I'm sorry we disturbed you." She felt his fingers tighten painfully on her arms, and when he pulled back the look in his eyes told her his words and actions had been for appearance' sake. Maddie missed him when he was gone, but each day they spent together made it harder to deny how much she enjoyed the closeness.

"Anthony and I have some more business to take care of. He'll be staying on for a few days until we've worked out the details. Aunt Bev, would you mind telling Sarah so she will be sure to have his room readied?"

"Of course," she said, taking Anthony's arm. "Come with me. Maddie and I made fresh cinnamon-raisin bread this morning. Devon's business will wait until you've had some refreshments."

Devon made to protest, but Beverly had already led Anthony from the room. He cleared his throat and faced his wife uncomfortably.

"I'm sorry, I should have warned you Anthony would be coming back with me."

"It's all right," Maddie lied, her embarrassment complete now that the moment had passed. "We were just . . ."

She waved her hand awkwardly and her voice trailed off. She realized there was no explanation she could offer Devon without reminding him she was different.

Devon saw her discomfort and assumed it was due to Anthony's presence. He hastened to reassure her.

"Maddie," he said, looking down at his boots and then over to the window. "I know it's asking a lot for you to put up this pretense around Anthony, but he's been my closest friend nearly all my life. Since everyone expected me to marry Elaine, they think ours was some whirlwind courtship. Anthony assumes, like everybody else, that we met and fell in love."

Maddie winced. Devon's words painfully yanked at her heart. She swallowed the hurt and nodded woodenly.

"I understand," she said. It was Devon who didn't understand that her discomfort came from trying to hide her love, not from any aversion to his touches and affection.

"Anthony has felt guilty since my wife died, and it's important to him that I'm happy now."

Suddenly Maddie thought she understood. And the implications were horrible! Could Anthony be . . .

She couldn't stop herself from asking the question her mind was dying to know the answer to. "Is he the one, Devon? Was Anthony Crystal's . . ."

"Lover?" Devon shook his head and tucked his hands in his trouser pockets. "No, she wasn't his lover. She was his sister."

"His sister!"

Devon nodded and glanced over his shoulder, making sure they were still alone. "Yes, we all grew up together." He stepped farther into the room and stared into the rays of sunshine coming through the window. "Crystal was so beautiful with her blonde hair and warm brown eyes. The summer she turned sixteen she blossomed, and I decided to marry her before any other man claimed her."

Maddie gulped and tried not to let her despair show. How could Devon tell her these things? How could he think his words wouldn't hurt her? But Maddie knew. Even after all their nights together, after all the glorious hours they'd spent in each other's arms, Devon still thought of their relationship in terms of their bargain. They'd agreed to a business arrangement with no emotions. It wasn't his fault she hadn't been able to keep that part of the bargain.

Maddie stifled those emotions. She willed her eyes not to show the love in her heart. And she prayed she wouldn't show her hand before she could get away from Devon.

"But I married her too young. Crystal hadn't even been courted by other men. She loved me in her own way, and she thought we'd be perfect for each other. But she soon realized her feelings for me weren't romantic. It was a small step from there to the end. She met someone she really did love, and you know the rest of the story."

"Yes."

"What you probably don't know is that Anthony has always felt responsible for what Crystal did. He's tried to pair me off with every other woman in the county in a misguided attempt to mend my broken heart. But I wasn't interested. I'd have never married again if it weren't for my father's will."

He pinned her with his engulfing black gaze and she felt paralyzed. Her feet wanted to run from the room, her ears wanted to shut out his confession. She realized she'd fallen in love with Devon Crowe and she wanted to cry out at the unfairness of it. Why him? A man who could never love her, and whom she would have to one day leave behind. In her mind she could almost imagine returning to her time, a time when Devon Crowe would be nothing but a vague name attached to a lake. Grief assailed her as though she'd passed that barrier and found her husband, and all she loved here, dead.

"So, for Anthony's sake," Devon was saying, "I'm asking you to continue the deception. Do you mind?"

Maddie wanted to shout—Yes! It would kill her for Devon to act as though he loved her when there was no real emotion on his part. Her feelings were too deeply involved to keep them in check much longer. She'd end up making a fool of herself by declaring her love, or begging him to stay the night with her.

But in the end, Devon's plea won her heart. She liked Anthony, a lot. If she could ease his guilt by pretending she and Devon were in love, she'd have to do it.

"All right," she whispered, dreading the days ahead.

"Thank you, Maddie. I wouldn't ask you to do this, but it means a lot to Anthony."

"I understand," she told him, trying to paste an obliging smile on her face.

Devon bent and planted a soft kiss on her mouth, and Maddie had to stop herself from leaning into him. She fought the urge to clasp her arms around his neck and she ignored the blaze of ever-present desire that smoldered just beneath the surface.

And, as Devon walked away, she blinked back the sting of tears in her eyes.

Chapter Fourteen

Maddie pounded the dough and tried to keep her mind busy. But even concentrating on making the cinnamon bread she loved couldn't keep her from thinking.

Two weeks didn't guarantee anything, she tried to tell herself. After all she'd been through, some delay was to be expected. Besides, it might just be a sign that her condition was progressing.

But a smile turned up the corners of Maddie's lips and she was lost in a world of wonder once more. The dough rose steadily as she leaned on the counter, imagining the possibilities.

She felt terrific. The dull ache in her abdomen and lower back had disappeared some days ago. She seemed to have shaken the fatigue which had plagued her for months. And, she recalled with a broad grin, she'd never been late in her life. Especially not two weeks!

Could it be? Was she already pregnant with Devon's child? A giggle threatened to escape even while tears seemed to come out of nowhere and fill her eyes. She dabbed them with the dish towel tied around her waist and let the giggle burst forth. Somehow, she knew it was true. Oh, how she longed for a modern, progressive home pregnancy test.

She wondered how long it would be before she could confirm her suspicions. When was pregnancy assured in this time? When two periods had been missed, or when the fetus could be felt during an exam? Should she wait that long to tell Devon? *Could* she wait? Her happiness bubbled over.

No, she couldn't tell him, or anyone, until she was certain. Under the circumstances it would be cruel to raise hopes. Devon needed this child desperately. Maddie realized how desperately she needed it, too. If her purpose for coming back in time had been to help Devon secure his inheritance while at the same time answering her prayer for a child, she knew she'd do it all over again, given the chance.

The fear, the confusion, even the homesickness she'd suffered could not dim her delight. She was going to have a baby. And not just any baby: Devon's baby. Warmth exploded through her and she hugged herself with her arms. She hadn't known she would feel this way. For so long she'd put off becoming involved with another man for fear of being hurt. And now she knew what the rest of the world already knew. The only joy in life greater than falling in love was discovering you are going to have a child with the one you love.

The only blight on the otherwise perfect horizon was the fact that Devon did not love her. But, she reminded herself, it was better that way. If she were to be swept back to her own time as soon as she'd fulfilled her part of the bargain, it was best only one of them suffered a broken heart. It was too late for her.

A wave of sadness replaced the glow of happiness for a moment, but Maddie refused to let it take root. This baby would not be touched by any negative feelings or emotions. She'd give him love enough for two parents when the time came and later, in the years ahead, she'd have a tale to tell him about his father.

And she would tell him. Because Maddie loved Devon, respected him, and considered herself lucky for having had him. If only for a brief time. He was a good man. Maybe too good, she thought, remembering how he'd cared for her even though he obviously thought her mad. Any son, or daughter, would be proud to have him as a father. She was only sorry her child would never know him personally. But that, too, seemed beyond her control and so she wouldn't dwell on it.

Humming a lively tune, she finished preparing the bread and set it into the waiting pans. As she bent to push them into the oven, she wondered how long it would be until her bulk would prevent such manuevers. Oddly, she even looked forward to that.

Maddie daydreamed until the smell of cinnamon drew her attention back to the oven. With a cry of alarm, she yanked open the oven door and drew out the loaves of bread, rescuing them just before their crusts grew too dark.

"Something smells delicious," a teasing voice said from the doorway. Maddie straightened and turned, smiling at the look of surprise on Devon's face.

"Maddie," he said, clearing his throat and glancing around as if looking for reinforcements. "I thought I smelled Aunt Beverly's cinnamon bread baking."

"You did. Only this time it's Maddie's cinnamon bread. Would you like some?" She held the loaf out to him and watched indecision battle longing on his face. His nostrils flared in appreciation and she knew hunger had won the day.

"If you don't mind me interrupting you."

"Of course not. I'll enjoy the company and take advantage of the excuse to have some of this myself."

She spread a dish towel on the table and set the bread down. She collected plates and a crock of butter from the counter as Devon pulled out a chair and sat.

"There's some coffee on the stove. Would you like a cup?"

He nodded, cutting into the bread and serving her a piece before placing a slice on his own plate. He slathered his own with lots of the thick, creamy butter and took a bite while she poured their coffee.

"Ummm," he murmured, closing his eyes. "I think this is even better than Aunt Bev's." He licked butter off his lip and smiled devilishly at Maddie. "But don't tell her I said that."

"Uh uh," she mumbled over a bite of bread. "My lips are sealed." She washed the treat down with a sip of coffee and glanced up to find Devon watching her lips closely. Her cheeks flushed and she lifted the cup to half cover her face, pretending to take another sip.

As though we are truly husband and wife. The thought popped into Maddie's head from out of the blue. But she realized that was how she felt at that moment. Sitting across the table from him, sipping coffee and eating homemade bread, accepting compliments and teasing one another. The warm glow returned to Maddie's heart and she smiled with pleasure behind her cup.

Devon silently finished his bread and accepted another slice from Maddie. "You've learned too well."

Maddie flushed at the compliment, choked down the suddenly dry bread, and turned her attention to some crumbs on the table. She wondered if Devon would question her about her health. Was he curious about their success? They'd been married over a month. Did he think it still too soon? Would he ask outright when the time came? Or would he adhere to strict mores of conduct and wait for her to broach the subject in some discreet way?

She longed to tell him of her suspicions, but she stuffed another bite of bread into her mouth to stem the urge. She'd decided to wait and she would. Even if it killed her.

"Misser Devon, Misser Devon," Sarah called frantically, bustling through the doorway of the kitchen with a disturbed look on her face. "You best come right quick. That woman's done come back and she brought your cousin wit her."

Devon's chair scraped the floor loudly as he jumped to his feet. "Elaine is here, with Edward?"

"Yessir, that's who it is."

Maddie saw the anger and loathing in Devon's hardened expression. "Excuse me, Maddie," he said curtly, tossing his napkin harder than necessary onto the table.

"That woman up to no good," Sarah fretted, wringing her hands in her apron. "I'd like to pull her hair out sometimes the way she act."

Maddie couldn't keep her dislike from showing. She knew just how Sarah felt. It was as though Elaine had sensed a warming between her and Devon and magically came out of nowhere to separate them. She lifted her cup

to her lips, but almost symbolically the coffee
had suddenly grown cold.

"I suppose I should go and meet Devon's
cousin," Maddie said, hoping Sarah would tell
her that it wasn't necessary. But to her dismay
Sarah nodded. The woman reached to take the
dish towel from around her waist. She dabbed a
speck of flour from Maddie's cheek and shooed
her out of the kitchen.

Maddie heard the raised voices before she'd
even reached the entry hall. They were coming from the parlor and she seriously considered turning around and going to her room
instead of interfering in the confrontation. But
she squared her shoulders and tipped her chin
up determinedly. She was Devon's wife; it was
her duty to stand beside him.

"You've never denied me a place in your
home, Devon," Maddie heard a masculine
voice say as she stepped through the parlor
doorway. The voice belonged to a tall, slender
man, about 30 years old. He was blond, not
bad looking in a GQ sort of way. His coat and
trousers were dusty but of good quality and
fit him in a way that announced they were
tailor-made.

"You're family, Edward. I would not turn
you out, as you know."

"Then your objection is with my companion?"

She saw Devon's jaw clench, and the dimple
she hadn't seen for some time returned to flash
out his annoyance.

213

"How unchivalrous of you to say so, Edward."

The blond man threw back his head and laughed, and Maddie noticed Elaine for the first time, standing off to one side smiling a wicked grin.

"But since you did say it, then yes. My objection is with your companion. As Elaine well knows I suggested she not return here the last time we spoke." Devon drew out the last word as though to remind the woman they'd done more than converse. Maddie remembered the heated argument, the slap Elaine had delivered, and the equally stinging barb she'd thrown at Devon's ego.

"But that's in the past, is it not?" Edward asked innocently. Maddie wasn't fooled by his ploy and she could see Devon hadn't bought it either.

"After all," he continued, "you are happily married now, are you not?"

The taunt sent dangerous sparks to Devon's dark eyes. At first he didn't respond; then Maddie saw him visibly relax. "Yes, I am," he said, looking from Edward to Elaine. "Maddie and I are very happy."

Elaine's smile soured, and Maddie thought the woman looked evil in her anger. She decided it was time to make her presence known, and in that moment she determined Edward and Elaine would see Devon's words brought to life. The little act they'd staged for Anthony had been a mere prelude to the one she was about to play out. And if they all saw the love shining in her eyes, all the better. She could convince Devon later it had been an Academy Award–winning performance.

"Darling," she cried, flowing into the room in a rustle of pink candy-striped poplin. "You didn't tell me we had guests." She went to Devon's side, her skirts swirling around his boots as she linked her arm through his.

She smiled at Elaine and held out her hand. "I believe I've met Miss Mason, but who is this handsome gentleman?"

Maddie's Southern accent oozed sweetness until she thought for sure she'd have a cavity before she was through. But her actions paid off as, without missing a beat, Devon smiled lovingly at her and brushed his lips across her cheek.

"Hello, darling," he said, holding Maddie's hand in the crook of his elbow. "Let me introduce you to my cousin, Edward Crowe. Edward, my wife, Madeline."

Edward stepped forward, his eyes alive with interest as they rudely inspected every inch of Maddie from her old-world coiffure to the toes of her heeled slippers. He took her hand and leaned over it, brushing wet lips across her knuckles. Maddie felt the urge to wipe her hand on the back of her skirt, but she forced herself to smile in return.

"Devon's cousin, how nice. Well, we're just delighted you could visit. Shall I show you to your rooms so you can freshen up and unpack?

How long can you stay?" She took Edward by the arm and waited while Elaine cast a long look at Devon. When he nodded his assent, Elaine turned away and sashayed out of the parlor to join Maddie and Edward.

"I'll be right back," Maddie told the pair, leaving them standing at the base of the wide staircase. "I'll just check with Sarah and see which rooms she plans to have made up for you."

Her teeth aching from the false smile she wore, Maddie hurried to the kitchen. When she returned, Elaine and Edward had their heads together, whispering in urgent tones. They caught sight of her and broke apart before she could catch a single word. Something told Maddie these two weren't on a social call, but she plastered the smile on her face and carried on the pretense.

It didn't take a genius to know Elaine had thrown her support to the other side in the battle for Devon's father's wealth. She'd lost Devon, and so she was here to judge Edward's chances of inheriting.

If Edward and Elaine were here to assess the situation between her and Devon, Maddie would give them their money's worth. And when they left, which she hoped would be soon, they'd go away with the knowledge they'd wasted their time.

After the two were properly delivered to their rooms, which Sarah had fortuitously assigned in the opposite wing from Maddie and Devon,

Maddie went down in search of Devon. She found him still standing in the parlor where she'd left him.

"They are settling in," she said, taking the glass from his hand and refilling it at the liquor cabinet. She handed it to him with a smile, noting the frown drawing his mouth down.

"Thank you, Maddie. I didn't know when I accepted your offer that we'd have to perform this little farce routinely. First Anthony, now Edward and Elaine."

Maddie seated herself in a floral brocade wing-back chair by the fireplace. She settled her skirts and smiled.

"I don't mind, Devon."

"No?" He came and took the matching chair beside her. "It can't have been pleasant for you. And it will only get worse, trust me."

"I do," she said, holding his gaze when he faced her. "And I know why they're here, so I don't mind doing whatever it takes to speed this little test along and send them on their way."

"It won't be easy, Maddie. Like vultures, they'll be looking for any weakness in my position. Edward covets all my father's holdings, but he especially wants this house."

"And he'll be the one who inherits if . . ."

"Yes," Devon said, reading the rest of her thought. "He had a child eight years ago by his second wife, Sandra. She died shortly after and he sent the boy to a boarding school as soon as he passed his fourth birthday."

217

"That's horrible! Four years old is little more than a baby."

"Yes, well, he's no doubt better off than he was before. Edward never cared a whit for the boy, and he was neglected and abandoned for the most part. The only reason Edward is taking any interest now is because the child makes him eligible to inherit if I don't produce an heir."

"That's sad," Maddie said, wishing there were something she could do for the boy. But she knew how impossible that thought was. After all, if her guess was right, then she would surely be swept back to her own time as soon as her goal here was accomplished.

"Yes, but that isn't all. When Elaine was here the last time, she slipped up and admitted she'd been in contact with Edward. It took some coercing, but I finally forced the truth out of her and she confessed they'd been having an affair."

Silently Maddie nodded. She'd wondered at the time why Elaine had been so foolish as to admit her infidelity. Maddie had thought she was just secure in her position as Devon's fiancée due to the time element and Devon's wish not to involve some romantic young girl in what he saw as a difficult scheme.

"I've wondered since if they weren't in league all along. It would be just like Edward to plot my failure by coercing Elaine to marry me and then somehow making sure she never produced the heir. No doubt her charms were designed to

blind me to her real character until I was well
and truly caught."

"But you didn't fall for her," Maddie said,
forcing the difficult words past the lump of
jealousy that had risen up to choke her with
its force.

"No, I didn't," he said, and he paused for a
moment to look deeply into Maddie's eyes. She
wished she could tell what he was thinking,
but his eyes grew black any time he showed
emotion, and so for once she couldn't be sure
which mood had caused the change. Anger,
passion, fear, she'd seen them all reflected in
his navy eyes during the last six weeks.

"And that is one more thing I have to thank
you for, Maddie," he told her sincerely. "If you
had not offered me another means to save all
this, I might have gone ahead and married
Elaine rather than involve another woman.
And, I imagine, I'd have lost it all in the end."

"Do you really think Elaine and Edward
planned to take your inheritance from the
beginning? Isn't it possible they've joined forces
now because they are both angry at you?"

"It's possible," he agreed, sipping his drink.
"But I want you to be careful while they're here
nevertheless."

"Me? Why should I be careful? It's you they
need to get out of the way, isn't it?"

Devon reached across the chair and ran his
finger down Maddie's cheek. His eyes grew soft
and dark, and this time Maddie knew exactly
what feeling stirred him. Her breath grew short

and she felt her breasts respond to his touch on the most basic level.

"No, love," he whispered, touching her lips. "That is why I wanted them gone as soon as I learned they'd arrived." He let his hand drop and he stared ahead for a long minute. "I'm no longer the threat, Maddie. You are the one who stands in the way of their plans now. You will be the one to produce the heir."

Maddie swallowed hard, wishing she'd allowed Devon to toss the two out the door. What had she done by attempting to fool them? Had she been naive to think they were only here to spy on Devon's marriage?

Her hand slid down to her stomach, where a million butterflies exploded in flight. Was Devon right? Was she in danger? And what would happen if they all found out about the secret she carried?

Chapter Fifteen

Maddie left her room the next morning, closing the door behind her, and ran straight into Elaine. The woman seemed to have been lying in wait for her, and Maddie steeled herself for another confrontation. Ever since Elaine and Edward arrived yesterday, the house had been in a state of tense anticipation. Each member waited anxiously for the next scene to be played out. It would seem Maddie was to be the star of this one.

"Good morning, Elaine. Can I help you with something?"

Elaine's tongue darted out at the corner of her mouth and she tried to suppress a smile. "No, thank you, Maddie. I was just on my way down to breakfast. I find I'm famished this morning." She chuckled and glanced over Maddie's shoulder in the direction of Devon's bedroom. Maddie longed to smack the smirk off Elaine's face, but she wouldn't give the woman the satisfaction. It was only too obvious what Elaine was up to and Maddie felt suddenly reassured. Maybe Devon had been wrong. Perhaps Edward and Elaine's only scheme was to try to drive the newlyweds apart.

Any fool could see Elaine had staged this little meeting. Her room was in the other wing, opposite the staircase. So Elaine thought Maddie would just assume she'd been with Devon and was therefore going to the stairs from this wing. How lame, Maddie thought with derision.

"Well, shall we walk down together?" she asked, her voice friendly and open.

Elaine hesitated as though she were caught, and her eyes went to the door of Devon's room once more. "I'll be right along. I think I'll wait for Devon to join us. He should be finished dressing by now."

As if you'd know! Maddie wanted to laugh in her face. "Oh, I don't think so, Elaine," she said instead, sweet as sugar. "Devon left almost an hour ago. He said he had business with Anthony and he wouldn't be back until dinner."

Elaine's face turned crimson with rage and she knew her ploy had failed, miserably. Maddie enjoyed her fury for a moment and then stepped away. Looking back over her shoulder she invited, "Coming, Elaine?"

The woman stomped past Maddie and tripped at the top of the stairs, where Maddie had almost met disaster herself that second day, stumbled down onto the first step, and turned her ankle with a little cry. Maddie bit her lip to keep from smiling.

"I really must speak to Devon about fixing that board," Maddie said, *tsk*ing as she watched Elaine. "I think it's warped or something." Maddie, and everyone else in the house, was accustomed to the uneven spot, and she thought no more about it.

Elaine smoothed her hair back into place, took hold of the banister, and preceded Maddie down the massive stairs.

The woman stayed several steps ahead of her and they made it to breakfast with no further incidents. Edward and Beverly were already there, and Devon's cousin rose as they entered.

"Good morning, ladies," he greeted cheerily. "I say, you both look stunning today."

He came and held a chair out for Maddie as she approached the table. Maddie glanced down at the chair and then back up to Edward.

"Thank you, Edward, but I think I'll fix my plate first. I'm famished this morning," she purposely repeated Elaine's taunt, and she saw the woman's lips thin angrily.

Edward looked nonplussed, but he quickly recovered and went to seat Elaine.

"Bring me some coffee, Edward," Elaine commanded. "And one of those tarts Sarah always makes."

Edward nodded and stepped toward the side-board, but Maddie turned back, a regretful look on her face.

"I'm sorry, Elaine, but Sarah didn't make tarts this morning. There's some cinnamon bread here. It's very good."

"I don't want cinnamon bread," Elaine complained, her voice edging to a whine. "Sarah knows how I like her tarts, why wouldn't she have made them today?"

"I'm afraid that's my fault. You see, I don't care for them. And so she's been trying a few new things since Devon and I married."

Maddie saw Beverly lift her cup to cover her smile of victory. It took a great deal of effort for Maddie to appear contrite when she, too, wanted to crow with triumph.

"Never mind," Elaine said testily. "I'll have toast. Aunt Bev, will you pass me the rack please?"

Beverly reached out and lifted the silver rack of toast. But as she turned to hand it to Elaine she bumped a goblet of water and spilled the bread and water onto the lap of Elaine's elaborate rose crepe dress.

Almost before the goblet hit the table, Beverly was apologizing. Elaine began to shriek and Maddie muttered sympathetic noises. Edward went to Elaine's side and attempted to mop up the mess with his napkin. The soggy bread clumped in the napkin and dropped back to her lap with a plop.

Elaine slapped Edward's hand away and

stood, shaking the whole mess onto the floor with an unladylike curse. She slammed her own napkin down on the table hard enough to rattle the silverware and stormed from the room in a huff.

Maddie tried to offer apologies to Edward, but he looked from one woman to the other and then followed Elaine from the room.

Maddie sat down at the table and listened as their footsteps faded up the stairs. She met Beverly's sparkling gaze and together they both dissolved into laughter.

"Aunt Bev," Maddie laughed. "That was a horrible thing to do." She tried to sound sufficiently shocked, but her giggles destroyed the effect.

Beverly slapped her hand against her bosom and her eyes widened. "Why, Maddie, you can't think I did that on purpose. That would be mean and spiteful and not at all like me."

Maddie burst into laughter again and dabbed her eyes with the corner of her napkin. "Don't play the innocent with me, Aunt Bev. I've never seen you accidentally knock anything over before."

"No," she confessed with a small chuckle. "And likely you never will again. But just this once . . ."

"I know. I'd have liked to do it myself," Maddie had to admit.

"That woman is impossible. Do you know she tried to sneak into Devon's room last night?"

Maddie's humor evaporated like alcohol in the sun. "What?"

"Yes, I thought you'd be interested to hear that. I heard her out in the hall after we'd all retired last night and I opened my door. I called your name, even though I knew it wasn't your footsteps I'd heard. The little witch let go of Devon's doorknob and tried to slink away down the hall, as though she thought I was deaf as well."

"How do you know she wasn't leaving Devon's room?" Maddie couldn't help asking.

Beverly's face tightened. "Because I know my nephew better than that. And you should, too," she said, disappointment evident in her tone.

Maddie immediately felt chagrined. "I'm sorry, Aunt Bev. But there are things—reasons—you don't understand."

"If you're referring to the fact that your husband doesn't stay with you all night, you can stop worrying."

"How could . . ."

"I just told you I can hear everything that goes on in the hall from my bedroom. I hear Devon leave his room each night, only to return sometime later."

Maddie's face flushed scarlet. She couldn't believe her and Devon's private life was common knowledge. Her humiliation was complete and she wished the floor would open up and swallow her.

"I'd rather not discuss this with you," she said shortly, pushing away from the table. Beverly's hand came out, and with her usual competence, landed directly on top of Maddie's.

"Wait, dear," she pleaded, tugging Maddie back into her chair. "I didn't mean to embarrass you. I should keep out of your affairs, but I'm a meddler and I always have been." Her words were matter-of-fact; not an ounce of contrition softened the excuse. "But I have that right, for it was Devon who meddled first."

Maddie sank back into her chair and picked up her coffee cup. She wanted to know what Beverly meant by that remark, but her feelings were still too close to the surface for her to ask. As usual Beverly seemed to sense this and she patted Maddie's hand before releasing it to lift her own cup to her lips. When she set the cup aside, Maddie's ears figuratively perked up.

"When I lost my sight in a carriage accident, Devon came to stay with me. I didn't want him there. I didn't want anyone, but Devon least of all. He was young and spirited and he reminded me of everything that was permanently behind me. But he came, and he stayed, and he pushed me when I wouldn't do anything but sit in bed feeling sorry for myself. And it was while he was with me that his father died."

Beverly's eyes clouded with tears and Maddie could see her brother's death still affected Beverly deeply.

"We never knew," she said, sadly. "I'm sure Olivia tried to contact us, but her letter must have gone astray somehow. So, after months of nursing my battered spirit, Devon returned home to find the house deserted and deteriorating. The servants had all disappeared, taking a great deal of silver and other valuables with them, no doubt, and no one knew what had become of Olivia, Devon's mother.

"It was the worst time of my life. Even without my sight I could see Devon die a little each day as he mourned his father and searched for his mother. And then he found her."

Maddie could tell by the change in Beverly that she was about to hear something important. Beverly stared directly into Maddie's eyes as she delivered the final blow.

"He found her in an asylum."

The sightless eyes seemed to be watching for her reaction. Maddie hoped she didn't look as horrified as she felt, for she knew Beverly would somehow know if she did.

"It was a place more horrid than anything your imagination could concoct, Maddie. And though he could never prove anything, Devon has always suspected Edward had something to do with the missing letter and his mother's incarceration."

"Dear God," Maddie breathed, wondering how Devon kept from strangling his cousin if it were true.

"Olivia was in a bad way, there's no doubt of that. Her grief over my brother's death, possibly multiplied by the absence of her son at the time, had affected her mind. But she was harmless—" Her voice broke and she swallowed hard. "And helpless."

Beverly took a moment to compose herself and Maddie surreptitiously wiped the tears from her own cheeks.

"She never spoke another word after Devon brought her home. I forgot my own troubles and spent all my time taking care of Olivia, but to no avail. She shrank into herself more each day until she seemed too small and frail to live. It didn't take long for her to follow her husband to the grave. Devon has been a different man since that day. He needs more love than most men, I think, but at the same time he sees himself as the strong one. The one who must protect everyone he cares for. The way he tried to do with Crystal."

"Just like he did for me," Maddie said, surprised to find she could fall more in love with her husband than she already was.

"Most especially you," Bev confirmed.

Maddie's head came up and she suddenly understood a great deal. "Because he really thought I was insane."

"No. Because he really thought you needed him. The way his mother had needed him. He wasn't there for Olivia at the beginning, but he was there for you and he'd have moved heaven and earth to see you came to no harm."

Voices shattered the moment and Maddie and Beverly fell silent, each toying with the food on their plates as Elaine and Edward came back into the room.

"Maddie, I'm glad you're still here," Edward said, shooting an odd look at Elaine. The woman seemed to force a smile to her lips, and Maddie felt like a chicken at a fox convention.

"Elaine and I thought we'd go for a ride this morning. Would you like to join us? Devon has some of the finest horses in the area."

A flash of alarm lit Beverly's eyes and Maddie was glad to see her own fear at the invitation wasn't just paranoia. She searched for a viable excuse.

"Oh, how sweet of you two to include me," she said, and saw their faces light up. "But I don't think that would be a good idea. About the most strenuous thing I do these days is walk."

She'd meant to leave them with no more information than that, but Elaine caught her arm as she walked by.

"Why, Maddie," she drawled, a thin white line around her lips signaling her fury. "Surely you don't mean what you're implying."

"Did I imply something?" Maddie exclaimed innocently. She believed the pair's only purpose here was to somehow come between her and Devon, but she decided to guard her words cautiously all the same. With a nod of farewell, she pulled away and left the room.

Maddie tucked her arms into the sleeves of Devon's black cotton shirt and inhaled deeply. He'd left it behind the previous night and she found it more comfortable than the elaborate gowns she normally wore. Besides, it still held his scent. If he wouldn't stay with her she'd at least be able to think about him after he'd gone.

A knock sounded and she checked her reflection in the cheval mirror before going to open it. Her smile died when she saw Elaine standing in the hall.

"Why, Maddie," she sneered, her lips curling as she surveyed the shirt Maddie wore. "If this is how you greet Devon each night it's no wonder he doesn't stay."

Maddie wanted to shout to the heavens that it was nobody's damn business what she and Devon did. She was tired of defending her and Devon's relationship to everyone in the house.

"What do you want, Elaine?" she snapped, not even trying to disguise her distaste any longer. The woman had made her life hell for two days with insults and innuendos and Maddie was sick to death of her. She'd come dangerously close to tossing the woman out on her ear more than once. Only her desire to find out what Elaine and Edward were up to kept her from doing just that.

"My goodness, you are cross this evening," Elaine said, clucking her tongue as she brushed past Maddie to enter the bedroom uninvited.

"I'm tired. So if we could make this brief."

Elaine turned slowly as though inventorying the room's contents and all pretense of civility fell away. She met Maddie's glare with a look full of hate and vengeance.

"I admire your mettle, Maddie. That's why I've decided to help you."

"Help me?" Maddie crossed her arms over her stomach to quell the urge to barf. The thought of her and Elaine in cahoots made her nauseated.

"I think you should leave, Maddie. You obviously don't know what you've gotten into and I'm sure you don't really care. You saw an opportunity to get your hands on some money by marrying Devon and you took the initiative. I can understand that." She smiled and Maddie felt as though a snake had slithered over her foot.

"Is that so."

"Yes. But you see, Maddie, Devon can't win. There isn't time now. I saw to that by postponing our wedding until the very last minute. And I don't believe a word of what you hinted at in the dining room this morning, either."

"Get to the point, Elaine. As I said, I'm tired." Actually Maddie was suddenly exhilarated. Devon had been right. Elaine and Edward were in league from the start and she'd saved him from ruin by showing up when she did. She thanked God, or fate, or whatever force had brought her here, because she'd have done anything to prevent these two slugs from destroying everything Devon held dear.

"My point is, Maddie, that Edward and I are prepared to offer you a sizable portion of this estate in exchange for your going away."

Yes! Maddie thought triumphantly. They had been trying to drive her and Devon apart. When that hadn't succeeded, they'd hit on the idea to pay her off. That meant they were desperate. Elaine must be to admit the things she had. She and Devon had them on the run now.

"That's ridiculous, Elaine," Maddie said calmly, fighting the desire to bask in her success. "All I have to do to get what I want is stay right where I am."

"Oh, Maddie, you're being foolish. Devon can't win, I told you that. Edward will inherit in the end and you and Devon will be left with nothing."

"You're the fool, Elaine," Maddie told her, all her anger and disgust now seething in her words. She decided to nip their nefarious plot in the bud. "I wasn't implying anything this morning. I was stating a fact. In less than nine months Devon will have his heir. Edward will never see a penny from this estate. And neither will you. So, Elaine," she said, stalking toward the other woman, feeling strangely powerful despite her skimpy attire and bare feet, "the only ones who'll be leaving here are you and Edward. And the sooner the better. In fact, why not now? I'll help you pack. No, I'll pack for you. It'll be my pleasure."

Elaine had been backed to the door and Maddie turned to see Devon standing just outside in the hall, a look of stunned disbelief on his face. His eyes darted to her stomach, seemed less than satisfied with what they saw, and sought her eyes. She tried to smile, but she felt paralyzed and she couldn't even manage that small reassurance.

"Is it true?" he asked, stepping further into the room.

Maddie glanced over at Elaine and saw the look of satisfaction light in the woman's eyes. If she denied it, Elaine would think she'd won. But could she confirm what was only a suspicion and end up hurting Devon?

She knew she had no choice and she nodded slowly, her eyes never leaving Devon's for a moment. Of all the things she'd thought to see there, she didn't expect the look of pure rage that filled his eyes, turning them a swirling black, like the depths of hell.

Chapter Sixteen

Devon took Maddie by the arm and backed her into the room. She looked surprised and alarmed and he wanted to comfort her, but first he had something more pressing to attend to. Something he should have done sooner.

"Maddie, I think you've had enough excitement for one day. Why don't you go on to bed."

"But, Devon . . ." she began, glancing toward Elaine. If he were going to confront his cousin and ex-fiancée, she thought they should do it together.

"No arguing for once, Maddie. Just do as I ask." He cut her off midsentence and his tone brooked no refusal.

She backed down with a wounded expression on her face and he swore to make it up to her later. As soon as he'd thrown Elaine and Edward out of his home. For good.

"Elaine, come with me."

Elaine's eyes widened at Devon's command; then she smiled. "Of course, Devon. I never could refuse you, you know."

Maddie didn't miss the implication. She did a slow burn thinking of this woman and Devon as lovers. The fact that her husband had more or less tossed her aside at a moment when they should appear united didn't calm her anger either.

"Good night, Maddie," Devon said, escorting Elaine out of the room ahead of him. He shut her door with a bang and Maddie sank to the bed in a fury.

"Oooh!" she fumed, pounding the pillows in frustration. She couldn't believe what that Neanderthal had just done to her. The nerve of the man, dismissing her like an insignificant child. She had a right to be a part of whatever lay ahead. She didn't need to be cocooned.

Real pain yanked at her heart. What's more, she thought, he'd dismissed the news of their child. He hadn't even acknowledged the fact that she was pregnant. After everything she'd done. After everything they'd done together, she amended.

Well, fine. Two could play that game. Let him come back. She'd give him a lesson in equality, especially concerning issues pertinent to her and her child.

She went back to the bed but was too pumped up to sleep now. Snatching the brush from the dressing table, she began to tug it through her hair ruthlessly. The second time she hit a snarl, nearly jerking herself bald, she put it down. He wasn't worth the pain. Not the pain in her heart or the pain on her scalp.

Devon propelled Elaine down the hall to the stairs. At the top he carefully skirted the warped board and released her. "Meet me in the parlor in one minute, Elaine. And if you try to come back up these stairs before then, I'll drag you down them myself."

She seemed pleased with the anger she'd managed to raise in him, but Devon ignored her smile.

"Whatever you say, Devon," she meekly complied.

Devon turned back and left her standing at the top step as he strode angrily to the west wing.

At the door to Edward's room he didn't even slow down. He opened the door and slammed it back against the wall. "Get dressed," he ordered a startled Edward. "And get down to the parlor in five minutes or I'll be back."

Edward made it to the parlor in three minutes. Devon and Elaine were already there. Devon paced before the fireplace, a drink in his hand. Elaine lounged comfortably on the settee.

"What the devil is going on, Devon?" Edward demanded in a wounded tone.

"I'm throwing you two out of my house."

Elaine sat up so quickly the folds of her robe draped open to reveal naked breasts beneath. Edward's attention passed over the sight to land deliberately on the drink in Devon's hand.

"Are you drunk?" he asked.

"No, Edward, I don't need artificial courage." To prove his point, or to vent his anger, he threw the glass against the back of the empty fireplace and let the shattering sound of breaking crystal echo around him while he gained control of his emotions.

"I'm doing what I should have done two days ago. If Maddie hadn't interfered I would have done it then. I want you out of my house. Off my property. And this time I want you to stay gone. Don't come back, either of you. You're not welcome here. I made that fact plain to Elaine the last time she was here. Now I'm making it clear to you, too, Edward."

"I'm family, Devon, you can't do this," Edward whined.

"Yes, I can. I allowed you to come in the past because you were family and because I could never prove any of my suspicions about you. But no more. I want you both out of here tonight. And I warn you, don't go anywhere near my wife again," he said, pinning Elaine with a murderous stare. "Just pack your things and get out."

"You'll pay for this, Devon. Beverly is my aunt, too. You can't refuse to allow me to see her."

"If Beverly wants to see you I'll put her on the right train. Until then, I don't even want to hear your name."

"You'll regret this, Devon." Edward looked from Elaine to Devon, rage in his eyes. "You'll regret it."

"I don't think so," Devon said coldly. "You've never been anything but a leech, Edward. You use people. Your parents, your wife, even your son. You used them up and walked away without a twinge of regret. I won't have you anywhere near my family."

Edward turned and sped from the room, his boots pounding loudly on the polished wood of the foyer.

Elaine watched her ally scurry away like a frightened mouse. Alone now, she stood and walked to Devon's side. She let her breast brush his arm as she leaned in close to whisper.

"He's never been anywhere near the man you are, Devon. I always knew he was weak."

Devon met her inviting smile with a look of disgust. "That never stopped you from climbing into his bed, though, did it, Elaine? You lie with swine, you're bound to start to smell." He wrinkled his nose and gazed into the opening of her robe with loathing. "And right now you reek."

He took her arm and led her to the door. "Get dressed and get out," he told her. "And this time, Elaine, don't make the mistake of coming back."

She snatched her arm out of his grasp and raised her hand to strike him. But Devon was on guard this time and he caught her wrist in a painful clench. "Never try to hit me again, Elaine."

He sent her into the foyer with a little push and kicked the door shut behind her. For several minutes his breath continued to come in short, sharp gasps. He'd never felt such rage in his life.

When he thought of all the months she'd gone from his bed to Edward's, all the while plotting to steal his inheritance, he could easily strangle her. Of course he hadn't believed Elaine loved him, but he'd never really thought her capable of such treachery either.

The only thing equal to his anger was the hate he felt for Edward. He'd known Edward was weak and spineless, and he'd suspected him of engineering his mother's incarceration. But without proof Edward had always been able to convince him he was mistaken.

Well, no more. He'd heard all he needed to from the hall outside Maddie's room. Thanks to Maddie, he finally knew the truth about Edward. He could accept the lengths to which his cousin would go to get what he wanted. She'd saved him from marrying Elaine and managed to secure his and Beverly's future at the same time.

And what had he done for her in return? He'd subjected her to Elaine's viciousness, Edward's deviousness, and his own foul temper. He'd agreed to her bargain, knowing he had no intentions of letting her take his child away from him. He'd taken all she'd offered in bed, but refused to engage his heart in the affair. He'd turned away from her in a desperate attempt to keep from falling in love with her.

Only it hadn't worked. Devon knew he loved his wife, had probably loved her since the moment in the field when she'd called him her angel.

When the baby arrived she'd have what she wanted, but what about until then? What could he do for her now? He couldn't tell her how he felt. He'd sworn an oath not to confuse their relationship with emotions.

No, he couldn't tell her he loved her, though it was certainly true. And, at the moment, only one other option came to mind. She'd fulfilled her part of the bargain. Now, he'd have to fulfill his. He'd leave her alone until the baby was born, though it would be the hardest thing he'd ever done. And when the time came, he'd help her find a place to live where she'd be happy. He'd keep his promise. He'd help her leave him.

He went to the liquor cabinet and poured another drink, deciding to get drunk for the first time in a long time.

The day was dreary and damp, and seemed custom-made to Maddie's mood. Even the sea-blue tea gown she wore couldn't brighten the dismal cloud hanging over her. She stared out the window at the drizzle just beginning to fall. Uncontrollable emotions took hold of her and she felt the matching drizzle of tears on her cheeks.

Why hadn't Devon come to her last night? she wondered again, glancing at the big, cold bed she'd slept in alone. For the first time since they returned from Gulf Island she'd had to try to fall asleep without Devon's strong warmth beside her. Was it any wonder she felt drained this morning and dark circles ringed her eyes?

She tried to remind herself that their deal had been to conceive a child and it wasn't surprising he'd considered his duties fulfilled once she'd told him she was pregnant. But she hadn't thought his attentions would stop so immediately. She felt emotionally whiplashed from the suddenness of his desertion.

But Maddie knew it was more than that. The fact that he'd left with Elaine was the salt on the canker. She'd seen the anger in his eyes, but she'd thought it was due to Elaine's confession. Had he heard all of it? she wondered now. Or only her own words stating she'd get what she wanted just by staying here? Did he now think she'd masterminded the situation to get her hands on his money as Elaine suggested? Or did he care nothing for her, disregarding Maddie completely now that his heir was assured?

Her head spun and ached with the effort to sort out this mess she'd gotten herself into.

She snatched the pins from her hair, trying to relieve the throbbing pressure, and let the length fall over her shoulders. Running her fingers over her scalp, she tried to think clearly. Something she feared she hadn't done since her turbulent trip through time.

Was she a fool to think there'd been some kind of cosmic intervention which sent her to this place? Could it be nothing more than a freak accident of nature? Could she have found her way back if she'd tried harder? Since the night she discovered Devon's need for a child, she'd accepted her presence here as destiny. Had she been wrong? Would she ever be swept back to her own time or would she remain here forever?

"Oooh," Maddie cried, snatching a ribbon off her dressing table. She quickly tied her hair back at her neck and left it to hang otherwise unfettered.

Not one to drift aimlessly like so much flotsam in a whirlpool, she took the handle of the door, and subsequently her own fate, into her hand.

A little breakfast would settle her stomach and ease the dull headache. Then she had some serious decisions to make. And she'd make them before another day passed.

"Good morning," Anthony greeted her as she swept determinedly into the dining room.

Maddie stopped, startled to see the doctor taking coffee at the large table. But instantly a smile lit her face and she swept forward.

"Anthony, what a pleasant surprise." He rose and took her hands, leaning over them in a bow. "I had no idea you'd returned. Are Edward and Elaine still here?"

He held a chair for her and brought her a cup of coffee. For some reason the smell of the brew made her stomach tighten, but she smiled in thanks anyway.

"Devon told me they'd left in something of a hurry. He also hinted congratulations might be in order." He quirked an eyebrow and it was obvious his last statement was meant as a query.

Maddie felt relieved knowing her nemeses were no longer in the house. But now she had to face Devon, and Anthony, with the truth that she wasn't as certain of her claim as she'd appeared. "I may have been premature," she confessed.

"Has something happened, then?"

"What? Oh, no, nothing like that. It's just that I'm afraid it's too early to know for sure. I wanted to wait a bit longer before I said anything but . . ."

"I understand," he told her, and Maddie felt sure he did. Obviously Devon had recounted the whole ugly scene. What if she wasn't pregnant? Would Devon think she'd purposely lied to him?

Anthony seemed to read her mind and he placed his hand over hers on the table. "Maddie, it's been my experience that a woman knows better than anyone in cases like this. Especially one as intelligent as you."

"I don't know how true that is," she admitted. "I don't have any real symptoms yet." She glanced at the coffee and experienced another twinge of nausea. She told herself that it might well be nothing more than a case of nerves. "And I'm sure it's too early to know anything definite."

"Probably," he agreed, slipping his hand off hers and wrapping it tightly around the handle of his coffee cup. "But why don't we just do an examination to be sure?"

"Did Devon bring you here to confirm what I told him?"

Anthony glanced down into his cup and then quickly back at her with an uneasy smile.

"He's concerned, Maddie."

"It's all right," Maddie told him. "I know how important this baby is to Devon. Devon told me everything before we were married. And I agreed saving his inheritance was very important. I'd like to know for sure myself."

Anthony looked relieved and he smiled. Maddie stared into his eyes and thought, for just a second, that she read something deeper than relief there. But he hid it quickly and so she wasn't sure it had ever really been there. He stood and pulled out her chair.

"Shall we?"

After a brief exam Anthony left Maddie to dress. He told her he'd be waiting in the parlor and they could talk then. She hurried down, anxious to learn what his verdict would be. When she arrived he met her with the mysterious look in his eyes, and once again he quickly masked it.

"Congratulations, Mrs. Crowe," he said, leaning forward to place a chaste kiss on her cheek.

"You mean it's true? I'm pregnant?"

"Well, I'd say it's very likely. We won't know for sure for some time, but you show all the signs."

Devon entered then and Maddie drew her hands out of Anthony's, too quickly. She realized she'd made the gesture look suspect somehow and she instantly regretted her jumpiness.

"I was just telling your beautiful wife that I think she will make a wonderful mother, Devon."

Devon's gaze went from Maddie to Anthony as though trying to gauge their thoughts.

"Isn't it a bit soon?" he asked, purposely avoiding Maddie's eyes as he stepped closer to Anthony.

"Yes, as I was about to say, it's too soon for a definite diagnosis. But after examining Maddie, I'd say it's a very good possibility."

Maddie watched as Devon seemed to throw off months of worry. How his situation must have weighed on him, she realized. To see his hardened features grow softer before her eyes seemed to reaffirm her belief in destiny. To know she was the one who'd secure his future made her believe in a higher power. The warmth of feeling that her love had saved him was almost too much to bear and she felt the all too frequent tears burn behind her eyes.

He turned to her then and surprised her with a giant hug that almost sent the tears flowing down her cheeks. He drew back slightly and touched her cheek.

"Thank you, love," he whispered, and she could almost forget that this was all supposed to be business. "I'll never be able to repay what you've done for me."

No reply could have escaped past the nugget of emotion trapped in Maddie's throat. She nodded and blinked rapidly to keep from further embarrassing herself.

Anthony broke the spell with an amused laugh. "Well, I can see I'm no longer needed here."

Devon quickly broke away from Maddie, but he kept one arm around her waist. She felt possessed by the love his gesture stirred in her. For the first time in her life, she felt connected to another human being in the most basic and instinctive way.

"Anthony, I intend to take Maddie and Beverly to Gulf Island for a little rest and celebration." He glanced down at Maddie and smiled. "We'd like it if you'd come along."

"That's a kind offer, Devon, but . . ."

"Oh, please," Maddie added her agreement, suddenly eager to see the island once more. "We'd love for you to go along. And I imagine you could use a rest as well."

"I won't deny that," he said, glancing from Devon to Maddie.

"Then we insist," Devon told him.

He looked pleased and he nodded quickly. "All right. I think I will, then. I'll have to make arrangements for a few of my patients to go to Lawrence for checkups, but things have slowed down a good bit this week."

"Then it's settled." Devon released Maddie and she missed the contact, wondering how things would be in their relationship now. The announcement that she was pregnant had taken him from her bed, but he seemed almost tender this morning. She realized she couldn't wait to see what the newest phase of their marriage would be.

She'd known his kindness, his compassion, and his desire. This morning she'd earned his devotion. It was almost like turning back the layers of an onion and finding each new bulb. With an anxious sigh she wondered what new facets of his personality the trip to Gulf Island would peel away.

Chapter Seventeen

As the ferry chugged toward Gulf Island, Maddie stood at the front, letting the bay breeze tousle her hair and warm her cheeks. She felt glorious, breathing in the fresh air and soaking the soothing sunshine into her skin. It had been too long since she'd lain on the bright white sand and let the sound of the surf wash away her troubles.

Victorian convention be damned, when she got to the island she intended to find a nice secluded dune, stretch out on the sand, and soak up some rays. She smiled. She'd even given in and brought along the silly bathing costume Sarah had altered for her.

This time there was nothing to keep her from enjoying the island she'd called home for so long. It seemed odd somehow, but her old life seemed like a distant memory.

Thoughts of time warps, destiny, and love had pushed aside thoughts of fabric swatches, current movies, and failed relationships. And thoughts of Devon had pushed aside everything else.

Her husband stood some distance away, conversing with a local farmer who'd been on the train with them. Aunt Beverly was sipping a cool drink in the salon below deck. Anthony had been with her earlier, but had wandered off without her notice some time ago. Maddie enjoyed the solitude and took the opportunity to put her concerns in order.

She was already pregnant, and she still hadn't had time to assess her emotions on that score. It was what she'd wanted, she told herself.

But had she been too hasty in tying herself to the past? Had she jumped to the conclusion that fate had had a hand in her arriving at Devon's just at the moment when he needed her because her sensible side had demanded an explanation? Had she somehow sealed her fate when she'd married Devon and conceived his child?

Again she wondered if she and the baby would return home when her purpose here was accomplished. And, she wondered sadly, why did that idea no longer hold the appeal it had for her just a few weeks ago?

The ferry bumped against the pier, jarring Maddie from her distracted wanderings. She glanced up and frowned, thinking something was odd but not able to place what it was. A murmur had begun to rise through the crowd of passengers and she turned to see them talking animatedly and gesturing toward the dock.

Mumbling apologies to the other passengers, she pushed her way back through the crowd in search of Devon. She found him, Anthony, and Beverly huddled in serious conversation.

"What is it?" she asked Devon.

He frowned and pointed toward the empty dock. "The carriages aren't here."

Remembrance stirred and Maddie finally realized why the dock had looked so different this time. The last time she and Devon had come to the island, several carriages from the hotel had been waiting to transport the guests. Today, the dock was deserted.

One of the crew lowered the gangplank, but no one wanted to exit the ferry until some explanation had been given for the lack of conveyances.

"I'll go and see if I can find out anything," Devon said, searching through the crowd for a clearing.

"I'll go along," Anthony told him.

"No, you stay with the women. I'll be back directly, hopefully with transportation."

"Devon, wait," Maddie called, as he prepared to clear his own path through the bustle. "I want to go along."

"I'd rather you stayed here," he told her, his gaze scanning the people between him and the gangplank.

"I'd rather go along," she countered stubbornly, eager to reach the island.

Devon's attention focused on her for a brief second, and then he nodded. "Come along, then."

He clutched her hand and led her through the crowd. The gangplank rattled as they hurried over it. Their footsteps echoed hollowly over the pier and then crunched through the shelled drive lining the dock. Devon peered up and down the long path, searching for late-arriving carriages.

When none seemed forthcoming, he took Maddie's hand again and they began to walk along the drive toward the small town Maddie had remembered seeing on their first trip through Gulf Island.

A rustle sounded in the brush next to Maddie, and she whipped around just as a young woman staggered forward out into the path. Maddie could see the wild brightness in her eyes. In her arms she carried a bundle wrapped in a blanket. As she approached Maddie her legs gave way and she fell to her knees. The blanket slipped back and Maddie cried out as a tiny head covered with black downy fuzz was exposed.

"Help me," the woman cried weakly. Maddie was already at her side, lifting the baby from her arms. The woman fell back and, moaning, began to retch on the crushed shells of the lane.

On her knees beside the ill woman, Maddie

could see the whiteness around her mouth. Frantically she searched her pockets for a handkerchief but found them empty. She lifted the hem of her dress and wiped the woman's brow awkwardly with one hand as she continued to hold the baby in her other arm.

"Don't touch her," Devon cried, grabbing Maddie's shoulders and trying to lift her away from the woman.

Maddie turned to look at him. "Help her," she pleaded, shifting the infant more securely into the curve of her elbow. The woman mumbled and rolled, cutting the flesh of her arms and face on the sharp shells beneath her.

"I'll get Anthony," he said, turning back toward the dock and racing away with ground-eating speed.

"Please hurry," Maddie said, trying to place a restraining hand on the woman without losing her grip on the baby.

"Hold on," Maddie entreated, dabbing the woman's brow again and feeling otherwise helpless. "Just hold on."

Maddie had seen the barely disguised fear in Devon's eyes and she shuddered. What sort of illnesses were still prevalent in the late nineteen hundreds? she wondered. Hadn't vaccines been developed for most of them by this time? Again she cursed her lack of historical knowledge.

"Maddie! Get back."

Maddie looked up and saw Anthony and Devon running toward her. Anthony suddenly drew to a halt and caught Devon's arm in a tight fist. "Wait here, Devon."

Devon shook off Anthony's hold and started forward again, but his friend took his arm once more and pulled him to a halt. "You can't go over there. It isn't safe."

Maddie looked from Anthony's sad eyes to Devon's fierce countenance. Her husband struggled to free himself as his gaze fell to the baby in her arms. For the first time Maddie glanced down at the infant, and she felt her heart break. The tiny head had lolled to one side, the mouth drooped open. The little blue eyes stared, fixed, at nothing. Wrenching sobs tightened Maddie's chest and throat and threatened to choke the breath out of her. She looked at Anthony, pleading with her eyes.

"Maddie, put him down," he told her gently.

Maddie looked from the baby to the woman still writhing on the lane. She rocked the bundle even though the child was beyond being soothed by the motion.

"Put him down," Devon implored, stepping forward again. "Put him down and come to me."

"No," Anthony shouted, holding his hand out to Maddie and grasping Devon's shoulder with the other. "Stay where you are, just put the baby down by the mother."

"I can't just leave them," she told the two men. Too well she realized the possible danger, but her heart refused to let her desert the pair.

Besides, she'd already been exposed to whatever sickness they had.

"Stay put," Anthony said to Devon, reinforcing his order with a studied look. When Devon seemed to comply, he picked up the black bag he'd dropped on the lane and walked toward Maddie.

"Can you help him?" she asked, even though she knew the answer.

Anthony looked down at the frozen features and shook his head. "I'll take care of him, Maddie. Hand him to me."

"No, I'll hold him," she said. "You'd better see about his mother."

"Maddie," Devon called, clearly enraged by his exiled position.

"It's too late, Devon. I might as well stay, I've been exposed already."

"She's right, Devon. I can't let her go back to the ferry now. Not until I know what we're dealing with here."

"I'm not leaving my wife in the middle of this, Anthony." Devon made to come closer and Anthony shot him a warning glare.

"Don't! If you come any closer you'll be quarantined here as well. And I need you to be able to come and go from the island to bring me supplies."

"He's right, Devon," Maddie agreed, covering the infant's face with the blanket as she struggled to put the horror of its death from her mind. The mother was still alive and she knew they'd have to fight to save her now.

"I'm not leaving without you, Maddie," Devon swore.

"You have to," she told him, trying to reassure him with a weak smile. "Someone has to take Beverly home. She can't stay here."

Anthony had opened the bag and was examining the woman in the road. She'd lost consciousness sometime in the last few minutes and Maddie thought it was just as well since the infant had died. Devon looked from Maddie to Anthony and back again.

"What is it, Anthony? Can you tell me anything?" Devon's voice sounded desperate as he stood, anxious and irate, in the lane.

"It's not the smallpox," Anthony said, moving closer to Maddie. He lifted the blanket and examined the infant as she held it on her lap. "It's not . . ."

He sat back, relief and fear battling in his eyes. "It's all right, Devon. Maddie will be all right." He seemed to visibly relax as he recovered the infant.

"What is it?" Maddie whispered.

"Cholera," he said, biting his lip. "It's spread through contaminated food and water, not by close contact." Then he lifted his head and told Devon, "Cholera."

Devon's mood seemed suddenly buoyant, even though Maddie could see the concern still present in his stiff shoulders and rigid stance.

"Thank God," he said, giving her a look that warmed her blood. He shook his head and ran his hand down his face as though wiping away the fear which had gripped him.

"I'll tell the others," Devon said. "I'm sure Taber Elkins and his wife will see Beverly home. Then I can come back and give you a hand."

"No, Devon. I'm going to need things from my office. I need you to go there and bring them back as quickly as you can. If everyone on the island is affected I'm going to need a hell of a lot more than what I brought with me."

"Wait!" Maddie cried, suddenly jumping to her feet as Devon turned away. Her mind was reeling with shock and hope. She'd been trying to remember what she'd heard of cholera and it had just come to her. Genevieve had explained this particular malady to her in great detail only recently because she'd said that the disease was one of many still prevalent in third world countries. And it had been one of the ailments her sister had anticipated she'd find on the medical mission. That would mean . . .

The possibilities were immense. And more than a little confusing at the moment, so Maddie focused on the main objective. "Devon, you must hurry. Go to the house and get my cases, the ones you recovered from the field after you found me. I can't explain now, but it's urgent. Go, as fast as you can, and bring them back here."

How could she have been so blind? Maddie wondered frantically. All the time she'd been in the past she'd had medical supplies which might save hundreds of lives and she'd never even considered that they might be important.

Devon and Anthony were sharing bewildered looks, but Maddie knew she could never explain. They'd have to see for themselves to believe and she wasn't sure even that would convince them once and for all that she was from the future. Also, it would mean revealing her secret to Anthony. He might think she was truly mad. Anthony was a doctor, with the ability to have her committed if he thought she was insane.

Looking down at the blanket-wrapped corpse in her arms, she knew it was a chance she'd have to take.

"I have something in my suitcases better than anything you have in your office," she told Anthony with such conviction he seemed convinced. He looked at Devon, who shrugged his shoulders, and then nodded.

"Lives are at stake, Maddie. I admit there isn't much I can do for these people. If you have some magic in your bags, I'm willing to try it."

"You'll think it's magic when you see it," she told him, a real smile on her face now. She didn't stop to analyze what this new development meant to her theory of why she'd been brought here. Later, she'd reassess her situation. Right now, these people needed her.

Chapter Eighteen

The next 12 hours were the longest of Maddie's life. She and Anthony worked around the clock, trying to see how many people were affected by the epidemic. Anthony had sent men from the town out to check the fresh water supply and he'd set up a hospital in the lobby of the Island Breeze Hotel. Maddie helped as much as she could, fetching boiled water, clean linens, and bedding.

They'd had 20 patients when they'd arrived at the hotel, including the woman from the lane. But since word had gotten out that the doctor was treating people in the lobby, 30 more had arrived.

Feather mattresses lay side by side with ratty pallets, wealthy resort patrons with poor islanders. All received the same treatment, as inadequate as it was, and two more died within hours of Anthony's arrival.

"Devon, Devon, please hurry," Maddie whispered, lifting one elderly lady up so she could pour water down her parched throat. Anthony had said the only thing to be done was to try to keep the patients from dehydration. Maddie struggled to get fluids into the most seriously affected ones and tried to offer comfort to the others.

The epidemic had started two days ago and most patients were well into the second phase by now. Anthony had explained each stage in depth so Maddie would recognize the signs. First, malaise, headache, diarrhea with possible fever. Next came the purging, vomiting, and muscle cramps. Finally, almost complete arrest of circulation, eyes sunken, cheeks hollow, skin dry and wrinkled.

Already several people had gone into coma, the last phase before death. If Devon didn't hurry, any effort would be useless.

As though in answer to her prayer, Maddie looked up and saw him standing in the doorway. His eyes hadn't adjusted to the dim lobby after being in the bright sunlight, so she saw him before he saw her. Her heartbeat quickened as she watched him scan the room. He looked exhausted, she thought. But so very handsome and strong to her. She longed to go to him, slip into his arms, and fall into a deep, untroubled sleep. She knew she could sleep for days if she allowed herself. But there was too much to be done and time was running out for many of the sick.

"Devon," she called softly, weaving through the makeshift beds toward him. He turned at the sound of her voice and his features softened. His eyes swept along the length of her and then came to rest on her face.

"You look tired," he said.

"So do you."

"Yes, well, I don't have the added worry of a baby to think about. Why don't you go up and get some rest?"

"Soon. You brought my cases?" she asked, eagerly changing the subject. He frowned, but nodded.

"Then we don't have time to wait. I'll get Anthony, you get the cases. I'll meet you upstairs in our room. It's number two-ten."

She forced herself to turn away from the lure of his arms, the welcomeness of his strength. Across the crowded lobby she spotted Anthony and she quickly went to his side.

Devon watched her go, pride and concern warring within him. He didn't know what his wife was up to now, but he felt certain he'd be amazed by whatever it was. She hadn't ceased to surprise him since her arrival. He hefted the cases, one in each hand, and proceeded up the massive center stairway.

He needed a bath and a shave, right after about eight hours sleep. He'd ridden all night and morning to deliver Beverly back home and fetch Maddie's suitcases. Now all he wanted was his wife beside him in the elaborate bed of their hotel suite.

No doubt she'd fight him if he tried to suggest that, though. Now that they'd succeeded in begetting the heir, he had no right to her favors. And even though the thought should have pleased him, he found his victory cold and hollow.

"Devon," Anthony said, as he and Maddie swept into the suite as though they hadn't been up the entire night. "I'm glad to see you. Maddie swears she has a miracle in store for us and I must admit that we're going to need one to stop this thing."

"You've had someone check the main food and water supplies?"

Anthony nodded. "Yes. The main water supply was affected—that's why so many took sick right away. Apparently the storm they had three days ago contaminated the groundwater. But they can't find the source of the contamination and we've had several new cases in the past few hours."

"Damn. I'll see if I can help as soon as I get a bite to eat and change my clothes."

"Thanks, Devon, but why don't you get some sleep first? You look worn out."

"Much like you two, I imagine," he told them with a small smile.

"Well, like I said, we need a miracle." He turned to Maddie. "I hope you haven't exaggerated the power in those suitcases." There wasn't much hope in his eyes as he faced the woman he'd come to admire a great deal in the past hours. She'd worked side by side with him, untiring, through the night and morning. But he was a doctor, and he knew there was damned little he could do for these people. He had to doubt Maddie's ability to do better.

"I think I should start by telling you how I came to be here, Anthony." Maddie saw the flash of shock and fear cross Devon's face, but she had no time to offer him assurances. "I'm certain Devon didn't tell you all there was to know at the time, and I was thankful for that. There were times I doubted my own sanity and I know he had serious concerns along that line."

"What has all this to do with your miracle cure, Maddie?" Anthony asked, glancing curiously from Maddie's determined expression to Devon's troubled one.

"Did Devon tell you I'd been hit by a car, Anthony? That when he found me in his field I thought I'd died?"

"Maddie, please," Devon cut in, stepping toward her, a warning in his eyes.

"I know you tried to protect me, Devon. I appreciate that. But we can't hide the facts now. As soon as I open those cases, you'll know I've been telling you the truth."

Devon's eyes shot wide and he took her arm. "Maddie, you can't. . . ."

"What's all this about?" Anthony asked anxiously.

Maddie knew Anthony needed to hurry back to his patients, but there was too much to explain to rush. He'd want all the answers when she presented him with the medicine anyway.

"I have to do this, Devon. Trust me. It will be all right."

He didn't look convinced and he raked his hand through his hair as he turned away from her. Maddie wished she could spare him the worry, but it was too late for that.

"I'm not the daughter of Beverly's friend, Grace. I'm not in any way connected to Devon or Beverly. In short, I'm not who they told everyone I was."

"I suspected as much. Devon said you were from Gulf Island, but it was obvious to anyone when we arrived that you weren't familiar with the island. And you didn't know a single person here."

"No, I didn't. That's because these people didn't live on Gulf Island when I did. In fact, all of them will be long dead by that time."

Devon groaned and paced before the window. Anthony looked at first startled and then dismayed. "Dead, from the epidemic?"

"No, Anthony," she told him, walking to the cases for the proof she knew she was about to need. "Dead from old age, probably."

Devon flattened his palms on the windowsill and bent at the waist, his head slumped between his arms. He was certain she'd just sealed both their fates. There was no way he'd be able to convince Anthony she wasn't a lunatic when this was over.

Maddie slid the cardboard tabs out of their slots and lifted the lid on the first case. "I know it's going to sound bizarre, Anthony. But I'm from the future. When I lived on Gulf Island it was nineteen hundred and ninety-two. I wasn't even born until nineteen hundred and sixty."

"Maddie, what the devil . . ."

A flash of annoyance crossed Anthony's face and she could see he thought she'd been wasting his time. But as she threw back the lid of the box, his eyes locked on the medical supplies. Confusion, surprise, amazement, they all sped quickly over his features. "My God, what is all that?"

Devon turned at the wonderment in Anthony's voice and his own eyes widened, then narrowed in astonishment.

"Well," Maddie said with a grin. "I'm no nurse, but I can identify most of this stuff. My sister, Genevieve, is a nurse. I was on my way to her house to deliver this when I had my accident and ended up here. She and some other people were planning a medical mission to Romania, a little country far away from here. I helped her pack the crates to be shipped."

She reached into the case and brought out a bubble pack of tetracycline and another of penicillin. "These are called antibiotics. And, although they're pretty common in my time, I'm sure they're going to seem like miracles to you."

She tossed them to Anthony and he caught them. He examined the package and then read the print on the foil backing. "This is impossible," he said.

Devon had come to inspect the odd-looking object Anthony held and he, too, read the writing.

"What is this?" he asked, fingering the round bumps covering each tablet. "I've never seen anything like this before."

"That's called plastic. And a lot of things are made from it in my time. Although they don't use it as much now for ecological reasons."

"Eco . . ."

"Never mind, I think we'd better take this one step at a time. These antibiotics are used to kill infection. Almost all kinds of infection. And even though cholera has been all but wiped out in the United States, it's still pretty active in small, out-of-the-way countries with inadequate sanitation facilities." See, I was paying attention, Genevieve, Maddie longed to tell her sister. She'd been thoroughly interested in the trip her sister had planned and she'd absorbed lots of details while she and Genevieve packed crates.

Finally, she thought. Something clicked and she understood all that had happened to her. Maybe there was someone important here who was going to die from this epidemic, and she'd been whisked back with Genny's medicine to save them. Or else . . .

A horrible thought occurred to her then and

her hand dropped automatically to her stomach. Had she made a terrible mistake? Had this been her mission all along? If so, she wasn't supposed to have conceived Devon's child. And if she was destined to return to her own time as soon as her job here was through, would she go before the baby's birth?

Her knees turned to jelly beneath her and she sank down on the sofa, grateful Devon and Anthony seemed so absorbed in the packages they were holding. Her face must have registered her shock. This never happened to the man on that television show. He always did the job he'd been sent to do, and then he leaped out. *Snap*, just like that. If her mission had been to save someone on the island . . .

"Maddie? Are you all right?"

Devon's voice came to her from a fog of terror. Suddenly she felt as though she were slipping out of the room and she couldn't control her body's movement, like she was floating above the sofa. The room spun dizzily, and she reached out to steady herself.

"Maddie?"

Devon's strong arms encircled her and laid her back on the cushions. He lifted her feet and set them on the sofa, then took her hands. "What is it, Maddie? What happened?"

"Devon?"

"Yes, Maddie. I'm right here. It's all right."

The room slowed to normal and her vision cleared. She hadn't been snatched back to her own time. Not yet. She was still in the room with Devon and Anthony leaning anxiously over her.

She forced a smile. "I'm fine, really. I just got a little dizzy."

"That's to be expected in your condition. Especially with no sleep. You *must* get some rest now."

"No!" Maddie sat up suddenly, fought another wave of dizziness, and rose to her feet. "This is too important." If this was her mission, she didn't intend to foul it up. She had to show Anthony the rest of the medical supplies.

"This," she said, digging through the box for a packet of solution, "is intravenous solution. I don't know if you know how to use this, but there should be . . ." She dug some more and quickly scanned the labels on each plastic pouch. "Here it is," she said triumphantly. "This is tubing. You have needles and the tubing and you mix the solution. It's saline. You inject it directly into the vein to replace lost fluids in the body. You can also use this stuff for blood transfusions, but we won't need it for that."

"Transfusions? Are they . . ." Anthony's voice trailed off. "Do they do transfusions successfully where you came from?"

"Routinely," she boasted, noting with some amusement he hadn't said anything about the future. "I'll tell you all about it later."

She rummaged through the box and came up with some antibiotic ointment, alcohol pads, suture kits, and even birth control devices. Too late for that, she thought wryly, quelling the urge to examine the possibility she'd erred. There'd be time for that later. Right now, they had lives to save.

"Maddie, I have to tell you I'm amazed by all this. Astounded, really. I don't recognize any of these things or even the materials they're stored in. But your story . . ."

"I don't blame you. I had trouble believing it had happened, and I was living it. I still don't know how I got here. I thought I knew why," she began, glancing at Devon with painful confusion. "But I'm not even certain of that anymore. And I'm really technologically ignorant, so don't expect me to come up with any startling answers. All I know is that I was driving down a country road in nineteen hundred and ninety-two when my car broke down. I got out to walk and was hit by another car. I fell over an embankment into a lake and woke up in Devon's field. I've been so busy just trying to adjust and adapt, I never even thought about all this until we arrived yesterday."

Devon looked at her and their eyes met for the first time since she'd opened the cases. She could read his thoughts in his eyes and she knew suddenly that he believed her. She should be rejoicing. Finally, an end to the pretense. But what she saw reflected in the too familiar eyes watching her was anger.

"Tell me more, Maddie. Quickly. Tell me everything you know about each item in here."

Thoughts of Devon's odd mood swing were

pushed to the side as Maddie and Anthony emptied both cases onto the sofa. She read each item off to him and told him as quickly and correctly as she could what they were used for. He raised an eyebrow at the birth control devices, nodded with approval at the ointment and alcohol pads, and grinned widely as he held the IV equipment, listening in facination while she explained the different types of blood and how they'd been able to perfect transfusions.

"My God, Maddie," he said, when all the items had been described to him. "This is a miracle. And if these things do what you say they will, it will be more than miraculous."

"I assure you, you won't be disappointed. But I'll leave the administering of the stuff to you. As I said, I'm no nurse. Blood and needles make me queasy."

"I think I understand all the theories behind these things, so I shouldn't run into any trouble. Of course, I don't know what I'll tell my patients. I'm quite sure they'll be suspicious."

"As soon as the first person responds, they'll be lining up to get their fair share. Just tell them it's all very secret and experimental."

"Yes, yes, of course." He began to load the supplies back into the cases, shaking his head. "I haven't the time to hear more now, Maddie. But when all this is over, would you mind if I asked you a few questions?"

"Only a few?" she teased.

Anthony laughed and threw back his head. "A few hundred, maybe."

"Sure, Anthony. I'll be happy to tell you anything you want to know, if I can."

"That's terrific. I'd better get this stuff down to my patients now." He lifted the two cases with no trace of his earlier exhaustion present. His eagerness made Maddie smile.

"Tell me one thing," he said, turning back to face her. "Have they found a cure for every illness in your time?"

Maddie thought of cancer and AIDS, and her smile died. "No, I'm afraid they haven't."

He looked a little sobered by her admission, but his smile quickly reappeared. "Well, I guess that would have been expecting too much."

Maddie nodded and watched him leave, her heart a little lighter. He'd save the people of Gulf Island. Because of her, and this crazy situation she was in, someone might live to make a very big difference. Her trials had not been in vain. She thought of the child she and Devon had produced and she couldn't regret a moment of her journey.

Devon's stare was trained on her back and Maddie could feel it boring into her. The time had come to face her husband. She suspected he wouldn't wait to voice his questions. As she turned to face him, she tried to anticipate what his reaction would be to this latest development. Would he be angry, bewildered, suspicious?

Her gaze met his and she felt a shiver of panic assault her. His eyes, black and dangerous, glowed with stark, vivid rage.

Chapter Nineteen

Maddie raised one eyebrow and smiled wryly at her husband. "Don't you want to ask me anything, Devon? Aren't there things you want to know about the future?" He didn't respond and the rage on his face made her swallow.

"You do believe me, don't you?"

"I can hardly ignore what I've seen with my own eyes."

"You're angry."

"For certain."

Tired of the clipped answers, Maddie went on the defensive. "Why? Because you were wrong? I told you . . ."

"A wild tale no one in their right mind would have believed."

"The truth, nevertheless."

"I thought you had lost your mind."

"For a time, I wasn't sure I hadn't," she said, defending herself and her actions the best way she could. "But I did try to explain."

He snorted derisively. "Oh, yes. I remember how you rambled on about automobiles and lakes that weren't there. No one would have believed such a bizarre story, Maddie."

"Maybe not, but that isn't my fault. I was honest."

"Were you? And what about our deal, Maddie? Did you plan to take my child back where you came from? Out of my reach as surely as if he were dead?"

"My condition was that the child would stay with me. You agreed."

"I thought you wanted a house somewhere," he shouted, causing her to jump. "I had no idea you meant to flit through time!" He raked his hands through his hair again and turned away. "God, I can't believe I'm even saying this. How can your story be true? How could something like this have happened?"

Unfortunately, she had no answers. She shook her head. "I told you, I don't know. I thought . . ."

She broke off, remembering her theory and the possible mistake she'd made. She couldn't lie to him, though. Devon deserved to know at least as much as she knew herself.

"I thought I was sent here to help you, by having the child I needed and wanted. That's why I agreed to marry you. It made sense at the time," she said, running her hands over her face to clear her thoughts. "Or at least it was the most sensible explanation I could come up with. But this . . ." She waved her arms out to her sides. "This epidemic changes everything. My real purpose must have been to help these people. And if that's true, if I wasn't sent here for you, then I'll probably be taken back soon."

"Taken back?" he said, frowning. "What the hell do you mean, taken back?"

"I didn't ask to come here, Devon. It stands to reason, if reason plays any part in this peculiar situation, that when my mission here is complete I'll be sent home. I think we should both be prepared for whatever happens next."

"Prepared," he repeated, startling her when she realized he'd come up close behind her. "What are you talking about?"

"I'm sorry, Devon. But if I was mistaken, and my mission didn't involve you, I probably won't stay long enough to give you the heir you need, and you'll lose your inheritance."

Maddie gasped as Devon's large hands descended on her shoulders, whirling her around to face him. He was so close the strands of hair stirred by her movements whipped across his face. He didn't seem to notice.

"The hell I will. You underestimate me, Maddie. Did you really think I would have let you take my child out of my reach?"

"We had a bargain," she said, accusation threading her tone.

"Yes. And I truly hated deceiving you, Maddie.

But as I said, this child is my heir."

Shock quickly gave way to anger. "You bastard!" she said, shoving his chest hard. He tightened his grip on her shoulders, successfully holding her in place. "You never intended to keep your end of the bargain, did you?"

"I never meant to take him away from you, if that's what you mean. But no, I never intended to let you disappear with him either. That has not changed."

She pushed again and he released her. He stood rooted to the floor. Maddie was deeply hurt by Devon's betrayal and she struck out the only way she could.

"You can't stop me," she told him, shoving past him, jarring her shoulder into his. "If I was brought here for a reason, then I'll leave when the time comes. Nothing you can do will change that."

"We'll see," he said, shaking his head determinedly. "We'll just see about that."

Maddie strode angrily through the door of her bedroom and slammed it behind her. She needed a long nap, and then she needed to get back down to the lobby and help Anthony. She was so tired; she didn't think she'd ever been so exhausted in her life. Physically, emotionally, mentally, she was drained. She didn't have another ounce of strength to draw from.

As she stretched across the coverlet on the bed, her tears slowly came. Devon had sworn to keep her here with him, at least until their child was born. But how could he? How could they control something they couldn't even understand?

Like roping the wind, she thought, sinking into the softness of the mattress. When the time came would Devon be able to hold her in the past? Did she want him to? The question came out of nowhere, surprising Maddie with its implications.

Had she been thinking of staying in this time permanently? Had her heart already accepted what her mind refused to? That she loved Devon. Loved him so deeply and completely that she'd give up everything she knew to be with him? Could she do it? Could she stay, knowing she'd never see Genevieve or her family again? Could she forsake all the familiar trappings of her own time and embrace a bygone era?

Her hands smoothed across her still-flat tummy and the answer was clear. Yes. If Devon loved her as much as she'd come to love him, Maddie knew she'd give the world, her world, to stay with him and raise this child.

But Devon didn't love her, and she couldn't be sure the choice would be hers to make. As she'd told Devon, when the time came she might just disappear as mysteriously as she'd arrived.

Maddie smiled at Anthony and they hugged each other close, propping their tired bodies against one another for support. The worst was over. The epidemic had been successfully put down with the antibiotics and IV solutions. No one else had died, and everyone was showing signs of improvement. It would be a few days before they'd be up and around, but the crisis had passed.

Maddie felt tears of relief and, she had to admit, anxiety. What would happen now? She felt stalked, as though fate waited behind the next corner to snatch her out of this time and place.

"Isn't it miraculous, Maddie?" Anthony said, giving her shoulder one last hug before releasing her. "I still can't believe it worked."

"I told you it would," she said, wishing she could enjoy his enthusiasm more.

"Yes, and there's still so much more I want to know. I know you're tired now, but after you've rested I want to get to those questions."

"Of course."

"I've been thinking about what you said," he continued, oblivious to her somber mood. "If you were sent here to help, perhaps you were meant to do more than just save these few lives."

"What? What are you saying?" She struggled to follow his exuberant chatter.

"We still have a few packets of the antibiotics. I kept samples of each along with the saline solution and some of the other things. I have a colleague in Boston—we went to university together. He specializes in research, Maddie. If we could get him these samples he could analyze them. With you there to answer questions he might be able to duplicate them. Oh, don't you see, Maddie? This epidemic is just a small part of what your mission here must have been. Surely if you're here for a reason it's to benefit people everywhere with your knowledge."

"But I told you, I don't know very much about these things. And I know next to nothing about the chemical makeup of medication."

"I'll wager you know more than you think. For instance, who invented this stuff, and how did it come about?"

Maddie tried to focus on the bubble pack in Anthony's hand. Penicillin. That was an easy one.

"A man named Fleming discovered it quite by accident. His experiment was contaminated by bread mold and he realized the mold was killing the bacteria."

"Bread mold! That's incredible." Anthony's enthusiasm threatened to race out of control. "You see, Maddie, you'd be a tremendous help to Miles."

"Miles?"

"Miles Landon, my friend in Boston."

"Anthony, I really don't think I'd be any help at all. That story about Fleming is common knowledge because it was so incredible. But other than that . . ."

"To you it's common knowledge, Maddie. To the rest of us, it's still years away. Don't you see, we'll need you."

"Oh, I don't know, Anthony. I'm too tired to think right now." She pressed her hand to her forehead and tried to bring her thoughts into focus. But it was no use. They twirled around in her head like leaves caught in a gale.

"I'm sorry, Maddie. Forgive me," Anthony said, taking her elbow in a more subdued manner. "You must be exhausted. Some fine physician I am, keeping my patient on her feet when she needs her rest. Go, get some sleep. There will be plenty of time to talk later."

"Yes, we'll talk," Maddie promised, happy to put the difficult decisions off until her mind could better deal with them. She turned toward the stairs automatically, inclined to take Anthony's advice. But she knew Devon would be in their suite and she couldn't face any more unpleasantness at the moment. They hadn't spoken since their argument and the tension built between them each time they came into contact with one another.

The beach had always been Maddie's escape. She sought its soothing sounds and simple joy now.

The Gulf had never let her down. Now was no exception. No matter the time or place, she could find solace in the monotony of the surf. The unchanging perfection of the endless blue-green of the water.

The breeze ruffled her hair and caressed her cheek like an old friend's touch. She strolled along the shore, unaware of the granules of sand flowing into her slippers to abrade her feet through her stockings.

She walked, on and on, until her legs burned from the exertion and her breath grew raspy from the salt air. With a gratified sigh, she sank down between two sand dunes and flopped onto her back.

She longed to lay there, dozing, not thinking, forever. Perhaps her mission was complete and she'd awake to find suntan lotion booths and brightly colored umbrellas dotting the shore for miles in either direction.

Maddie did sleep. Something woke her and she stirred to find a large shadow blocking the sun. She squinted up and met Devon's irritated gaze.

"I have been looking everywhere for you."

Maddie sat up, brushing the sand from her arms and hands. "I must have fallen asleep."

"Don't apologize, you needed it."

"I wasn't apologizing," she said coolly, looking away to shake her skirt out.

Devon's heavy sigh caught her off guard and she stared at him as he dropped down beside her. He took her hand in his.

"Let me start again," he said. "It is I who owe you an apology. For my outburst earlier, for not believing you. For a lot of things."

She quirked an eyebrow and stared down at their joined hands, not making any attempt to draw away.

Devon took Maddie's compliance as a good sign. He felt reassured, and he knew he'd need assurance to see this through.

"At first it was easy to discount the things you told me," he said, staring out at the glassy blue water. "I thought you were suffering from delusions, or making the tale up because you were running from something. Later, when I was convinced you weren't insane, it was simpler to just forget your claims and pretend you were exactly what we'd decided to tell people you were. A family friend."

"Easier?" she asked. His admission took her by surprise and she wasn't sure how to respond. Where had his anger gone? Where had this placidity come from?

"Easier for me," he admitted. Facing her, Devon decided to forge ahead. "You see, I'd already become very fond of you by that time."

"You had?" Maddie's eyes lit with question. And hope. Could there be more to Devon's feelings for her than kindness and gratitude for her part in their bargain? Of course, she'd long ago admitted to their attraction for one another, but Devon seemed to be saying his feelings went beyond that.

He nodded and squeezed her fingers lightly. "From the moment I found you in my field, I was intrigued by you. When you asked me if I was your angel I almost said yes. I soon found I wanted to be whatever you needed.

"If ever anyone was in need of rescuing, I thought, surely it was you. You seemed so fragile and bewildered, I wanted to take care of you."

"You have," she confessed. She didn't want to think what she'd have done if Devon and his aunt hadn't taken her under their wings.

She'd been little more than a babe in this time, incapable of even the smallest task, like finding food.

"No, you would have done all right on your own, I suspect. You have pluck, lady. And spirit. And you have given me more than I ever thought I needed."

"Devon," she began, moving so she could see his face better in the fading light.

"What I'm trying to say, Maddie, is that I love you. I'm not doing a very good job of it. . . ."

"You're doing just fine," she told him, tears suddenly filling her eyes.

"I thought you needed me, Maddie. But the truth is, I needed you. And I didn't even know how much until now. I don't know how you came to be here, or why. I may never understand the things you've told me. But you have already made a difference in my life, and I can't imagine it without you now."

Maddie was crying now, tears rolling unchecked down her cheeks. "Oh, Devon . . ."

"I can't let you leave me," he said, his voice shaky. "And it's not just because of the baby. Maybe you weren't sent here for me. I won't pretend to understand any of what has happened. But even if your reason for coming here didn't involve me, that doesn't necessarily mean you'll be taken from me now, does it? It's possible you might stay, isn't it? That you might never return to your world?" He steadied his shaking hands and cleared his throat. "If that's what you want, I mean."

"I do," she said, the tears sliding off her chin onto the bodice of her dress. "But I don't know how to make sure that happens."

"Just stay with me, Maddie. Don't leave me. Somehow we'll find a way to keep you here."

"It isn't that simple. Anthony wants me to go to Boston with him. He thinks I was sent here to help with the discovery of antibiotics. I have to go. I have to help if I can."

"But if you leave me, Maddie, what will happen?"

"I don't know," she whispered. "I'll come back, if I can. That much I promise you."

"I don't want to let you out of my sight." He drew her close, she thought for comfort. But when he spoke again she realized it was so she couldn't see his face.

"I'm frightened, Maddie. I'm terrified you'll disappear and I'll never see you or our child again."

"I'll come back, Devon," she swore, not knowing if she would, but needing to reassure them both nevertheless.

"I have a better idea," he said, leaning back to look into her eyes. "I'll go with you."

"Would you?" She turned to meet his gaze and felt all the love in his eyes wash over her.

"Of course. There's no reason I can't."

"What about your work, and someone will have to be here to oversee the hospital project with Anthony gone."

"I don't care about any of that. It isn't important."

But Maddie knew it was important. "Someone has to take care of things here."

"I'll get Taber Elkins to take over the hospital project until we return. I'll explain everything to Beverly, hire a man to look after the crops and oversee the workers, and then we can go. It shouldn't take more than a week."

"But Anthony wants to leave right away."

"Anthony can go ahead and we'll follow as soon as we can." She could see his enthusiasm catch fire and race out of control. She felt the same flame ignite in her own heart. Their future might very well depend on the outcome of this trip. She'd come here for a purpose, of that she was sure. And she'd do whatever she was meant to do. And maybe, if she succeeded, she'd be given a choice about staying.

"I want to get this over with as soon as possible, Devon. I'll go along with Anthony and you can meet us in Boston as soon as you've settled your affairs here."

Devon wanted to argue, but Maddie wouldn't be swayed on this point. "It will only be a few days," she told him, reveling in the closeness they could now share, when only hours ago they'd seemed miles apart. Finally, Devon relented.

"Take care of yourself until I get there," he entreated, his mouth pressed tenderly against her hair. "And take care of my child while we're apart."

She assured him she would and he eased her back against his chest. They sat that way for a long time, adjusting to the newness of their love. She tried to memorize every sensation of being in his arms. The sound of his heart beating beneath her ear, the feel of his muscles twitching and shifting under her fingers as they played over his back, the smell of his warm skin.

She etched it all on the slate of her mind so she could recapture it when they parted. The trip to Boston must surely decide the issue of her fate. Once she delivered the samples to Miles Landon she would either return to her own time, or she would be returned to Devon.

Please God, she prayed, let it be the latter.

The maid hurried along the corridor, careful not to be seen by the other employees still able to work. It had been a madhouse around the hotel since that nice-looking doctor had opened his hospital, and she'd had no trouble slipping out the night before. But things were settling down now and she knew she'd be questioned if she were caught leaving the hotel while she was on duty.

But her mother had been one of the sick ones and they'd need the money more now than ever. If that fancy lady wanted to pay good coin for mere gossip, who was she to refuse?

Gathering her skirts, she ran away from the hotel toward the woods separating the resort from the edge of town. It took nearly an hour for her to reach the bungalow at the old pier.

Her breath heaved from her lungs and she had to lean against the weathered wood of the house for a moment before knocking.

"It's about time you came back. One more minute and you could have forgotten getting paid."

"I'm sorry, ma'am," the girl panted. "But that lady disappeared and I had to wait for her and her man to come back."

Elaine sneered as the little maid referred to Devon as Maddie's man. Damn the bitch. She'd be sorry she ever tried to take what belonged to Elaine before this was over. Elaine vowed to make her regret butting in where she didn't belong. If it hadn't been for Madeline St. Thomas, she'd be Devon's wife now, and forever. She'd have had the man she wanted and, when the deadline passed without an heir, she'd have had half of the fortune Edward stood to inherit for her part in the scheme.

Now, she stood to lose it all if that little slut delivered a child before the deadline. She'd already lost Devon; she didn't intend to lose the money as well. Somehow, she swore, she'd get rid of that child. She escorted the maid into the bungalow, eager to hear what the girl had learned about Maddie.

As the maid relayed the details of Maddie's planned trip to Boston, Elaine smiled. This might be easier than she'd expected, after all.

Chapter Twenty

He couldn't believe she was gone. Devon paced the hotel suite and wished he'd gone to the train station with Maddie and Anthony. He missed her already. He could see her in his mind, but the memory wasn't enough. He wanted to hold her, to touch her, to assure himself she would always be with him.

What if she wasn't? he wondered. What would he do if she disappeared from his life? How would he go on without her? He'd never felt this way about anyone, not even Crystal, and it scared the hell out of him. He alternated between his anger that their future was threatened and his desire to hurry and be with her again.

He'd prayed for the first time in a long time

that morning, asking God to let her stay with him. He hadn't lied when he'd told her how much he needed her. Maddie and the baby were his whole life now. He shouldn't have let her go ahead. But he knew he couldn't have stopped her. Dammit, he should be with her now instead of waiting for the afternoon ferry to take him home. But Maddie hadn't wanted that. He understood why, but it didn't make him like the situation any better.

In a week, maybe less, he'd be with her again. Until then at least he'd have his work to keep him busy. But for now all he had were memories, sweet and bittersweet, to torment him.

A knock drew him out of his reverie. "Who is it?" he called, not turning away from the window.

"It's the maid, Mr. Crowe," a soft voice answered.

"Come back later," he said absently.

"I was wondering if I could speak with you a minute, sir," the voice continued, soft and subdued behind the thick door.

Devon frowned, running his hands through his hair and tugging his suspenders back over his shoulders. He went to the door and drew it open. Outside was a young, meek-looking girl about 13 years of age in the dark blouse and skirt worn by the hotel staff.

"Yes?"

"I don't mean to be forward, sir, but if we could speak inside," she pleaded, glancing over her shoulder anxiously.

Devon found himself following her nervous gaze down the hall but he didn't see anything. "What is this about?" he asked.

She darted another hasty look down the hall and leaned close. Instinctively, Devon leaned forward also.

"It's about your wife, sir."

Devon thought she must be another of Maddie's admirers. They'd swarmed around him all day, singing his wife's praises. And Lord knew no one was more proud of Maddie than he was. But he'd rather not get into a discussion about how she'd conquered the epidemic. The answers they'd managed to come up with were awkward at best.

"Look, miss . . ."

"I know it isn't proper for me to come, but it's terribly urgent. Please," she whispered, twisting her hands.

Devon relented grudgingly. He stepped aside and made room for her to enter the suite. She whisked past him so fast he found himself checking the hall for pursuers again.

"Now, what can I do for you?"

To Devon's chagrin, the girl burst into tears. He was so taken aback, he didn't move for a long moment. Finally, chivalry kicked in and he fumbled for a handkerchief.

The girl mopped her face, but she continued to cry. After a long, seemingly endless flow of tears, she began to speak.

"My mother was so ill, we thought she'd die. And then this morning when we took her home, all she could talk about was how good your wife had been to her. How she'd saved her from dying and all."

Just as he'd thought, another grateful soul. He tried to appear patient, but his sympathy had been depleted. "That's nice," he mumbled. "But I'm . . ."

She turned toward the window and paced, just the way he had minutes ago. "I guess Mother must have seen the truth in my eyes," she continued. "She asked me what was troubling me. I never could lie to her, you know. She always could read me too good."

"Miss . . ."

The tears began anew and Devon found himself patting his pockets before he realized she still had his handkerchief.

"I thought I was helping, you understand. We needed the money. My father, he drinks," she admitted, hanging her head as though it were her shame. "But my mother said we'd never stooped to hurting anyone before and we sure wasn't gonna start on Miss Madeline."

Suddenly Devon's full attention was directed at the girl. "What do you mean?" he asked, his voice gruffer than he'd intended. The maid jumped and looked guiltily toward the door as though gauging the distance to freedom.

"Mind you I'm not sure what the lady meant to do with the information, but my mother said it couldn't have been needed for any good. I was only trying to help," she wailed, snapping Devon's tenuous hold on his patience.

"What in the name of all that's holy are you trying to say, girl? Spit it out and be done with it."

"I took money to tell the comings and goings of your wife," she blurted. "I'm as sorry as I can be, truly I am. But I didn't see no harm. All the lady wanted was a bit of gossip."

A shiver of apprehension feathered up Devon's spine, raising the growth of hair on his neck. "What woman?"

"Some fancy lady, I don't know her name. Honest," she added, when he narrowed his eyes menacingly.

"What did this lady look like?"

She mumbled a few details, not very coherently but enough for Devon to know who she meant. Damn! he cursed. Elaine. What was she up to?

"Sit, please," he said, leading the sobbing girl to a chair by the window. "Tell me everything this woman said to you."

"I don't remember every detail," she said, looking as though she'd burst into tears again.

"All right," he told her, trying to keep the impatience out of his voice. "Then tell me everything you can remember."

"Well, she came to me the first time you and your missus stayed here."

"On our honeymoon?" he asked, astounded to think Elaine had followed them.

The girl blushed. "I wouldn't know, sir."

"Of course. Go on."

"Well, she asked me if I was cleaning the

293

room and I told her I was. She gave me a dollar and told me if I heard anything to tell her."

That didn't sound so bad, Devon thought with relief. Maybe Elaine just wanted to find out the details of his marriage. It was disgusting, but hardly dangerous.

"Is that all?"

"No, sir. She came back this time, too. Only this time she wanted me to ask questions. Find out things."

"What things?"

"Well." She blushed scarlet and her gaze fell to her hands clasped in her lap. "Personal things."

"Can you tell me?" he asked, wondering if he'd have to offer her some more incentive to get her to repeat what she'd told Elaine.

"She wanted to know if both beds were being slept in," she whispered, tucking her chin further into her chest. "And if your wife was showing any signs of—well, expecting."

Definitely disgusting, Devon thought, rage coloring his vision. When he got his hands on Elaine . . .

"There's more."

He looked up and the girl was watching him now. Her eyes looked hollowed and sunken from crying, but there was a determination in them he hadn't seen before.

"She paid me good this time to listen in on your wife's conversation with the doctor. She seemed mightily pleased to learn your wife would be going away. I thought maybe she was your—well, you know. I thought she wanted to spend time with you. But she left right behind your wife and she was with another man."

"A man?" he coaxed, sitting on the edge of his seat now.

"Yes, sir. She called him Edward."

Just what he'd been afraid of. Elaine by herself was bad enough, but when she joined forces with his cousin, nothing would be beyond the realm of their revenge. Maddie might very well be in danger if Elaine and Edward were plotting something.

"Is that all?" Devon asked hopefully.

"No, sir. She said . . ."

The girl hung her head again and Devon longed to tell her not to get shy on him now. He held his tongue and waited for her to continue.

"She said there wouldn't be no baby if she had her way."

Devon choked back panic and struggled to remain calm. Surely she couldn't mean . . .

"I reckon she was going to do something to break you and Miss Madeline up before you could—you know."

"My wife is already pregnant," Devon said, the fear sweeping through him now like a wildfire out of control. Cold sweat broke out on his palms and ran in rivulets down his back. "And Elaine knows it."

The maid's eyes widened and she twisted her hands faster and faster in her lap. "I'm sorry," she sobbed, her tears flowing freely down her face once more. "I'm so sorry. I never meant to do nothing to hurt your missus. You got to believe me." She jumped off the chair and began to pull coins from her pockets. "Here, that's all the money I got left of what she gave me. Take it, please. Oh Lordy, I never meant to hurt nobody."

Devon pushed the money back into the girl's hands and tried to calm her. "It's all right," he said, not at all sure if what he said was meant to reassure her or himself. "Keep the money. You couldn't have known what Elaine was up to."

"No, sir, I didn't. But I don't want any part of this money. If she was to hurt your wife . . ."

"She isn't going to hurt my wife. And if you can have my bag packed in less than five minutes, I'll match whatever Elaine gave you."

He set her aside briskly, deciding he didn't have any more time to waste. They had a full day's head start on him and he'd play hell catching up as it was. But he would catch up, he swore. He'd finally found what he needed, wanted, in his life. He refused to let anything, or anyone, take it from him. He'd get to Maddie first and he'd make damn sure not one hair on her head was harmed. He had to.

The train rumbled on, cramped and belching black smoke. Maddie tried to find a measure of comfort in the small compartment, but the motion had brought on nausea and headache. She'd taken the peppermint spirits Anthony had assured her would settle her stomach, but to no avail. The only cure for what ailed her was for the interminable trip to end.

They could have been there in a few hours if they'd been flying. Instead, she and Anthony had traveled days.

She needed a bath. She longed to wash her hair. And she'd have sold her soul for a soft bed.

Anthony fretted over her like a mother hen, making sure she rested and ate properly. Physically, she was all right.

But she missed Devon. More than she'd ever thought possible. And if she'd had any doubts about staying with him, they'd all been banished by their separation. She loved him more than she'd ever loved anyone in her life. And as much as she grieved knowing she'd never see her sister again, she would fight to stay in this time if it meant being with her husband.

She remembered the way he'd looked, sleeping in the elaborate bed in the hotel suite. That was how she wanted to remember him. He'd offered to go with her to the train station, but she could see he didn't want to part that way. So they'd said their good-byes in private and she'd left him looking tousled from sleep and loving.

Closing her eyes, she could picture every detail of his face. If they were apart for a hundred years she knew the memory would be as strong.

"Maddie?"

Maddie opened her eyes and smiled at Anthony. He hovered by the compartment door, worry etched on his features.

"How are you doing?"

"Fine," she lied. There was no use telling Anthony she'd never been so miserable in her life. He'd only blame himself and this misery came from her heart, not her health.

"We should be pulling into the station any minute now," he told her, coming in to sit on the faded leather seat. "I wired ahead from the last station, so Miles should be waiting for us. It's a short drive to his town house from the station."

"That's fine," she said, tucking her hair into place and smoothing the wrinkles out of her serge skirt. She would put the heavy jacket back on when they reached the station, but for now she was more comfortable in just the blouse. She realized with a hint of amusement how quickly she'd gotten used to the confining clothing. She'd have felt almost naked wearing her silk shorts and tank top now.

The smoke from the engine billowed around the train and the wind caught it, tossing it back across the heads of the passengers as they disembarked. Maddie didn't care how polluted the air smelled; she was just grateful to be in the open again.

"This way," Anthony shouted over the noise of the train and the bustle of people coming and going.

"Anthony!"

Maddie and Anthony stopped, scanning the crowd for whoever had called his name.

"Anthony, over here."

Maddie spotted the man first, waving his hat in an arc over his head.

"There," she said, pointing him out to Anthony.

Anthony took her arm and cleared a path through the crowd. "Miles, how are you?" he greeted the man when they'd reached him.

"It's been too long," Miles said, clasping Anthony's hand and shoulder at the same time. The two shook hands and then patted each other's backs, all smiles.

Maddie stood to one side, waiting for the reunion to be over. Miles noticed her and a broad smile crossed his face.

"My God, man, you didn't tell me you'd married."

Maddie coughed—the smoke must be getting to her—and shook her head. "No," she said huskily, looking to Anthony for help.

"I wish I'd had the honor," Anthony said, holding her elbow and bringing her close to his side. "But I'm afraid someone else found her first. This is Madeline Crowe. I didn't have a chance to explain everything. I hope it isn't a problem."

"Of course not, we have plenty of room."

"If it's too much trouble . . ." Maddie began.

"No, I insist you both stay at my house. Tiffany will be thrilled."

"Tiffany?" Anthony questioned, one eyebrow raised in speculation.

"My sister. She's been staying with me. Keeps me in line. You'll meet her when we arrive."

He hefted Maddie's bags in his large hands and nodded toward a carriage. "Shall we?" he said, waiting for them to lead the way.

"I can't wait to hear all about this important breakthrough, Anthony. Your wire certainly aroused my curiosity, as I imagine you intended it to."

"Yes, indeed," Anthony admitted, smiling gleefully at Maddie. "But I must warn you, you're going to hear things they never taught us about in university."

Maddie laughed, the first real laugh she'd felt since leaving Devon. What an understatement. The tale they had to tell Miles and the samples they'd brought to show him would knock his socks off.

Chapter Twenty-one

Maddie came downstairs from her nap refreshed and eager to begin fulfilling her mission. A fervent desire to do something for the people of this time had overcome her, and her need to do all she could to put a stop to such tragedies as cholera burned in her.

If Miles Landon could analyze the samples she and Anthony had brought along, she knew it would be the most important thing she'd ever done in her life. For as long as she could remember, Genevieve was the humanitarian, the one who visited nursing homes and children's wings at the hospitals. Maddie had her designing, but it had never fulfilled the need in her to help others. She prayed this trip would.

The town house where Miles Landon lived
with his sister Tiffany was lush and rich
with period detail. Maddie admired the lav-
ishly carved rosewood furniture and the plush
fabrics of the heavy velvet drapes, tapestried
pillows, and chair cushions. She marveled at
the works of art hanging from wire suspended
from the top of the walls. Ancestral portraits
mingled with popular artists' works of the day
and a few older collector's pieces.

Her journey through the streets of Boston
had been astounding with the mixture of people
walking, carriages passing, and wooden, horse-
drawn buses. They'd arrived at the brownstone
town house, one of several like structures, and
Miles had ushered them into his home.

The introductions had been brief and hurried,
and then Tiffany showed Maddie to her room,
where she was invited to nap until teatime.

The floor plan of the town house had been
easy enough to memorize on her walk upstairs.
The street-level floor held a parlor, a dining room, and the adjoining kitchen area.
The lower level, Miles had told them, held
his lab and apartments. He liked to sleep
near his equipment for those times when
he awakened with a sudden desire to try
some new experiment. The third floor contained Tiffany's suite of rooms and two guest
rooms where Maddie and Anthony would be
staying. The upper floor used to be servants' quarters, but as they had only a housekeeper and two maids now who went home

to their families in the evenings, these were vacant.

Maddie easily found her way to the parlor, where Anthony and Tiffany were already waiting.

As she entered, she couldn't help noticing the blush of pleasure on Tiffany's face or the look of heated interest in Anthony's eyes. The couple stepped apart, a little too quickly, and Maddie felt certain romance was in the air. She hadn't formed much of an opinion about Tiffany Landon earlier—there hadn't been time—but she considered the woman now and decided she liked what she saw.

Tiffany had an open face, expressive eyes, and a mouth quick to smile. She had shown her kindness by insisting Maddie take a nap after the long journey, and she'd displayed her generosity when she welcomed the pair unhesitatingly despite no prior warning.

Maddie smiled easily at her hostess.

"How do you feel?" Tiffany asked, waving Maddie to the fashionable horsehair sofa. Maddie sat, and Tiffany immediately poured her tea and filled a small china plate with finger sandwiches and slices of sweet cake.

Maddie nibbled the sandwich and sipped her tea as Tiffany and Anthony shared a few brief remembrances of Miles's and Anthony's university days. Maddie found herself amused and would have been content in her surroundings if it weren't for missing Devon. The ache had dulled to an ever-present throb in her chest. She

303

knew if she were whisked back to the future when her job here was complete, it would be a pain she'd live with for the rest of her life.

"I apologize for my brother, Mrs. Crowe," Tiffany Landon said, offering Maddie another slice of cake. "When he's in the middle of a project it's difficult to get him to put it aside, even for a short time."

Maddie shook her head at the offer of cake and smiled. "That's quite all right. I understand."

A door closed in the entryway, just off the stairs, and Tiffany looked relieved. "There he is now," she said, rising. Maddie and Anthony rose together and the three greeted a rumpled-looking Miles Landon as he entered the parlor, his eyes troubled and somewhat dazed, as though he'd left his work physically but not yet mentally.

"I'm sorry to keep you waiting," he said.

"Not at all," Anthony told him. "You've been more than generous to allow us to descend on you without explanation."

"So, what is this explanation you've promised me? I must say you know how to whet the appetite of my curiosity."

Anthony looked from Maddie to Tiffany. Maddie knew he was wondering if she objected to Miles's sister being part of her secret. Maddie didn't feel threatened any longer by the truth and she nodded.

"Tell me, Miles, what do you know about time-travel?" Anthony began.

Their host looked puzzled but he nodded. "There are some who believe all time runs in parallel lines like train tracks and when you pass a particular place where the curtain between the different planes is thin or non-existent, you can, theoretically, glimpse other worlds."

"And pass from one to the other?" Anthony asked, smiling at Maddie.

"Well now, I don't know about that. I haven't formed any theories along those lines. I'm only repeating what I've heard and read. My specialty is pharmaceutical research."

"Yes," Anthony said, "that's why we're here." He reached into the breast pocket of his coat and drew out one of the sample packets of penicillin. He handed it to Miles, who lowered his glasses from his forehead and peered through them at the odd-looking item.

"What would you say if I told you I just saved close to fifty lives with what's in that packet?"

Miles's eyes sharpened and narrowed. "What is it?"

"It's called penicillin, and it's an antibiotic derived, somehow, from the mold on regular household bread."

Miles glanced up quickly, his gaze honed to attention. "Go on," he coaxed calmly. His expression gave away his enthusiasm though, and Anthony grinned.

"I can't. I don't know how this particular drug was processed or investigated. All I know is that it arrested a cholera epidemic within hours of being administered."

305

"Cholera!" Tiffany cried, pressing her hand to her heart.

"Yes. There was a storm on Gulf Island. A sewage line broke and contaminated the fresh water supply. By the time I arrived, a few people had already died and close to fifty more had been affected. Maddie gave me this, along with something called tetracycline, and she showed me how an intravenous solution can be used to replace body fluids. We did not lose another patient and the epidemic began to subside almost immediately."

"Amazing," Miles said, eyeing first the packet in his hand and then Maddie. "If anyone else had told me this, I'd be doubtful. But I know you, Anthony, and I must assume you're speaking the truth. Tell me, how did you know these things?"

Maddie cleared her throat and prayed the look of interest in Miles's eyes wouldn't fade to skepticism, or worse, anger, when she'd spoken.

"I slipped through one of those curtains of time you talked about. I don't know how it happened, but it did. And I brought that with me."

"Are you saying you aren't from this time period? That you lived in another era previous to coming here?"

Tiffany's mouth had dropped open and Maddie wondered if she should tell the woman it was an unattractive position. Instead, she stared hard into Miles's eyes, trying to read his thoughts. She saw a glint of disbelief but not the outright denial she'd feared.

"Yes, that's what I'm saying. I was born in nineteen hundred and sixty. Before I came to be here, in this time, the year was nineteen hundred and ninety-two."

Tiffany's mouth snapped shut with an audible click and her cup rattled noisily on its saucer as she struggled to set it down without mishap.

"I see," was all Miles said. He removed his glasses, took out a handkerchief, and polished the tiny round lenses. The packet of penicillin sat boldly on his knee, its foil backing gleaming in the afternoon sunlight streaming through the full-length window.

"Can you tell me about this period in which you lived?" he asked, as though troubling her for the time of day.

"I'll answer any questions I can." Maddie saw the tea in her cup rippling and realized she was trembling. She dabbed her mouth with the corner of her napkin and set the implements of their refreshments aside.

After a moment Miles looked up and met her gaze. "Start with some modern inventions. Anything you can think of that might be helpful."

"That's a tall order," she told him, smiling. "I could list for days the discoveries modern science made in a single year. We have automobiles, of course."

"Horseless carriages." He nodded, not too impressed, Maddie thought.

"And we have airplanes. Flying machines which carry people from one place to another through the air."

Tiffany looked as though she'd faint, and Maddie noticed the glint of surprise in Miles's eyes as well.

"And we've even put a man on the moon."

Tiffany gasped, sputtered, and sank back against the back of the sofa. Miles quirked an eyebrow in stunned interest and Anthony grinned. He'd already heard most of this from Maddie on the train.

"And of course there are the medical miracles. A vaccine for everything from chicken pox to polio. There is laser surgery, organ transplants, and even cryogenics, which I still have doubts about."

"Cryogenics?"

"That's where they freeze you until a later date when they can thaw you out and cure whatever disease you had."

Tiffany's curiosity peaked and she sat on the edge of the sofa, apparently over her swoon. Miles could only sit, silent, shaking his head. Anthony inched forward, replacing his own cup and plate on the low table.

"Pretty amazing, isn't it?" he grinned, barely able to contain his excitement.

"Interesting," Miles said blandly. Maddie feared he didn't believe a word of her tale and she felt her heart lurch. How would she be able to convince him the medicine was real if she couldn't convince him she was telling the truth? Anthony's laughter surprised her.

"Stop acting so blasted nonchalant. I've known you long enough to know that spark in your eyes means you're dying to know more, so don't try to appear casual."

"I don't deny I'm interested. But I'm also cautious with my enthusiasm. You must admit this is all a bit much to take in."

"You'd better believe it's a bit much. A cure for cholera, tetanus, maybe even the plague. Don't you see what this means?"

"Yes, yes of course. If all of this is fact . . ."

"It is, I assure you."

"Then it would be the most important medical breakthrough in history."

"Yes, I do believe it was," Maddie cut in, drawing both men's attention to her. "I can't imagine a time when antibiotics weren't commonplace, but as frequently as they are used in my time they must have been thought some kind of miracle when they were first discovered."

"I tell you, Miles, it *is* a miracle. You should have seen my patients. After only one dose, most of them showed immediate improvement. By the next day they were all conscious, coherent, and able to take nourishment by mouth."

"One dose?" Miles studied the packet more closely.

"Only one. It was incredible."

"You say you don't know how you came to be here," Miles said to Maddie. "Can you tell me what you do remember?"

Maddie relayed the story of how she'd found herself in 1892. Miles nodded, shook his head, and seemed thoroughly engrossed in her description.

"Fascinating. And you don't know how to go back where you came from? You haven't discovered any kind of passage or key to the phenomenon?"

"No, nothing. I assumed, rightly or wrongly I don't know, that I'd been sent here on a mission. Now I wonder if I will be directed back to this door or whatever when I've completed the job I was sent here to do."

"And you think it was your mission to bring me this antibiotic?"

Maddie thought of Devon, his inheritance, her need for a baby, the cholera epidemic and all the lives she'd helped to save. Suddenly, she was no longer sure of anything. Even to her own ears her theory sounded wilder than her tale. Finally, she could only shake her head.

"I just don't know anymore. I thought I wanted to go back and so I tried to rationalize my being here. I managed to keep from losing my sanity at first by telling myself all I had to do was fulfill my mission and I'd be swept home. It gave me something to focus on. A goal. And I worked toward that goal in the hopes that I was somehow right."

To her chagrin, tears welled in her eyes and she had to clear her throat before she could finish. "Now I don't know anymore."

Tiffany's arm came around Maddie's shoulder and Maddie smiled at her new friend. She thought of Devon and their baby and the tears disappeared as quickly as they'd come. She didn't regret a minute of her time here, even if she'd been wrong, and she had to admit she wouldn't change a thing that had happened even if she could.

"Why don't you visit with Tiffany while Anthony and I go down to the lab and take a look at what we have here," Miles said gently, fingering the bubble pack of penicillin.

Anthony and Miles rose, and the ladies excused them to return to Miles's lab. Tiffany reminded her brother that dinner would be served shortly, and Miles gave Maddie one last smile of encouragement.

Devon leaned out the window of the cab and silently urged the man to a faster pace. He'd wasted precious time in locating the doctor's house in Boston and now his urgency roiled to a full boil.

"Please, hurry," he entreated the horses, slapping his own gloves impatiently against his thigh. He'd ridden hard for two days trying to catch Maddie and Anthony's train before it neared Boston, but he'd missed them by only hours each time. Finally, he'd settled for the next train leaving a small Georgia town, and so he'd been one step behind them the whole way.

He prayed Edward and Elaine had no better luck than he had.

311

As the hired hack swiftly turned the corner of Main, Devon saw another cab draw near, heading in the opposite direction. A familiar face stared back at him and time seemed to slow. Elaine's eyes were at first surprised, then stunned, and finally horrified as her cab and Devon's came within inches of one another.

She opened her mouth and, it appeared to Devon, uttered a silent cry of dismay. Her head whipped around, and her gaze locked on a brownstone town house just down the block. Devon turned to follow her line of vision.

As the hack neared the brownstone, he saw Edward lob a bottle, set ablaze with a rag in the neck, through an alley window into the basement floor of the house.

The crash of broken glass was quickly followed by the whoosh of an igniting inferno. Devon leapt from the carriage as it drew close to the brownstone. The horses smelled the acrid smoke first and reared and shrieked in panic, almost overturning the carriage. Devon raced forward, intent on overtaking Edward.

His cousin looked up at the sound of the frenzied horses and saw Devon. He turned to run down the alley and Devon saw that Elaine had circled back and awaited her accomplice at the other end of the narrow space between houses.

Devon pumped his legs harder. Smoke now billowed from the window of the basement and surrounded him as he raced toward Edward. He had only a few yards to go. His hands reached out for his cousin's shoulders. Suddenly an explosion blew the remaining windows out of the basement of the brownstone. The force of the blast propelled him forward and he felt himself being tossed through the air like a windswept leaf.

He hit the ground hard, his bones seeming to jar together on impact. Smoke billowed out in torrents and he had to squint to see. Edward looked back, skidded to a halt, and smiled triumphantly. He caught the side of the waiting carriage and hopped onto the step beside the door. The hack raced off with him clinging to its side.

Chapter Twenty-two

Maddie and Tiffany had just stepped into the entryway when they heard the door to Miles's lab open. Anthony stepped out to join them, a smile on his face.

"Good news, ladies," he said, a look of triumph lighting his face all the way to his eyes. "It looks as if . . ."

A crash stopped the trio in midstep, followed by a strange roaring.

"The lab!" Anthony cried, turning back to the door he'd just closed behind him. His hand closed on the knob and he yanked, but the heavy door stuck. In the next second the fire reached the chemicals in the lab and an explosion ripped through the lower floor of the house, flinging the door wide and knocking Anthony back into the ladies. They toppled like bowling pins onto the slick marble floor of the hall.

The heavy oak door slammed into Anthony with the force of a locomotive and he slumped atop Maddie and Tiffany like a rag doll.

Maddie felt something warm and sticky trickle over her cheek. She struggled to remove Anthony from her chest. Unconscious, he felt like a felled tree. She couldn't budge him. Through the thick smoke filling the hall Maddie saw Tiffany, likewise pinned beneath Anthony's legs.

His chest pressed her down. The weight pinned her hands at her sides. Maddie couldn't get leverage to throw him off. Tiffany had less to contend with and managed to squirm from her trap. She raced on hands and knees to Maddie's side and shoved at Anthony with all her strength.

He shifted enough for Maddie to free her arms, and she and Tiffany finally rolled him to the floor.

"Miles!" Tiffany cried, looking toward the open portal where the door of the basement used to be. A strange reddish glow lit the hole with an unearthly light.

"No, Tiffany, you can't go in there," Maddie cried. She grasped the other woman's arm and restrained her.

"But Miles," Tiffany screamed.

Maddie feared it was too late for Miles Landon. Already the flames licked at the doorjamb. She glanced around and tried to get her bearings. Pressing her hands to her stomach, she prayed the baby hadn't been hurt in the fall. Blood seeped into her eyes, momentarily blinding her. She scrubbed at her eyes to clear them.

"We've got to get Anthony out," she entreated. Tiffany sat, stunned, for another moment. Maddie shook her arm. The thick smoke prevented any long-winded conversations. Time was running out. She motioned wildly to Anthony's prone form on the marble. "Help me!"

Tiffany glanced at the basement doorway. The first flash of fire circled up from below. The reddish orange blaze rolled over the top of the doorway and encased the first rungs of the stair railing.

"Hurry," Maddie cried, tugging on Anthony's arms in an attempt to drag him to safety.

Tiffany scampered to her knees, wrapped her arms around his booted feet, and lifted his heavy legs to her sides. After several aborted attempts, the two women had Anthony halfway across the foyer. Another blast from the basement toppled them. Maddie hit the wall of the entryway with enough force to knock the breath from her. Blackness swirled and dipped before her eyes. She shook her head and struggled to see Tiffany through the thick blanket of black smoke.

"Tiffany?" she called, choking on the smoke as she pushed to her feet once more. "Tiffany, are you all right?"

She received no reply. Finally, she could wait no longer. The smoke blinded her and tears streamed from her eyes. Already, she could feel the marble heat to a dangerous degree.

Positioning her hands under Anthony's arm-pits, she planted her feet and tugged. Maddie felt the resistance ease. Tiffany must have been alerted by her movements. Together, Maddie and Tiffany carried their burden in the direction of the door. With the billowing black fog sur-rounding them now, Maddie could only guess at the way. Twice she encountered a barrier and had to change her direction.

The fumes threatened to choke the breath from her. Her lungs burned with each breath and she could feel the heat char her throat. The flames were an encroaching beast, inching closer and closer until Maddie felt the sweat on her face grow warm.

A sudden whoosh of air and light startled Maddie, causing her to topple beneath the weight of her burden once more. The air ignited the blaze anew, sending the flames raging in a crazed dance of destruction. She pressed against the wall only to look up and see the tongues of fire licking along the ceiling over her head.

Propelled with terror, she scrambled toward the light, dragging Anthony along behind her. She longed to call out to Tiffany to assure herself the woman was still with her. But the oxygen had been swallowed by the inferno. She couldn't draw breath enough to speak. Already, her eyes burned and her lungs ached from coughing. So she tugged and crept along, praying her new friend had managed to retain consciousness.

"Maddie!"

Maddie slumped, dazed by the sound filling her ears. Had that been Devon's voice? Impossible. She knew, even as she renewed her efforts to reach the door, that it couldn't be Devon.

"Maddie!"

This time Maddie knew she hadn't imagined the voice. Through the cloud encasing her she sought the direction of her husband's call.

"Devon," she attempted to answer, but her cry was muffled by the roar of the fire and the dryness of her throat. Her tongue felt thick and large, and she couldn't make it form the words she longed to say.

"Maddie, can you hear me?"

The voice drew closer and Maddie scrambled to her knees. "Devon," she croaked. Knowing she'd lost all sense of direction, she struggled to cry out. It might be their only hope.

"Devon!" Finally, her throat managed to pump enough saliva into her mouth for her to form the word. She wanted to weep with relief.

"Maddie, keep talking, love. I can't see you."

Through the blackness a slice of light shone and Maddie focused on it, thinking it must be where Devon was.

"Here," she said, fighting for air. Thinking quickly, she pounded the wall behind her. Within moments, a form leapt out of the smoke and staggered to her side. Devon's hands reached out and grasped her shoulders.

"Oh, Devon," she said, her words mere movements of her lips.

"Love, love," he whispered, clasping her close against his chest. "I've got to get you out of here."

"Anthony." She motioned toward the form lying next to her. "And Tiffany and Miles."

"I'll come back for them."

Maddie shook her head. Determined, she forced the words from her scorched throat. "Take Anthony. I'll follow."

"No . . ."

"Take him," she said, pushing Devon toward his friend.

"Hold my hand," he insisted, and Maddie nodded.

Devon hefted Anthony over his shoulder and rose to his feet, hunching to keep his head out of the thickest part of the smoke. Maddie took his hand and with her other reached into the darkness.

"Tiffany," she choked out. "Tiffany, can you hear me? Take my hand." She felt another body and grasped the hot flesh with her fingers.

Tiffany responded by squeezing Maddie's hand and the three, each grasping one another in turn, stumbled toward the door, and life.

The air outside scalded Maddie's damaged lungs as she drank it in. Her head cleared as she sucked in great gulps of oxygen. She scanned the steps outside the burning brownstone and saw Devon, Anthony, and Tiffany. Bent at the waist, they tried to regain their breath.

Anthony had come to at the first touch of the cool, crisp air, and Devon had him propped against the wrought-iron railing. Tiffany coughed steadily, her face bloodred and soaked with black rivulets of sweat. Smut smudged her cheeks and Maddie thought she saw several burns on the woman's clothing.

Taking all this in took only a second and Maddie felt relief, followed immediately by terror. It took Tiffany only a split second longer to have the same thought.

"Miles!" The woman cried, turning back toward the engulfed building. Devon caught her around the waist before she could rush back into the house and he lifted her off her feet in an effort to restrain her. He choked, coughed, and pushed her aside.

"I'll go," he said, whipping a handkerchief from his pocket to tie it across his nose and mouth.

"No!" Maddie screamed, clutching his arm and trying to stop him. Even Tiffany seemed reluctant to let this stranger risk everything and reenter the house.

"I'll be all right," Devon said through the cloth, his eyes reassuring Maddie. Then he'd released her and was gone before she could stop him.

Maddie slumped against the rail, her hands folded over the slight mound of her stomach protectively. She closed her eyes and prayed steadily.

After what seemed like an eternity Anthony started for the door. She closed her hand quietly over his arm and shook her head. Tears poured silently from her eyes, diluting the soot on her cheeks, turning it from black to gray.

Anthony's eyes met Maddie's and she could read the pain and regret there. "No," she whispered, her voice hoarse and husky. "He'll be back," she told them. "He'll be back."

Behind her she heard the wail of the fire wagon making its way through the bustle of the Boston streets and the hum of voices as the neighbors gathered around, but she focused on her litany. "He'll be back," she assured herself, desperate to make it true.

The fire brigade drew to a wild halt in front of the town house, its occupants bustling with activity. Hoses were unfurled and pumps primed.

Two of the oddly dressed men grabbed the end of the hose and raced toward the front door.

"Wait," Maddie called, blocking the doorway. "There are still two men in there."

"Sorry, miss," the heaviest of the two said. "But we got to get at it right away. This building is connected to the whole row. If we don't hurry we'll lose the block."

"But . . ."

Devon burst forth from the house, his clothing smoking and his face purple from exertion.

The other fireman caught him and covered the burden he carried with a blanket. Tiffany ran forward, but was halted by Anthony's hands on her shoulders. He drew her into his arms and she realized for the first time the form was completely covered and still. She dissolved into tears and Anthony cradled her in his sympathetic embrace. Devon bypassed the fireman and stepped in front of Maddie. She felt her lower lip tremble on a sob and he opened his arms. Gratefully, she fell into them.

All around them the sudden activity of the fire fighters abounded. But Maddie's eyes were trained on Devon. He was safe, unhurt, and she was in his arms. Where she belonged. She wrapped her arms around his back and hugged him close, to imprint the feel of his body against hers.

"Are you all right?" she asked, looking up at him without loosening her grip.

"The fire had blown itself out in the basement. It's mainly upstairs now. The lower floors are gutted, but no longer burning. He was on the floor of the basement."

The thought of Miles's body, burned, had Maddie struggling to keep from passing out. How long ago had he been watching her intently as she told her story? An hour, two? No more. Now he was dead. And so was her hope of fulfilling her mission. And what of his future? Had it been his destiny to die so young? Or had her appearance in his life brought about his untimely death?

Quivers of fear shook her. Her rubbery legs threatened to give way beneath the waves of shock and regret. Devon swooped her into his arms and carried her away from the brownstone. Anthony followed, Tiffany still held tightly against his side.

"Maddie, are you hurt, is the baby—"

"Everything seems to be fine," she told him, cupping his jaw lovingly.

A woman came from behind the fire wagon and draped a blanket around Tiffany's shoulders. A young girl joined her carrying a tray of cups filled with tea. Devon, Maddie, Anthony, and Tiffany seated themselves on the tailgate of the wagon and gratefully accepted the soothing beverage. The hot liquid burned their already raw throats, but none of them seemed to notice. Each was beyond feeling their own discomfort.

Tiffany's glance kept returning to the wrapped bundle lying on the ground some yards away, and finally she rose, letting the blanket fall from her shoulders. Anthony followed as she went to the body of her brother. He knelt beside her on the ground as she bent over the blanket and wept.

Devon's arm went around Maddie's shoulder and she leaned into his warmth. They were alive, and well. But somehow she couldn't feel any joy in that fact just yet. Miles Landon had died. Why, she didn't know. But somehow, Maddie felt it was her fault. And instead of saving lives as she'd intended, she'd caused one to be lost.

What had gone wrong? Was it a chemical explosion? A gas leak set off by the use of a flame? In any case, Miles had been in that basement at that exact moment because of her. If she and Anthony hadn't shown up on his doorstep out of the blue with their outlandish claims, he'd have probably been in the dining room at that precise moment. And he'd probably be alive now.

"Maddie, love, are you sure you and the baby are all right?"

Devon's concerned voice drew her back to the grisly scene around her. She tried to paste a reassuring look on her face, but it felt wooden and strained. "I think so. Besides, I should be asking you that question. You scared me half to death when you went back into that house."

"I wouldn't have taken any unnecessary chances. I would have come straight back out if the blaze had still been raging downstairs. I'm sorry I frightened you."

"You were very brave," she said, touching his flushed, smudged cheek with her fingertips. She wanted to add, "And I love you."

"I only wish I could have saved him. But it was too late." His eyes took on a haunted look and Maddie could see the horrors he'd seen reflected there. "It was too late," he repeated.

"You did all you could. If you hadn't shown up, it could have been a lot worse. I don't know how you managed to arrive just in time, but I'm sure glad you did."

Devon merely nodded. But his arm tightened on Maddie's shoulder and she felt him tremble. She'd never been so frightened in her life and she slid her arms around him once more, trying to reassure herself he was truly there and safe.

She laid her head against his chest and listened to his heart beat beneath her ear as they watched the firemen battling the last vestiges of the fire.

If she'd ever wondered how much she loved Devon, Maddie now had her answer. She loved him more than she loved the life she'd left behind. She loved him enough to fight the forces of fate to stay with him. And she loved him enough to stay with him forever.

Suddenly, Maddie knew she had to tell Devon how she felt. The knowledge that she could have lost him gave her courage and determination she hadn't known she possessed. Life was too short, and she'd wasted enough time as it was.

"Devon," she said, looking up into his face.

He pressed a kiss against the cut on her brow and met her gaze. "Yes, love?"

"I want you to know I—"

He kissed her tender lips and tucked his head into the curve of her neck. "I love you, too," he said, holding her close. "I love you more than I ever thought it possible to love anyone. And I died a thousand times searching for you in that house. If anything had happened to you . . ."

"I know. I felt the same way."

They stared at one another for a long time; then he kissed her, slow and sweet. Maddie melted into his arms.

"I don't want to leave you, Devon. I want to stay with you forever. I want to have this baby and a dozen more. I want to grow old with you. Here, in your time."

He smiled. "I was going to tell you I'd go back with you to your time if you wanted. I would, you know. I'd give up everything I thought was important to me. You and our baby are all that matters to me now."

"Oh, Devon, I do love you. I never thought I'd find anyone like you. I thought I'd be alone all my life. I don't know how I came to be here, but if this is what I had to do to find you, I'd do it all again. Gladly."

Maddie and Devon hugged each other close for a long time. The fire sputtered to a spark and died beneath the onslaught of water from the firemen's hoses. Anthony led Tiffany away and Maddie saw them huddled together watching the macabre tableau. A black carriage arrived and collected the body of Miles Landon. And all around them people buzzed like flies. But Maddie felt secure in her husband's arms and she faced the nightmare by drawing strength from his support.

Chapter Twenty-three

It had been nearly five months since the fire in Boston. Devon and Maddie never missed an opportunity to tell one another their thoughts or feelings. Their brush with death had made them both aware of the tenuousness of life and they clutched at happiness now with both fists.

The death of her brother had affected Tiffany a great deal, and she'd agreed to come to Alabama with Devon, Maddie, and Anthony. She'd worked as Anthony's assistant for nearly four months and only last week the pair had announced their engagement.

Maddie slipped into the bright pink gown of ruched satin and adjusted the folds over her burgeoning stomach. "Fasten me, darling," she said, turning her back on Devon as he strug-

gled with a bow tie. Devon's lips closed over
Maddie's neck in a playful love-bite, and she
suspected they'd be a bit late arriving.

Devon loved her gently, always concerned
now for the child growing beneath her heart.
He'd tried to stay away once she began expand-
ing, but their love would not be denied. Neither
would their passion. Maddie assured him it
would be safe if they were careful, and Devon
was easily convinced.

Now, as she lay with her backside pressed
against Devon, one hand beneath her head and
the other gently massaging the mound of her
belly, she felt joy well in her heart. To never have
known such contentment was unthinkable. But
Maddie never forgot how close she'd come to
living her life without the joy of fulfilled love.
Each day she thanked God for bringing her here
and prayed he'd let her stay.

All was not rosy with Maddie and Devon,
despite their vow not to discuss what they
couldn't change. Elaine and Edward had been
charged with the death of Miles Landon, but
since they'd fled without a trace the warrant
issued was worth little more than the paper
it was written on. And always looming on the
horizon was the question of Maddie's departure.
Would she leave this century when the baby was
born as she'd first thought? And if that was the
great plan, was there any way to change it?

Devon tightened his arm across her and bur-
ied his face in the pile of hair spread across the
pillow.

"What was that for?" he mumbled, nudging her neck with his lips.

"What?"

"That long sigh. What are you thinking to bring on such a forlorn sound?"

Maddie tucked her behind closer against Devon's lap and wiggled. "Nothing important," she hedged, smiling when she felt his answering arousal.

"Then I suggest we leave this bed while I am still able or we will not make it to Anthony's before the party ends."

"Oh, we can't do that," she teased, caressing him one last time. "How would it look if the maid of honor and best man didn't show up for the engagement party?"

"Scandalous," he confirmed, patting her rump and then giving it a small squeeze as though he couldn't get enough of the feel of her.

"Definitely."

She slid from the bed, comfortable with her husband's heated gaze as she moved, nude, across to the dresser. She ran her brush through her hair, aware of Devon's close scrutiny, and tucked the long strands back into her combs.

"You grow lovelier with each day," he told her, letting his eyes touch on every part of her.

"Bigger, maybe. I don't know about lovelier." She listened to the sound of Devon's formal, polished tones and let them wrap around her like a favorite quilt. How she'd grown accustomed to his voice in the past months. It no longer took her by surprise when he called her his beloved wife, or some similarly old-fashioned term. In fact, she thought there was a lot to be said for chivalry in its truest form.

"Come here, wife," he drawled sexily.

"Uh uh," she scolded lightly. "You get yourself out of that bed so we can get going. I don't want to do anything to spoil this night for Anthony or Tiffany."

Devon heaved a long-suffering sigh and ducked when Maddie hurled a powder puff at his head. He strode boldly to her and clutched her from behind. His body burned its imprint into her naked flesh as his hands reached around to caress her.

"I will go along, for Tiffany and Anthony," he said, his tone charitable. "But just you wait until tonight."

His words brought shivers of anticipation to her and she felt her nipples pucker and tighten. He saw the change in her body and his hands slid up to cup her full breasts.

"Ah," he breathed into her ear. "That is what I like to see. To know that I can still arouse you with mere words after all this time is an aphrodisiac."

"As though you need one, you rogue," she said, playfully slapping his hands away before she lost her resolve and went with him back to the bed.

"Fasten my dress?"

"With pleasure," he said, handing her the garment. "And a little regret," he admitted, watching her cover her body with the blush-colored gown.

"That was one of the most beautiful weddings I've ever seen," Maddie breathed, tossing her gloves and bag onto the parson's bench in the foyer. Devon took her coat and Beverly's and laid them on the bench.

"Let me get you folks a warm drink," Sarah said, bustling forward to welcome them home.

"I can't believe how cold it is for March," Devon said, leading the way into the parlor. "You'd think we were up North instead of in southern Alabama."

Maddie went to the fireplace and held out her hands toward the warmth. Beverly followed her.

"I can remember years when I was a child it would stay cold past Easter," Maddie said, accepting the brandy-laced tea Devon offered her.

"Yes, we don't have many cold days, but we do have a few cold snaps now and again," Beverly agreed, sipping her own drink.

"It didn't affect the wedding, thank goodness," Maddie said, her eyes still dreamy from the happy day. Tiffany had made a beautiful bride and Maddie couldn't remember seeing Anthony look happier.

"Ah, I hope the honeymoon goes as well."

Devon's words brought silence to the group. Maddie knew Tiffany had asked Anthony to take her back to Boston for their honeymoon.

She was ready to face her brother's death now, and the loss of all she held dear. And she'd wanted Anthony beside her, as her husband, when she went back for the first time.

Since the hospital had been completed just a week ago, Anthony was now free to go. It would be a solemn trip, but one the pair needed to make before starting their lives anew.

Maddie pressed her hand against her protruding stomach and frowned. The niggling threat of Elaine and Edward had weighed heavily on her mind of late. She suspected it was the onslaught of maternal instincts, but it was a feeling of foreboding she couldn't shake.

"Are you all right?" Devon asked, placing a comforting hand on her stomach. The baby jumped, kicked, and settled back into place. They laughed.

"For a woman who's being so badly abused, I'm fine."

"It won't be long, darling. And you can hold him in your arms while he practices his kicks and punches."

"I can't wait," she breathed, placing her hand over his where it lay on the bulge of their child. "I hope he looks just like his father," she said honestly, fighting the wave of fear that always came on the heels of her joy. The baby's birth would be the final test of her theory. If she didn't leap back to the future after the birth, she'd finally be able to relax and feel secure here in Devon's time.

"Shall we retire? You look tired."

Maddie lifted Devon's hand and pressed a kiss against his knuckles. "I'm beyond tired. Yes, let's call it a night."

Devon smiled at her modern phrase. Just as she'd been fascinated by his formal speech, he was amused by her casual terms. They held hands as they bid Aunt Beverly good night and made their way upstairs.

But Maddie found she couldn't sleep. Despite her exhaustion, she felt restless. Not wanting to wake Devon, she paced before the window. Her nightgown had long since grown tight and it stretched across her tummy. Her feet were swollen, and ached constantly. Thankfully she'd only gotten a few of the tiny stretch marks so many women dreaded, but she feared their number would increase if she got much bigger.

Only three weeks to go, she thought. It seemed like an eternity, but she knew it would be over before long. She kept her spirits up by imagining the day she'd hold her child in her arms. She told herself any amount of discomfort was well worth the result.

But as her restlessness grew into achiness, she wondered how much more she'd be expected to bear. A sharp pain stabbed her lower back and she decided she'd better forgo the walking for the remainder of the night.

Softly she slid into bed next to Devon, trying not to awaken him. She snuggled against his back, but the baby began a rollicking rendition of the two-step and Devon mumbled irritably in his sleep.

Wide awake now, Maddie climbed back out of bed. She went to the chair by the fireplace and decided she'd rest better if she could just sit comfortably and stare out at the night from the window.

The chair was small, not too heavy, and she decided she could pull it under the open window. But as she bent to grasp the chair back, a warm wash of water flowed down her legs, puddling on the floor.

It was too dark to see clearly, but Maddie had no doubt what had happened. In her excitement, she shouted.

Devon bolted upright in the bed, his eyes wide but confused, as though he had no idea what had yanked him from a sound sleep.

"What . . . where . . . Maddie?"

"Devon," she said, her voice trembling now with anxiety and anticipation. "Devon, it's time."

Devon's gaze darted around the room until he finally adjusted to the dark enough to spot Maddie by the fireplace. He focused on her for a long moment as the importance of her words sank in. With a muttered oath, he threw aside the blankets and bolted from the bed.

His foot caught in the tangle of bedclothes and he stumbled, righting himself at the last moment with another curse. "What in the name of all that's holy are you doing over there?" he asked.

Maddie felt a mixture of tears and laughter at the familiar phrase. Laughter won out and she giggled. "Oh, Devon, I love you."

He stopped, frozen, as he saw the tears in her eyes sparkle in the moonlight. "I love you, too, darling," he whispered, coming to her side and leading her back to the bed. "I love you, with my very heart and soul."

"Devon," Maddie said, clutching his hand as he adjusted the blanket over her tummy. "Everything's going to be all right."

Devon wasn't sure if it was a question or a statement. He stared down into the anxious face of the woman who'd crossed a span of time to love him and his own eyes burned. "Of course, love. Everything is going to be fine."

But Devon felt his spine tickle with fear. He and Maddie had agreed not to talk about this day. They both understood that she wasn't guaranteed a place in his life. She'd appeared like magic, and they understood she could well disappear the same way. It was something they hadn't wanted to think about. A black cloud they hadn't allowed to shadow their happiness.

But the storm of truth raged near, and Devon dreaded the birth of his child even as he looked forward to it with a fervor he'd felt for few other things in his life.

He jerked open the bedroom door and ran headlong into Beverly.

"What is it?" she asked, clutching his bare shoulders to steady herself. Devon realized he hadn't taken time to dress and he was thankful his aunt couldn't see him at that moment.

"It's the baby. Send someone after Anthony,

quickly. Then come back." He placed his hand on her arm and squeezed, looking for assurance himself.

"I'll be right there. Meanwhile, you'd better get some clothes on before anyone else sees you that way."

Devon smiled and stepped back into the bedroom with a chuckle. "That woman is amazing," he said, shaking his head.

"I've thought so for some time," Maddie agreed.

Devon lit the lamp and quickly located his trousers and shirt. Maddie giggled when she saw his embarrassed flush and he tweaked her nose. "We'll see who's giggling a few weeks from now when that unquenchable passion of yours gets the best of you."

She patted her stomach and sighed. "I think it already has."

He looked amused, but tried to appear stern. Finally, he gave up the effort and slid onto the bed beside her. "Come here, you saucy wench," he teased, easing her back against his chest. He encircled her stomach and slowly caressed it.

As the first contraction slid painfully from her back to her abdomen, he gently rubbed the hardened mound. It helped ease the discomfort and from then on he made sure he was within reach each time a contraction gripped her.

By the time Anthony arrived, rumpled and frowning, Maddie's pain could not be soothed. Devon had raked his hands through his hair so many times, it was plastered against his head.

"You couldn't wait for this, Maddie Crowe," Anthony teased, a look of mock anger on his lean face.

Maddie laughed. "Sorry, Doc. I didn't mean to interrupt anything."

Anthony flushed scarlet and Devon laughed. "Saucy wench," he repeated, laughing at his friend's discomfort.

"Well, I'm here now. Let's get this show on the road."

"Oh, no," Devon said, chuckling. "She's got you talking like her now."

"I can't help it," Anthony defended himself. "Some of the things she says are so catchy."

Maddie looked at Devon's horrified expression and laughed. But their humor was short-lived as another contraction engulfed her. Beverly came through the door with a pile of clean blankets. Sarah followed, a basin of warm water in her ample arms.

"Okay, Devon, time for you to kiss your wife good-bye."

Devon and Maddie both stared, shocked and stunned by the implication of Anthony's words. Anthony saw their reactions and winced.

"I'm sorry, Dev, Maddie. I meant . . ."

"I'm not going anywhere," Devon vowed.

As if to prove his point he took Maddie's hand and stepped to her side.

"But, Devon . . ."

"I said I'm not leaving. Get on with whatever you have to do."

"Devon, you can't be here," Bev said, taking his arm. But Devon shook off her grasp gently and met Anthony's gaze. "I won't go."

Anthony stared at his friend for a long moment, then nodded. "All right, but step back out of the way. I have work to do. I don't have time to look out for you."

"Don't worry about me," Devon said, releasing Maddie's hand and stepping back a few feet from the bed. "Just take care of my wife."

"I'll do my best," Anthony said, tying a length of torn bedsheet to the post at the foot of the bed. "You know I'll do my best."

Devon looked from Anthony to Maddie. Her face was drawn and white as another contraction gripped her. As the pain eased she met his gaze and smiled weakly.

Let it be enough, he thought. Let Anthony's experience be enough to help her. And let my love be enough to keep her, he added on a prayer.

Chapter Twenty-four

At 6:47 the next morning, Jeremy Michael Crowe was born. His mother's doctor estimated his weight at six and a half pounds. Not bad for a preemie, his mother thought, staring down at the tiny red face.

By noon of the same day, Maddie could no longer hold her son. She'd continued to bleed following the birth. A hemorrhage, she'd heard Anthony tell Devon. All Maddie knew was that her bones felt like water and her eyelids like lead.

Devon's worried face loomed above her each time she opened her eyes. She tried to smile, to tell him everything would be all right. But the effort was too great. In the distance she heard the baby cry and felt the thickening in her breasts. She needed to feed him, her baby. He must be hungry. But the lethargy took a deeper hold and Maddie soon slipped into unconsciousness.

"I don't know what else to do. The bleeding has slowed, but I fear it's too late. She's lost so much blood already it would take a miracle to save her now."

Anthony laid his hand on his friend's shoulder and shook his head. Devon remained silent, staring down at the bed where Maddie lay, unaware even that he was in the room. Tiffany had arrived and she and Beverly stood to one side, their faces stricken, their eyes damp. Sarah held the baby, wrapped in a blanket, and dabbed constantly at the corner of her eyes with her apron.

"It can't end this way," Devon said, his voice haunted. "Not after all we've been through. Not after all she's done to help save other lives. It just can't simply end this way."

"I know how you feel," Anthony told him, glancing toward his own wife. "But there aren't any miracles left in Maddie's bag of tricks. Between the epidemic and what we took to Boston, all that's left are a few odd supplies. Nothing that will help her now."

"Dammit," Devon cursed, shaking off Anthony's hand. "Why should Maddie have to die? Hasn't she done enough? She saved my home, she gave me a son. She risked her own life to help the people of the epidemic, and she traveled all the way to Boston to try to save others. She's done everything she thought she was supposed to do. Without any guarantees in return. And all she wanted in exchange was a child."

He walked slowly toward Sarah, his eyes blurred with tears. He took his son and pushed the blanket aside. The infant squirmed and turned his head hungrily toward Devon's chest. Maddie hadn't even gotten to feed him, Devon thought sadly. She'd barely had time to get a glimpse of their child.

"Do you know," he whispered, leaning his head down to nudge the baby's cheek with his own. "Your mother wanted you so much, she journeyed through time just to have you. No baby—" His voice broke and he cleared it roughly. "No baby was ever wanted or loved as much as you."

"Devon."

Devon kissed his son's cheek and handed the bundle back to Sarah. With a discreet cough he turned to face Anthony. "What is it?"

"Maddie's heart rate has dropped again. I'm afraid it won't be long now."

Devon's face was impassive as he stepped hesitantly toward the bed he'd shared with Maddie all these months. He knelt beside the bed and took her hand in his. "Don't leave me, beloved," he entreated. "Please, Maddie, don't leave me now. I've only just realized how truly wonderful life can be. But it will be a never-ending torture without you."

343

Anthony held Maddie's other hand in his, his fingers pressed to her wrist to constantly monitor the steadily slowing beat of her heart.

"I was thinking, Dev," he said, a catch in his own voice. "Maddie said once she thought perhaps she'd died in her own time."

Devon nodded, his gaze never leaving Maddie's white face. He stroked the hair back from her brow and let it twine around his hand.

"Perhaps," Anthony continued, disturbed by his friend's grief. "Perhaps she is just returning to her own time. You thought—that is, the both of you wondered if she would go back once her mission here was complete. If she was sent to help you, then her job here is finished."

"But she was so certain she'd return *with* the baby when the time came. If," he added dejectedly, "the time came at all. We so hoped . . ."

Suddenly Devon stood, carefully tucking Maddie's hand back beneath the covers on the bed. "Anthony, don't let her die before I return."

"Devon, I can't. . . ." Anthony blinked in surprise and stared at his friend. "Where are you going?"

"You just make sure she stays alive until I get back."

With only that cryptic statement, Devon darted from the room, ignoring the startled looks on everyone's faces.

"I can't keep her alive," Anthony told the women helplessly. "I tried to tell him. . . ."

Devon raced through the house, out the door, and across the yard. His heart was pounding against his chest when he finally stopped. He bent over, clutching his knees in an effort to catch his breath. His eyes scanned the innocent-looking field. It had to work. It just had to.

Maddie experienced an odd floating sensation. She was in a dark place, but not a room. The darkness was open and expansive. Like being adrift in the night sky. She tried to call out to Devon. Where had he gone? Where was her baby? She could hear him crying in the distance and she tried to reach out to him, but her arms wouldn't respond to her brain's command.

In the distance she could see a faint light and she tried to will herself to move toward it. The glimmer brightened and flickered, and she could see it growing larger.

Her strength returned in a flash, like being submerged in water. The light called to her now. Maddie spiraled toward it, flying as she had in her childhood dreams, and thinking no more of it now than she had then. Couldn't everyone do this? she thought, enjoying the feeling of freedom.

The voice in the light grew clearer and Maddie was surprised to hear Genevieve's soft tones speaking anxiously. She entered the light and settled to the ground. Waves of shock and dismay rippled through her. She turned slowly, taking in the horrific scene around her.

Red and blue lights flashed, casting eerie patterns along the trees and off the water's surface. Two police cars were blocking the paved road, holding traffic back as the ambulance attendants loaded the driver of another car onto a stretcher. They drew the sheet over the older man's face and shook their heads at Genevieve and John. Genny turned her face into her husband's chest and he cradled her in his arms.

One of the police officers held a pad and pen in his hand and waited uncomfortably for Genny to regain her composure. Maddie called out to her sister, but her voice didn't carry across the distance. Genny wiped her eyes and nodded.

"Genny," Maddie called again, louder this time. The officer motioned toward her and for a moment she thought they'd heard. Then she looked down and gasped. The lake was all around her, its glassy surface undisturbed. But where she stood, one small spot of ground in the center of the lake, was familiar to her. Devon's field!

So she hadn't gone back, not completely. A wave of horror followed on the heels of a quick and disturbing thought. She had fallen into the lake after the accident. So she wouldn't return completely until her body was found. Until then, she seemed to be locked in some sort of limbo, not officially dead in her own time, yet not in the past any longer.

She'd never be able to speak with Genny, and she'd never see Devon again. Panic threatened to paralyze her. Her chest hurt and she realized in her fear she'd forgotten to breathe.

"Oh, Devon," she cried. "Help me. I don't want to go back. I don't want to die. I want to live. I want to hold you and our son."

"Maddie?"

A frightened voice startled her and she whirled, sucking in a startled gasp. "Devon?"

Through a haze Maddie could see the form of her husband. His hands were reaching out beseechingly. She stepped forward and was stopped short. There was a barrier, a solid boundary she couldn't pass through.

"Devon!"

Devon's widened eyes seemed to be looking past her, toward the accident scene on the highway. Realizing he couldn't see her either, Maddie followed his stunned gaze and saw that the crowd was inching toward the lake.

"No," she heard Genny whisper, tears coursing down her cheeks.

"It looks as if she made it to the embankment and then collapsed. See, there's a pattern in the grass here. And it leads right to the edge of the water." The officer's tone was apologetic and Maddie felt her sister's pain as Genny edged closer to the lake.

"You mean . . ." Genny's words trailed off as the group gazed down into the depths of the water.

347

This is it, Maddie thought. They'd wade in and find her body. Any minute now she'd be discovered and it would all be over. She'd miss her sister. She regretted never having the chance to say good-bye. But her thoughts were on Devon now. Her husband and son were the most important things in her life. Her mind spun in a crazy mixture of hope and fear. Would she be returned to Devon? Or would she simply cease to exist at all? And did she have any control over the outcome?

"Devon," she cried, facing her husband, knowing, if she were about to die, that she wanted his face to be the last thing she saw.

"Maddie," he called, still not seeing her behind the invisible barrier. "Maddie, if you can hear me, help me get through if you can."

Maddie focused on his words and for the first time paused to wonder what he was doing in the field.

"Help me get to your time. I know I can find something there to help you, if only you'll help me get there." He tried to step forward again, only to be brought up short. Maddie realized he couldn't see her at all. She was in limbo, not visible to Genny or Devon, either. He assumed she was back in her own time, though, and he was pleading for her to help him get there as well.

"Damn!" he shouted, raising his fists.

"Hey, Chief," Maddie heard someone shout behind her. She whipped around, for a split second, and saw the looks of fear and excitement on the faces of her would-be rescuers. "I found something."

Maddie looked down and saw the reflection of her brightly colored silk shorts beneath the water's surface. This was it. They'd spotted her.

"Devon!"

Devon turned to see Anthony hurrying across the field toward him. He looked over his shoulder and cursed. Gone! The crazy tableau he'd been watching was gone. If it had really been there at all.

"Devon, come quick."

Devon glanced back one last time, but now saw only the rolling green field and pasture stretched out before him.

With regret, he took a step toward Anthony. "She's gone, isn't she?"

Anthony's eyes widened and he sobered. "Not yet." Suddenly he brightened. "That's why we have to hurry."

"Hurry?"

"Yes. Devon, I looked in Maddie's boxes again. I didn't think there was anything there that could help her, but I needed to do something. Anyway, I found some of the tubing we used to administer the saline during the epidemic and I got to thinking. Maddie said the IVs were used for medications *and* transfusions."

"Transfusions?"

"Yes. Of course I knew about blood transfusions, but they're risky. If you give a person the wrong type of blood you can kill them."

Devon's look of hope died slowly. "Then why are we talking about this? We're trying to save Maddie, not kill her."

"Yes, but, you see, that's when I remembered what Maddie said. She said blood transfusions are common in her time because they can type blood easily. She mentioned, in passing, that she knew this because she was type AB. Which means that she is a universal recipient."

"A what!?"

"That means that she can safely accept any type of blood. With the rubber hosing and some other supplies we can transfuse. . . ."

But Devon had already caught the importance of Anthony's statement and he grabbed his friend by the arm. "Hurry, Anthony," he called, dragging the physician along behind him. "Hurry."

It took Anthony the better part of 15 minutes to set up the needles and tubing which would carry Devon's lifeblood to his wife. Devon reclined on a chaise longue they'd carried over from Beverly's bedroom and set up next to Maddie's bed. He clenched his fists in anxious anticipation. Anthony monitored Maddie's heart rate with his stethoscope and occasionally crimped the tube so as not to administer the blood too quickly.

After the first hour no improvement could be detected, and Anthony began to wonder if he'd waited too long. He cursed himself for not remembering what Maddie had told him sooner. He pressed his stethoscope to her chest and shook his head.

Devon leaned anxiously to the side, trying to catch some sign from Maddie that the treatment was working. But she continued to lie still, her face too white, her lips colorless.

In the next room he could hear the cries of his son. Sarah had fed the baby, but Jeremy wanted his mother and would not be appeased.

"Come on, Maddie," Devon whispered. "You wanted this baby more than anything in the world. You were willing to cross a chasm of time to get him. Don't give up yet. Don't let us go so easily."

But Maddie showed no signs of hearing his pleas. Her eyelids never fluttered. Her chest rose and fell shallowly.

He laid back and relaxed his fists. It would work. It *would* work. He just had to be patient a bit longer. Maddie always had been a stubborn thing, never relenting, never giving up on what she wanted.

The next hour passed slowly. Anthony continued to listen for any change. Devon prayed and thought of the scene he'd viewed from his field earlier. Had all that he'd seen been real? He knew it had. But what could he make of the flashing automobiles and odd-looking equipment? From the manner of dress on the people he knew they were from the future.

The future he'd been willing to venture into to try to find help for his wife. He'd been desperate to save Maddie. Desperate enough to travel to her time, if possible, and bring back help. He'd had no idea how to get help, or even if he'd be able to get back should he find it, but with no other option he'd been ready to take the risk.

He looked down at the vacant expression on Maddie's face and felt his heart sink. Maybe Maddie was already back in that world. Could she have been reaching for him, trying to draw him with her? Was that why he'd been able to see the things he had? If Anthony hadn't called him back, would he have gone with her?

"Devon."

Anthony's voice was low, but filled with promise. Devon's attention snapped back to Maddie. Was it his imagination, or did she look better? Her color was still not good. Her lips had dried, and they were pale and cracked. But there was something different about her. As though her spirit had returned. As though her soul was once more in residence within the weakened body.

"Maddie," he called softly. Her eyelids twitched and he sucked his breath in sharply. Had Anthony noticed the movement? he wondered.

Anthony smiled back at him. "It's coming up," he said, lifting the stethoscope and repositioning it on her chest. He tipped his head and grinned. "Her heart rate is definitely coming up."

Behind him Devon heard the grateful sighs and whispered thanks from Beverly and Tiffany. Their smiles lit the room and it was all Devon could do to lie still instead of jumping to his feet and shouting. He turned, gently, to watch his wife's face. If she made a sound, a movement, he wanted to be the first to know it.

Nothing happened for several minutes, and Anthony picked up her hand and placed his fingers against her wrist.

"I can feel her pulse better now," he said. "It's stronger."

Beverly and Tiffany shared a hug, but all Devon wanted was to see some sign. Then he could be certain Maddie was all right.

"Talk to her, Devon," Anthony instructed.

Ignoring the tube still attached to his arm, Devon reached across to take Maddie's hand. "Maddie," he said, trying to keep his voice steady. "Maddie, love, can you hear me?"

Another flicker. Devon was sure she'd heard him. Again he called her name and again he was rewarded with the small flutter of her eyelids. Anthony's grin confirmed that it was a good sign.

Deciding to take another direction, Devon leaned closer. "Maddie," he said sternly. "The baby's hungry. Wake up, Maddie. Your son needs you."

Almost immediately the flicker became a blink and Maddie's eyes opened once and closed again.

Tiffany laughed and hugged Beverly's arm to her side tightly. Anthony smiled encouragingly at his friend.

"Maddie," Devon called again. "Maddie, wake up. The baby is hungry. He needs you." Then, because he had never wanted anything as much as he wanted to see his wife's eyes at that moment he added, "I need you, love."

Maddie opened her eyes and met his worried, tired gaze. She tried to smile, but was too weak.

Devon saw the movement of her mouth and knew her joy at seeing him again. He squeezed her hand and his smile lit his whole face. "Hello," he whispered.

Maddie's eyes filled with tears and she moved her mouth. Devon leaned closer and barely caught her words.

"I'm back," she said. And then fell back to sleep.

Chapter Twenty-five

Devon rolled to his side, holding Maddie close beside him. He pressed a kiss to her brow and tightened his arms around her.

"Are you all right?" he whispered into her hair.

"Perfect," she purred, running her leg up the length of his calf.

"Are you sure? I didn't hurt you?"

"You could never hurt me, Devon," she told him, gazing into his dark eyes with love and tenderness.

"But it's only been a month. Anthony said . . ."

"I know what Anthony said, but I told you before I felt fine. Truly," she assured him. "And now I feel better than fine."

"I can't believe how sassy you've gotten," he

teased her. "A month ago you nearly died and now you're taking walks and entertaining guests." He paused and ran his hand along her thigh to cup her buttocks. "And making love," he added huskily.

"Umm, and not a minute too soon. I missed you. I love you."

"I love you," he said, holding her too tightly as he sometimes did since he'd nearly lost her.

"Besides, the walks are good for me. I'm getting my strength back quicker. And Jeremy loves them. And I didn't intend to wait another day to make love to you. What Anthony doesn't know . . ." Her voice trailed off as Devon's caresses turned bold.

"What Anthony doesn't know he'll soon discover. When his own wife gives birth."

"Is Tiffany . . ."

"No, not yet. But the way those two sit and gaze at one another produces enough heat to wilt the flowers in their vases. I don't imagine it will be too long."

Maddie laughed and stayed his hand on her hip. He quirked an eyebrow in question and she laid it boldly on her breast.

"Twice?"

She nodded.

He shook his head. "Not this time, love. It really is too soon for that. But perhaps I can ease that ache you seek to appease."

He rolled her to her back and placed hot kisses along the length of her neck. Maddie's head tipped back, allowing him better access.

She tried to draw his lips to her own, but he shook his head.

Trailing his mouth across her heated skin, he found first one nipple and then the other. Stopping long enough to draw each peak into his mouth for a suckle, he traveled on to her navel. And lower.

"Devon, what are . . ." She arched as his lips found the center of her desire. "Devon, no."

"Yes, oh yes," he moaned, burying his face in the apex of her thighs. Maddie fell back against the bed, writhing beneath the sensual onslaught of his mouth.

The pleasure built until she couldn't lie still. She rolled, and he followed. She arched, and he moved with her. She cried out, and he matched her rhythm with the motion of his tongue.

Maddie sank back, exhausted. Her chest rose and fell rapidly. Her eyes couldn't focus for the bright lights whirling in her head.

"Heavens," she exclaimed, spent.

"Did you say heaven?" he teased, touching the dampness where he'd loved her.

Maddie stilled his hand and drew his face up to hers. She kissed him and felt a rush of embarrassed pleasure as she tasted herself on his lips.

"Yes," she said. "It was heaven."

"Shall I repeat the performance?"

Maddie chuckled and kissed him soundly again. "No." He looked disappointed and she had to laugh. "Not that I wouldn't enjoy it, but we're expecting Anthony and Tiffany for dinner. If I don't get up, I won't be ready when they arrive."

Devon moaned and gave her a wounded look. "Tonight, then," he promised, touching her to seal the vow.

"Tonight," she agreed. "And every night from now until forever."

"Thank you for coming back to me, Maddie," he said, turning serious again.

"Thank you for saving my life," she countered.

"I still can't believe the things I saw," Devon said, relaxing against the pillows and drawing her to lie across his chest. Maddie's fingers drew lazy circles around his nipples and he felt himself grow hard again.

"I can't believe you couldn't see me," she said, rehashing the whole thing even though they'd discussed it more times than she could remember. The amazing events of that day never failed to astound her.

"What I saw was incredible enough. If I'd seen you as well, I'd have probably fainted dead away."

Maddie giggled at the thought. "Yes, I know what you mean. When I saw where I was I nearly did faint. What I can't figure out is why no time had passed in that world even though I'd been here for months."

"That was all you could think?" he asked, aghast. "After everything that's happened that seems like such a minor detail."

"All right, I admit it was a crazy thought at

the time. But so much has happened, the odd seems almost commonplace now. It just threw me when I realized for Genny, John, and the others no time had passed."

"Yes, I admit that is odd. But I won't pretend I understand any of it. I'm still puzzled by your appearance here. All I know is, I will always be thankful you came, and grateful you stayed with me."

Maddie snuggled closer, letting her senses take in the essence of her husband. The smell of male and female blended in love, the feel of hair-roughened skin on smooth flesh, the salty taste of his neck on her tongue.

"Did I thank you for thinking of the letter?" she asked, nibbling his shoulder.

"Yes, and it was my pleasure. My attorney has assured me that no matter what happens it will be delivered. And, as he already has a son in business with him and several grandchildren to follow in his footsteps, I expect there's no danger of failure."

"It was ingenious," she told him, praising him with her kisses. She thought of her sister's shock when she received the hundred-year-old missive.

Maddie had written down everything that had happened to her, along with several little-known facts which would prove her identity to her sister. Devon had delivered the letter to his attorney with instructions that it be delivered to a certain address, provided by Maddie, on a certain date.

That, he told her, had caused more than a few raised eyebrows in the lawyer's office. But the old attorney had agreed to comply with their unusual request and had refrained from asking the questions Devon knew he longed to ask.

Maddie settled back, comforted by the knowledge that Genny would know what had become of her. The letter was scheduled to be delivered the day after her accident. And so, the last obstacle to happiness had been removed. Maddie knew she'd made the right decision, to come back to Devon.

"The house has already been sold and the new owners are rebuilding. You won't be able to tell there had ever been a fire when they are finished," Tiffany told Maddie and Devon at dinner.

Maddie saw Anthony take his wife's hand and gently squeeze it. She was pleased they'd found one another, despite their tragic beginning. She'd never been so happy or fulfilled in her life, and she wanted everyone around her to share her joy.

Her eyes met Devon's across the table as she sipped her wine, and the heated look he gave her made her blood warm. If anyone had told her a year ago that she would be content to live in the nineteenth century, without benefit of microwaves, cellular phones, and rapid transportation, she'd have split her sides laughing. She'd never been one to "rough it."

But somehow, with Devon and Jeremy, Tiffany, Anthony, and Beverly, life didn't seem tough at all. She knew the tough part would have been living without them.

She lifted her wineglass slightly, in silent salute to her husband, and he smiled in return.

"So," she said, clearing her throat of the huskiness brought on by desire. "Tell us how things went at the hospital without you for two weeks."

Anthony went on for another half hour talking about the new hospital he and Devon had been responsible for building. Maddie marveled at having been present for the groundbreaking, since she knew Genny's hometown of Brewster, Alabama would arise around the perimeter of the Seth Brewster Memorial Hospital. Already someone had opened an apothecary next door to the hospital and there was talk of a boardinghouse opening soon.

And Maddie knew she'd be there to see it all come to fruition. She felt almost like a pioneer, settling new territory and establishing areas which would live on to prosper long after she was gone.

"What do you think of that?" someone asked Maddie. She blinked and smiled, realizing her mind had drifted from the dining room.

"I'm sorry," she said. "I guess I was woolgathering. What did you say?" She directed the question to the table in general, since she wasn't even certain who had spoken.

"Tiffany is thinking of starting a school to train nurses."

Maddie's smile was a mixture of bittersweet memories and eager anticipation. "The Brewster Academy of Nursing," she murmured, remembering Genny's graduation and how she'd chosen Maddie to cap her. They'd cried and laughed and hugged so much that day. Tears stung her eyes.

"What a wonderful name," Tiffany said. "I'd been wondering what to call it. Your idea is perfect. Don't you think, Anthony?"

Anthony glanced at Maddie's odd expression. Maddie smiled and knew he understood her thoughts.

"What?" Tiffany asked, glancing from her husband to her friend. Devon caught the looks and smiled.

"Let me guess," he said, reaching across the table for Maddie's hand. "Genny?"

Maddie nodded and dabbed discreetly at a tear pooled at the corner of her eye. She turned to Tiffany and said, "My sister is a nurse. She graduated from the Brewster Academy of Nursing eight years ago." She shook her head and laughed. "Or rather, eight years before the time . . ."

Her words failed her and she couldn't think of the right thing to say to explain her meaning to Tiffany. Tiffany furrowed her brow and looked from Maddie to Anthony. Finally, her face brightened and her eyes grew wide.

"Oh, you mean before you came here. But

that means that you knew the name because the place existed in your time. But if that's the case how could you have been the one to choose the name?"

The four stared at one another silently for a minute; then Anthony broke the stillness. "That's just one of many things we may never understand about time-travel," he said, even his scientific mind unable to unravel this particular mystery. "One of many."

The magnitude of the situation sank in slowly on the friends gathered around the dinner table that night. Each took a moment to try to assess his thoughts. Finally, Devon raised his glass in a toast. The others followed suit.

"To Maddie, who made the ultimate journey. And in doing so, saved lives and brought joy to all she encountered."

Maddie nodded a slight acknowledgment and touched her glass to the three held in her honor. Could any woman be so happy? she thought. Had anyone ever had such a perfect life?

The dinner was marvelous and Maddie enjoyed the company, but as the hour grew late she ached to go up to the nursery and see Jeremy. Her breasts were full; he'd be waking soon to eat. Devon usually sat with her when she nursed, and it was a private time she'd come to look forward to. She hoped her son would hold out until their guests had left so his father could join them.

Anthony seemed anxious to leave and soon after dinner the newlyweds departed. Devon smiled at his friend's eagerness, but as he remembered the scene with Maddie earlier, he felt no less ardent. He'd missed making love to Maddie, and they had some catching up to do from the last month.

As Anthony and Tiffany took their leave, Maddie went ahead to the nursery. Devon told Sarah he'd lock up and then join his wife and son.

"I'm all done in the kitchen, Misser Devon," she told him as he bolted the front door, something he'd gotten in the habit of doing since their return from Boston.

"You need anythin' else 'fore I turn in?"

"No, thank you, Sarah," he said, extinguishing the gas lamps beside the front door. "Good night."

"Night," she murmured, turning to shuffle back through the kitchen to her room.

Devon took the stairs two at a time, in a hurry to see his wife and son once more. He passed the door to their bedroom, knowing she'd already be in the nursery. He found her there, her hair loose around her shoulders, her breast bare above the bodice of her nightgown. The moon came in the parted draperies and bathed her in its blue-tinged light.

Captivated anew, he stopped to stare at the sight. Jeremy was still drowsy and Maddie was gently patting his cheek in an effort to rouse him enough to eat. The baby turned his head without opening his eyes and found her nipple, latching onto it with zeal.

"This is my favorite time of the day," Devon said, coming into the room and drawing the matching rocker up beside Maddie's. He sank into it, facing his wife and son, and relaxed.

"Umm, mine too," she answered, leaning forward to receive a kiss while not disturbing the nursing baby.

"No regrets?" Devon asked, thinking of her earlier sadness at the thought of her sister.

Maddie shook her head. "Genny would be the first one to tell me to grab happiness with both hands and hang on. And that is just what I intend to do. Genny has her family, and while I know she'll miss me as much as I'll miss her, she would understand my decision. She'll do fine once she gets my letter."

"Good. Because I want you with me for the rest of our days. And I think I'd have done anything to keep you. But if you'd really wanted to go back . . ."

"No, I don't. And I never will."

The wind blew and the curtains fanned out from the window. Maddie shivered—the nights were still cool—and glanced over her shoulder.

"Devon, would you close that window? It's too chilly for the baby."

Devon stood and latched the window as Maddie shifted Jeremy to her other breast. He began to doze soon after and his father took him and laid him in his cradle.

Maddie kissed her baby good night and Devon extinguished the light. They left, leaving the door to the nursery ajar, and went to their own room next door.

"I can't believe Sarah would leave that window open," Maddie said, brushing her hair as Devon stripped off his shirt and trousers. She felt heat pool in the core of her womanhood as he strode behind her, naked.

"Shall we continue where we left off earlier?" he said, taking her by the shoulders and drawing her to stand in front of him.

"That sounds like a wonderful idea," she agreed, twining her arms around his waist. She pressed her body against his and soaked in the feel of him, absorbing every nuance of being in his arms.

"But first," she added, stepping out of his arms, "I think I'll run down and tell Sarah not to open the window in the nursery if she should get up during the night. I really wouldn't want Jeremy to catch cold—he's still so tiny."

"I'll wait for you," he said, knowing it was no use trying to convince her not to leave him just yet. He knew she wouldn't relax until she'd settled the baby for the night.

"Be right back," she whispered, kissing him quickly and smiling at his easy compliance.

Maddie swept down the stairs, a bright smile on her face. She couldn't wait to get back to Devon. Their physical relationship had always been more than healthy, even when neither of them wanted to admit to their real emotions. And the month of abstinence following Jeremy's birth had been the hardest 30 days of her life. She'd wanted Devon with a passion she'd only recently discovered.

She skipped over the last steps and padded lightly to Sarah's door.

"Sarah," she called softly, tapping on the housekeeper's door. "Are you up?"

The door was opened immediately and Maddie had to struggle to keep the smile from her face. The woman's hair was wrapped in rag rollers and her bosom, beneath the thin cotton gown and robe, sagged to her waist. Her feet were encased in scuffed slippers with most of their plushness worn off. If she didn't know better, she'd think the woman had no money. But she knew the amount Devon paid her and it was more than generous. Apparently, Sarah just had her favorite items and she wore them regardless of their appearance.

"I'm sorry to bother you, Sarah," Maddie said, fighting a smile. "But I wanted to ask you not to open the window in the baby's room again. At least not until it gets a little warmer out."

Maddie smiled again, just so the woman wouldn't think she'd been reprimanded. Maddie trusted Sarah with her life, and her baby's care. She didn't want to offend the woman. She was a great help to Maddie.

Sarah tipped her head and planted her hands firmly on her ample hips.

"What you talkin' about? I wouldn't never leave that chile's winder open. Why, he'd catch his death in this weather."

Maddie's smile died on her suddenly tense

367

lips. "What are you talking about? The window was open." But even as she said the words she could see by Sarah's expression that the woman didn't know anything about the window.

"Beverly . . ." She started feeling a bit of the tension ease from her bones. Sarah's negative shake of her head sent the foreboding racing back through her with a vengeance.

"I checked that young 'un after Miss Beverly done went to bed. He was sound asleep and I know his winder weren't open. Why I—"

But she never finished. Maddie whirled, her legs pumping faster and faster as she raced toward the stairs. Somehow she knew, even before she reached the nursery, what she'd find. As she slammed the door back on its hinges, the gently rocking cradle caught her eye.

"No," she prayed, afraid to even look inside. "God, no, please."

She inched toward the cradle and glanced down. Suddenly her shrieks filled the silent night.

"Devon!" she screamed, clutching the sides of the empty cradle. "Devon!" she called, over and over.

Chapter Twenty-six

Devon ran into the hall, hopping on one foot as he tugged on his trousers. He managed to get them in place before Sarah reached the landing. Beverly darted out of her room and ran into the two of them and the three swayed drunkenly as each tried to gain the lead. Finally, Devon broke ahead and slid through the door of the nursery.

"Maddie?" he called, his eyes not yet adjusted to the dark.

Sobs drew him and he rushed to the window where Maddie hung over the ledge, looking out.

His voice seemed to galvanize her and she swung around, grabbing his arms in a death hold.

"He's gone, Devon," she cried. "He's gone."

"Who?" Devon asked, trying to take in what Maddie was saying. It took only a split second for realization to dawn. He shoved her aside and gazed down into the empty cradle.

"My God," he swore, shaking his head as though he couldn't believe his eyes. Sarah and Beverly entered, both looking rumpled and confused.

"Devon, Maddie," Beverly called. She stepped forward, not hindered by the darkness, and reached out for them.

Maddie whirled to face her husband. "We've got to do something. They must be out there somewhere."

Sarah went to the lamp and soon the room filled with light. Devon blinked and scanned the nursery, looking for a clue to where his son might be. Terror boggled his mind and it was a minute before the pieces fell into place.

"Edward and Elaine," he whispered, drawing a frightened gasp from Maddie.

"No," she said, shaking her head. "They wouldn't come here. Not after Boston."

"They're desperate now. Edward has almost gone through the money his father left him. With the authorities after them, they're going to need to get their hands on my father's money to try to get out of trouble. The only way to do that . . ."

"Is to kill Jeremy," Maddie finished for him. Beverly clutched Maddie's cold hand in hers, but Maddie was beyond feeling. She'd gone numb with fear and shock. Her baby, her son. They couldn't hurt him. No one could be that cruel. She thought of Miles Landon, and her body began to tremble.

"I'll find them," Devon said, clutching her shoulders and giving her a gentle shake. "They can't have gone far. I swear to you, I'll find them."

He kissed her hard on the mouth, then released her. Without another glance back into the somber nursery which had held such joy so short a time ago, he strode off.

He donned his clothes in record time and raced down the stairs. In the library he snatched open the bottom desk drawer and grabbed the case containing his father's pistol. He checked it quickly, loaded it, and tucked it into his waistband.

He had to reach them in time. There was no way he would allow them to hurt his son. And he'd kill them, he swore, for ever laying a hand on Jeremy in the first place. Both of them would pay for this mistake.

He slammed back the bolt on the front door and yanked it open, startled when he came face-to-face with Anthony. Already Devon's hand rested on the butt of the gun.

Anthony's eyes widened and he took a step back. "Dev, you startled me," he said, his gaze locking on the gun. "Tiffany forgot her purse," he added. "What the hell's going on here?"

"Edward and Elaine are back," Devon told him, certain he spoke the truth. He saw the hate and rage register in Anthony's eyes. "They've taken Jeremy."

"Dear God," Anthony said, aghast. "Where have they gone? Do you have any idea what their plans are?"

"I can guess at their plans. But I have no idea where they've gone or how they intend to accomplish it."

"We just drove up the drive; no one passed us on the way in. Are you sure they've left the grounds?"

Devon scanned the dark yard. "No. I'm not sure of anything. Except that I have to find them." He raked his hand through his hair and let his dread show on his face. "I have to find them," he repeated woodenly.

"Well, let's stop wasting time, then," Anthony said, stepping aside to let Devon pass. He raced forward to the carriage and quickly informed Tiffany of the situation. She leapt down and went into the house, in search of Maddie, as the men began their search of the yard.

"I'm going to get dressed," Beverly said. "You'd better do the same. Sarah has sent someone to alert the sheriff and he'll be here soon."

"Yes, all right," Maddie said, not yet ready to leave her son's room. She stood near the cradle, clutching the tiny pillow he'd laid his head on. The soft cotton still held his scent and she could barely keep the terrifying panic at bay.

There had to be something she could do, she thought. She couldn't just stay here, doing nothing. But what? Her brain refused to function on a level capable of coming up with a plan. All she could think of was her baby, scared, or cold, or, God forbid, dead.

No, she wouldn't think that way. She refused to even consider that her son might be lost to her forever. She would do something, she told herself determinedly. Beverly had left her alone to go and dress. Maddie took one last look at the empty cradle and started for the door. A thought snagged her attention and she went to the window.

Locked. Just as Devon had left it when they were in here earlier. But if they came in through the window, how did they get out? They couldn't have gone down the stairs without passing her and Devon's room and besides, she was on her way to Sarah's room at that time. Then how had they gotten away?

The undeniable truth stuck in her brain and she stood frozen to the floor for a full minute. They hadn't left the house. There was no way they could have. And since she had covered the hall, stairs, and lower floor on her way to see Sarah, that only left the opposite wing. The place where Elaine and Edward had stayed on their last visit.

Thinking Devon had already gone after the kidnappers, she knew she couldn't wait for his return. She had to find them before they had a chance to harm Jeremy.

Bare feet flying, she left the nursery and raced along the hall. Passing the stairs at a dead run, she didn't see Tiffany's approach or hear her call out.

Her mind focused on only one thought. She still had time. They hadn't had a chance to do whatever they'd come to do. Apparently she and Devon had arrived in time to frighten them off. Or maybe they'd been in the nursery the whole time, hiding behind the door or in the huge chifforobe. Two adults could hide and remain silent for as long as it took Maddie to feed the baby.

And then they'd taken Jeremy from the cradle. Spirited him away to another part of the house, perhaps so his cries wouldn't draw attention if he should wake up.

She slowed her steps as she drew close to the first door. For the first time she realized she was unarmed and wished she'd thought to grab something she could use for a weapon. But it was too late now. There wasn't any way she'd go back. Not as long as there was a chance her baby was in this part of the house with those murderers.

She tiptoed to the door and listened for a moment. Nothing. Slowly, she turned the knob, wincing when the door clicked open. Peering around the edge, she could see the outline of furniture in the pale moonlight. The room was decorated in heavy, masculine pieces, but she didn't see anything out of place.

Edward and Elaine had planned something,

but what? Maddie racked her brain, trying to think the way the nefarious pair would think.

They had to get rid of Jeremy in order to gain Devon's fortune. That was the given. But how? If he disappeared, there would be no proof he was dead and Devon would still inherit on his thirty-fifth birthday as scheduled. Therefore, the baby would have to be irrefutably dead. A cold shiver raised the hair on her neck, and her knees trembled violently. She steadied herself against the door frame and tried to control her rapidly growing panic. She had to think clearly. Her baby's life depended on it.

With strength born out of maternal love and instinct, she put together what she thought must have been their plan. They would have to make Jeremy's death look natural somehow, or else they'd be suspected. And they'd have to do it in the house where he'd be sure to be found. So they'd waited for Maddie and Devon to leave, took Jeremy, and planned to return him to his crib after . . . what?

Her mind couldn't begin to contemplate the horrors of that thought.

She fought back the waves of hysteria and inched further down the blackened corridor. Once, she knocked against a table set beneath a portrait, and she had to grab frantically for the items on top to keep them from falling noisily to the floor. Had anyone heard the scrape of the table legs? Was anyone really in this part of the house at all? Was she on a wild-goose chase?

She continued on, determined to check every inch of the wing before giving up her theory. Because, somehow, she felt a little better thinking Jeremy was somewhere in the house than imagining him out in the pitch of night.

The next room, and the next, proved as unfruitful as the first. By the fifth door, she'd nearly given up hope. Then she spotted a tiny slice of pale light at the end of the hall. She eased forward, approaching that room with added caution. She could see the door was ajar, and there was some sort of light coming from the other side. It was dim, too dim for a lamp or gaslight. Perhaps a match.

Pressing herself against the wall, she crept to the opening and peered in. A hand snaked out from the small crack and grasped her arm, jerking her into the room.

Maddie cried out, but a hand came down on her mouth before she could complete the sound. The door shut firmly behind her, and she jerked free. Edward stood behind her. He'd been waiting for her. So they had heard the noise she'd made with the table. She whipped around and came face-to-face with Elaine. The bundle in her arms could not be mistaken. Maddie stepped forward.

"Don't try it," Edward said, grabbing her hair and yanking her back. "And if you scream we'll snap his neck like a twig."

There was no danger of her crying out, Maddie thought. Her mouth had gone bone-dry. Her throat worked to produce some sound, but nothing could get past the lump of horror wedged there.

"I should have known you'd get in the way," Elaine told her, her high, sharp voice cracking with anger. "You've managed to ruin everything since you came here. Who the hell are you, anyway? I don't believe a word of that ridiculous story Devon told everyone about your being the daughter of Beverly's friend."

"I'm Devon's wife now," Maddie finally managed to say. "That's all that matters."

Elaine's nostrils flared in rage and she gripped the blanket-wrapped bundle more tightly. Maddie saw her baby shift and wished she could take back the words that had so inflamed Elaine.

"That was supposed to be my place," Elaine whispered through clenched teeth. "I would be his wife now," she said, her arms closing in on the baby. "I'd be the one lying beside him at night. Do you think I don't know what a wonderful lover he is? Do you think you were the only one he took to his bed?"

Maddie felt jealousy rise like bile in her throat, but she vowed not to do anything to further anger Elaine. So she swallowed hard and remained silent.

"And when it was all over, I'd have had the money, too. Then he'd have done whatever I wanted, because I would hold the purse strings."

"He'd have known you betrayed him, Elaine. He never would have had anything more to do with you."

"That isn't so. I can be sweet, if I need to. I can make him forget his anger. And now, when this is over, I can make him forget you."

"Do you think he'll forget if you harm his son?" Maddie asked, astonished.

"He'll have no proof I was involved. Neither of you would have suspected a thing if our idea had gone on as we intended."

Maddie knew Devon would not return to the house until he'd found something, so she couldn't hope he'd come to her aid. But Beverly was in the house, and Sarah, and they'd wonder where she'd gone. And when the sheriff arrived they might find her. She doubted she could keep Elaine talking long enough for that, but she knew she had to stall for as long as she could.

"And just what did you plan?" she asked, hoping she seemed interested enough that they wouldn't suspect what she was doing.

"It was dreadfully simple, really," Elaine said, gloating. "We were going to sneak in, smother the child in his crib, and leave without anyone being the wiser. When your baby was found, his death would be put down as natural causes. Then Edward could show up to claim his inheritance and use the money to buy his way out of that sticky situation in Boston."

"Just like that," Maddie said, horrified because the simplicity of the plan would have guaranteed its success. She could see herself and Devon, waking in the morning and wondering why Jeremy hadn't roused them. They'd go to the nursery, and their precious little boy would have been gone. His life snuffed out for some land and money.

Chills swept over her and she could feel the downy hair on her arms stand up. These two were monsters, refusing to let anything stand in their way. But it hadn't worked. She was here now and, she realized with a start, she too stood in their way.

Elaine watched the emotions play across her face and she jiggled the baby lightly in her arms. "Yes. If you hadn't noticed that damned window being open. I knew you wouldn't rest until you'd settled that problem. And so we had to alter our plans a bit. But they'll still work, despite your butting in where you don't belong."

"That is my baby," Maddie said, angered at Elaine's careless handling of Jeremy. "How can you say I don't belong here? I'd die before I'd let you harm him."

"Don't worry," Elaine taunted, seeing how her movements were affecting Maddie and taking pleasure in jiggling the baby more casually. "You'll have the chance to do just that. Soon."

Edward stepped forward, impatient with the conversation. "Stop gloating, Elaine. We still have to decide what to do with her now."

"I've already figured that out. We can take care of her and the brat both by pushing them out the window here. It won't be as neat as the original plan, but by the time Devon returns and finds their bodies, we'll be long gone. And

379

no matter what anyone suspects, there won't be any proof."

She smiled, an icy, evil little grin, and tossed her head defiantly. "You see, Maddie. We took precautions just in case you and Devon thought to accuse us in your grief. We rented a private vessel to bring us back from England and we took care to silence the captain when we arrived. So no one knows we're here. We'll make a grand show of our return when the time comes to claim Edward's inheritance and no one will be able to prove we weren't in England all along."

"Devon will know you did it," Maddie told them confidently. "He already knows you're here. He won't care what the official decision is, he'll kill you both if you hurt me or Jeremy."

"He won't get the chance. Once Edward inherits, he'll be destitute. I think, considering the life he's accustomed to, Devon will put aside his doubts when I generously agree to support him and his beloved Aunt Bev. With my love, and the money I'll get from my share of the inheritance."

"It'll never work. Devon will never let you near him or anyone he loves again."

Elaine shrugged. "Perhaps not, but I'm sure I won't be lonely. It won't be the same as it would have been with Devon, but I'll make the best of it."

Maddie knew time was running out, but she couldn't think of a single thing to do.

She couldn't hope to overpower Edward and Elaine, and she feared rushing Elaine while she held Jeremy. The baby stirred and she glanced down at his tiny head, just visible over the edge of the blanket.

"Can I hold him, just for a minute? Surely you can't deny me that."

Elaine looked as if she might comply; then the wicked smile returned and she threw back her head with a throaty laugh.

"Nice try, but I'm not that foolish, Maddie."

Maddie felt her heart plummet. She grasped for any straw that might delay what Elaine had planned. Help came in an unusual form.

"Let her hold him. We don't want him waking up and raising a fuss," Edward said.

Elaine looked as startled as Maddie felt. She eyed her co-conspirator coldly and shook her head.

"No. She's up to something."

"She just wants a chance to hold her baby. She can't escape. What harm can it do?"

Maddie took advantage of the power struggle to make her move. "I promise," she said, easing toward Elaine. "I won't try anything. I just want to hold him. Please."

It galled her to have to beg this witch, but she knew she couldn't do anything as long as Elaine held Jeremy.

Elaine stood stiffly as Maddie reached out and took her baby. She clutched Jeremy close, fighting the urge to turn and dart from the room. They'd stop her before she made it two feet. And then they'd take Jeremy and . . .

Her love overflowed as her son opened his eyes and looked up at her. He'd slept through the whole thing; he had no idea of danger or evil. Such a wealth of emotion bubbled up in her she couldn't fight it. She'd do anything, *anything* to make certain he wasn't harmed.

"Please," she begged, no longer concerned with the indignity of what she was doing. "Please don't hurt him. He's only a baby. He's so helpless."

Tears welled up and ran down her cheeks. She stepped back, away from Edward, Elaine, and, unfortunately, the door. But she couldn't just let them kill him without a fight.

"Dammit, Edward," Elaine sneered. "I told you she'd make trouble. Now get that kid before she starts screaming and brings everyone running."

"I will," Maddie threatened, glancing over her shoulder. There was no escape. Her back was nearly pressed against the window now. Her captors stood between her and any chance of freedom. "I'll scream so loud they'll hear me in the next state."

Elaine gave Edward a disgusted look and stepped toward Maddie. "You hand him over now and I'll kill him mercifully. If you open your mouth I'll take great pleasure in seeing him suffer."

"You monster," Maddie said, clutching the baby against her chest. "How can you be so cruel?"

"Where money is involved, I can be anything I have to be."

Maddie looked to Edward for some kind of support. Maybe she could divide and conquer. He was weak, insipid. She knew Elaine had to be the mastermind of the plot.

But Edward's eyes were cold, blank, and she realized if he'd ever possessed a heart, it had long since withered and died beneath his greed. He wouldn't stop Elaine from doing whatever she chose to do.

It looked hopeless, and she gazed down into Jeremy's sweet face once more. With a silent prayer, she bent to place her lips on the powder-soft cheek.

"I love you, darling," she whispered, her own heart breaking. And then, because she wasn't a quitter, or a coward, she did the only thing left for her to do.

She charged Elaine and Edward, catching them off guard as she barreled between them. Edward grabbed for her, but his hand caught the thin fabric of her gown and she heard the material rip as she raced for the door. She tucked her arms around Jeremy and clutched at the knob, trying to turn it.

Elaine screeched as she lunged for Maddie, grabbing a handful of hair. Maddie yanked the door open, but Edward was there, slamming it shut again. He shoved it with such force it bounced open again, but it was too late for Maddie. Elaine jerked her arm hard, almost causing her to drop the baby. She shoved her toward the window, cursing and wrenching her hair in painful tugs. Maddie ignored the pain, focusing on the precarious hold she had on Jeremy.

Elaine opened the window wide and stepped back, her breath coming in short, rapid gasps. "I warned you," she said, fighting for breath. "Now I'll take great pleasure in watching that brat suffer before I kill him. It's just a shame you won't be here to see it."

She reached for the baby and Maddie struck out, landing a stinging blow to the other woman's jaw.

"Don't you touch my baby," she screamed, frantic now. She might not stand a chance, but she'd be damned if she'd go out without a fight.

Elaine stumbled back and clapped her hand to her cheek. "You bitch," she screamed, flying at Maddie, fingers curled into claws.

The door slammed back on its hinges, stopping her in midswing. She whirled and gaped.

Devon and Edward were already locked in a fierce hold, each struggling to overpower the other. Maddie could see Devon's hand, still holding the gun. He'd stormed the door, but Edward had been in a position to grab him as soon as he entered. If the gun went off there was no telling who'd be shot.

Longing to help Devon, but torn between doing that and protecting her son, Maddie glanced around for a safe place to put the baby. Elaine stepped toward her once more and she knew she couldn't let him go, not even for an instant. Devon had to fight this battle alone.

Elaine watched Maddie back away with the baby. Maddie could see defeat register in her eyes. The woman knew her plan had failed. Escape was the only thing on Elaine's mind now.

Suddenly the room was filled with the roar of a gunshot and time stood still as Maddie held her breath, waiting to see which man had been hit. Elaine seemed equally paralyzed by the scene being acted out before them. When Edward sank to his knees, Maddie heard her choked cry of dismay. Before she could make a move, Elaine lifted her skirts and darted from the room.

Maddie rushed forward, anxious to make sure Devon hadn't been injured. He turned to face her and she saw the blood on his chest. For one frightened moment she thought it was his. Then she realized it had come from Edward.

She cast a hurried glance at the man on the floor. The bullet had pierced his chest, right where his heart should have been. She felt no sorrow to realize he was dead.

"Oh, Devon," she cried, stumbling forward into her husband's arms. "Thank God you got here when you did."

"Elaine," he forced out raggedly, battling to catch his breath.

"She's getting away," Maddie cried, knowing they'd never rest as long as that woman was roaming free. She and Devon hurried down the hall toward the landing. Halfway there, a high-pitched wail split the air, going on for what seemed like an eternity before abruptly halting.

Chapter Twenty-seven

Maddie and Devon glanced at one another and then raced toward the stairs. At the bottom they saw Anthony, bent over Elaine's twisted body. Maddie turned her face into Devon's shoulder and he placed his arm around her.

"Devon, thank God you two are all right."

Tiffany raced up the stairs, sparing not a glance for the dead woman. She grabbed Maddie in a bear hug and then took the baby, who'd begun to fuss.

"I'll put Jeremy back in his cradle," she offered. "You two will have a long night ahead of you."

Maddie caught her friend's arm. "You'll stay with him?"

"Every minute," she promised, squeezing Maddie's arm reassuringly.

Anthony stood and faced them. "She's dead," he said coldly.

Devon nodded. Maddie couldn't help herself and she whispered, "Good."

That woman possessed a black soul and Maddie was not sorry she was out of their lives for good. Devon turned to her and brushed the tangled hair back from her face.

"You don't have to go down," he told her. "I'll handle things here."

Maddie shook her head. "No," she said, grasping his hand and pressing it against her lips. "I want to be by your side for this."

"Then we'll stand together," he said, tucking her hand into his.

Beverly rushed into the entryway at that moment and stopped dead. "Sarah and I were watching for the sheriff," she said, out of breath and clutching her chest. "He's just arrived."

Maddie looked at Devon and he reassured her with a small smile. She felt her heart flutter and soar. "How did you know where I was?" she asked, knowing they'd be tied up with the authorities for the remainder of the night and wanting to settle this one detail in her mind.

"Tiffany saw you run across the landing. She felt certain you had found something and she didn't want Anthony and me to get away from the house in case it was something important. She came outside and found me first. When she told me what she'd seen, I put the pieces together and came up with the same thought I'm sure you had."

"That they were still in the house."

"Yes. I cursed myself for ten kinds of a fool for not realizing it sooner. I came as fast as I could. But I had to go slow since I didn't know if they were armed or where exactly they would be. And I deduced by that time that you'd be with them."

"Edward had a gun, but I never saw him take it from his belt," Maddie said.

"Then he was even more foolish than I was," Devon told her, the rage he'd felt as he'd attacked his cousin still evident in his navy eyes.

"Thank God," she whispered, hugging him close as she faced the fact that she could have lost him, their child, and her own life that night if things had gone differently.

"We have a lot to be thankful for," he agreed.

They started down the stairs, each with their arm around the other. At the bottom, Sarah had fetched a blanket and Anthony was draping it over Elaine. Beverly and the sheriff stood to one side, conversing in low tones.

"Sheriff," Devon said, holding his hand out. The other man took his proffered hand and shook it.

"Heard you had some trouble here tonight," he said, looking past Devon to the blanket-draped body.

"Yes. Come into the study. My wife and I will tell you all about it."

*   *   *

As the sun came over the horizon, tinting the morning sky in hues of cerise and salmon, Maddie watched the sleeping faces of her husband and son. The three lay together in Devon's bed, wrapped in love and blankets to ward off the chill of morning and memories.

Thoughts of the previous night started her legs quivering and she snuggled closer to the men in her life. Their warmth radiated out and cocooned her in its reassuring embrace. They were all fine, healthy, unhurt. The threat hanging over them had died with Edward and Elaine.

Nothing loomed on the horizon to disturb their happiness any longer. Maddie felt her eyes grow heavy and she fought sleep for one final moment. Just long enough to tip her head to the heavens.

"Thank you," she whispered. "Thank you for everything."

She drifted into a dreamlike state, but before she crossed the barrier into complete repose she thought she heard a celestial voice whisper in return.

"You're welcome."

Author's Note

The condition endometriosis—which Maddie suffers from in *Time's Healing Heart*—its treatments, and symptoms are all factual.

Medical missions to Romania, such as the one Genevieve planned in *Time's Healing Heart*, actually took place in May of 1991 and July of 1992.